$\mathscr{L}$OVE ON
THE TITANIC

———— ◆ ————

JUSTIN LOVE

DEDICATION

For those who still feel the heartbeat of a ship long gone.

For the ones who believe love can bloom in impossible places, across decks, between glances, in the final hush before dawn.

This is for the romantics who keep searching the sea for what history forgot. For the believers in second chances, secret touches, and stories that refuse to sink.

To all who carry the *Titanic* not just as a tragedy, but as a place where hearts once dared to hope—this story is for you.

With all my heart,
J. L.

ABOUT THE AUTHOR

Justin Love writes queer historical romance about people who loved boldly in times that didn't always allow it. He's drawn to stories hidden between the lines of history—moments of tenderness, risk, and connection that were rarely recorded but deeply felt.

Love on the Titanic imagines one such love, shaped by class, duty, and a ship the world thought unsinkable. Justin believes history is more than dates and disasters—it's also made of glances, whispered promises, and love that refuses to sink.

He lives in Denver, Colorado, with his partner and their two dogs, Max and Teddy. When he's not writing, he can usually be found hiking or camping in the mountains, exploring new places, seeking out a good brewery or distillery, visiting any *Titanic* museum he can find, or getting lost in research, old photographs, and thinking far too much about fictional characters.

AUTHOR'S NOTE

Love on the Titanic is a work of fiction.

While the RMS *Titanic* and its tragic voyage are very real and steeped in historical record, the characters, events, and relationships portrayed in this novel are entirely imagined. Henry, Oliver, Madeleine, and their story are products of creative interpretation and are not intended to represent any real individuals who sailed aboard the *Titanic*.

This book was written with the utmost reverence for the lives lost and forever changed on that fateful night in April 1912. I deeply respect the historical accounts, survivor testimonies, and the legacy of those who were part of that voyage. My intention is not to rewrite history, but to explore what could have been—through the lens of love, identity, and humanity.

Thank you for stepping into this fictional journey with care, imagination, and an open heart.

ACKNOWLEDGMENTS

Writing this story has been a journey through time, memory, and imagination, and I could not have taken it alone.

To the real *Titanic* and all who sailed her: Your stories—both remembered and lost—were the spark. Your courage, your lives, and the silence you left behind gave shape to every page. May we continue to honor you not just with fact, but with feeling.

To the LGBTQ+ community: Thank you for being living proof that love has always existed in every corner of history, even when the world refused to see it. This book is a tribute to the love stories that never made the headlines, but should have.

To my readers—romantics, historians, dreamers, and the ones who believe in love that defies the odds: Thank you for opening your hearts to Henry and Oliver. You make stories like this worth telling.

To my early readers, supporters, and friends who reminded me that this story mattered: Your encouragement kept this book afloat through every draft, every doubt.

To Madeleine—for her fire, her friendship, and her place between. You were the anchor no one expected but everyone needed.

And finally, to the boy I once was—the one who believed love should be whispered in secret and dreamed of seeing it written into the stars: This one's for you.

Thank you.
J. L.

CONTENTS

CHAPTER 1

The Biggest Ship in the World

HENRY

"The biggest ship in the world," I said, breathless. Madeleine and I stepped onto the gangway, pausing beneath the towering hull of the RMS *Titanic*. The sea breeze stung our cheeks, thick with the scent of brine and coal. Dockhands shouted over the screech of pulleys and the groan of cargo being loaded. Around us, people clutched bundles of belongings and tickets, but we were frozen in place—two young souls from different corners of the world, gazing up at the future shaped in steel.

Madeleine whistled softly. "*Mon Dieu*. I didn't think it would be so big. The papers said it was grand, but this?" She shook her head. "This is a floating city."

"They say third class on this ship is finer than second on most others," she murmured. Her voice carried the softness of her French accent, delicate and certain all at once. She tightened her grip on her satchel, brown eyes wide with wonder and something else I couldn't quite name. Hope, maybe. Or fear.

I watched her closely. She was trying to sound composed, but the awe in her gaze betrayed her. I felt it too—something vast and shifting beneath our feet. The sense that our lives had split in two: before the *Titanic*, and whatever came after.

"I wonder if it'll still feel this big when we're in the middle of the Atlantic," she said, almost to herself.

"I think it's going to feel even bigger," I replied, nudging her.

Madeleine was a quiet force—striking in the kind of beauty that didn't ask for attention. Her black curls tumbled loose around her shoulders, unruly as ever. Her skin, fair and freckled, told stories of summers spent working with her hands—carving, sketching, and building. She had the soul of a craftsman and the eyes of a dreamer. Even when dressed simply, as she always did, she carried herself with a grace that felt older than her nineteen years.

We'd met in Montmartre, in a crooked, colorful corner of Paris where art and work and music collided. I'd come from New York, born in the crowded tenements of Lower Manhattan to Irish immigrant parents. Carpentry had been my way out and a trade that gave my hands purpose when the world didn't offer much else. I'd journeyed to Europe to sharpen my skills and landed in the workshop of Madeleine's father, a respected woodworker.

She and I became fast friends, drawn together by long days at the workbench, shared silences, and the way we both looked at the world with a kind of wary wonder. We talked about art, family, and how sometimes belonging had less to do with place and more to do with people. And through it all, she accepted me, fully and unflinchingly, even when society didn't at the time. Her friendship was a sanctuary where I could be myself.

But Madeleine's story was always bigger than ours. Not long before I received the telegram about my mother's illness—an urgent call home—Madeleine had met a young American man passing through Paris, a painter with a travel-stained coat and a sketchbook full of jazz clubs and rooftops. He had a way of seeing the world that lit something in her. They spent days walking the Seine and nights in cafés lit by candlelight. He left as suddenly as he arrived, promising he'd write and telling her he'd wait in New York if she ever came. And she believed him.

I didn't ask many questions. Some things you could see without being told. The change in her was subtle but certain, like someone who'd glimpsed a door they never knew existed. She wasn't chasing him, but rather the possibility of a life not mapped by other people's expectations.

When I told her I was heading back to New York, she asked if I'd mind the company. Her voice didn't waver. She had sold a few carvings, saved what she could, and packed only what she needed. The plan was for her to stay with me until we could find a place together—somewhere modest and ours—where we could finally settle into the rhythms of a new life in New York.

It hadn't been easy for her to convince her parents. They

clung to tradition and the idea that a young woman's future should be carefully mapped, not chased across an ocean with a suitcase full of hope. But Madeleine had always been a free spirit, more wind than root, more brushstroke than outline. Once her mind was made up, not even her father's stern silence or her mother's anxious pleading could sway her.

She was going, and that was that.

And now, here we stood. Two third-class passengers, bound for America. I was going home. Madeleine was risking everything to chase a boy she might never find again, in a city ten times the size of Paris. As simple as that.

"I wonder if he'll be waiting at the pier," she said suddenly, her voice barely above the din. "I did write to him, letting him know when I'd be arriving."

I glanced at her. "If he's smart, he will be."

She smirked. "And if he's not?"

"Then he's a fool," I said. "And he doesn't deserve you."

She looked down at her satchel, then back at the ship. "I'm scared, you know. I didn't think I would be, but I am."

"I know," I said. "Me too."

She smiled, eyes fixed on the shining promise of the ship. "Even if I don't find him, I may still build a life there anyway."

That was Madeleine. Braver than she knew.

The gangway swayed under our feet as we moved forward with the crowd. The *Titanic* rose above us, immense and immaculate, like something out of a dream. Around us, hundreds of stories were beginning. Ours were just two.

As we stepped inside, the scent of fresh paint and polished wood wrapped around us like a hush. Everything gleamed—new, untouched, and full of promise. The air carried a faint sweetness, like a stage waiting for its first act. Though we boarded through the third-class entrance, shoulder to shoulder with families from Ireland, Scandinavia, and Southern Europe, it didn't feel like we were being ushered into steerage. Not at all. The corridors were brighter than I expected, the walls paneled in warm oak, and the floors scrubbed so clean they reflected the light from the small, steady electric lamps lining the passage.

Madeleine slowed, her boots tapping lightly. "*Parbleu*," she whispered. "It's beautiful."

I nodded. "This isn't like the steerage I imagined."

She touched the wall, trailing her fingers across the wood. "It's hard to take it all in."

The hum of the engines vibrated faintly beneath our feet, like a heartbeat in the floorboards. Somewhere in the distance, languages I couldn't place echoed, along with the shuffle of feet, the occasional clink of luggage, and soft laughter from a nearby cabin. We passed a steward pushing a cart of folded linens. He nodded politely as we slipped aside. A cluster of children darted past, giggling, with a woman chasing them with a scolding in Italian.

"I wonder what they'll make of this ship," Madeleine said, gazing down the corridor.

I shrugged, grinning. "Everything, probably. The lights, the shine of the wood, the way it smells like varnish and metal and steam all at once." I swept a hand ahead of us.

"All this space—enough to get lost in. It's the biggest place most of them have ever set foot in."

She laughed softly, eyes bright.

"It feels endless," I went on. "So new and full of promise, like it was built to astonish."

She slipped her arm through mine, and together we kept walking, carried forward by the hum of the ship and the thrill of what lay ahead.

Soon, we reached a junction pointing toward E Deck. The corridor narrowed. The carpet faded. The elegance dulled, but only slightly. Even the plainest corners of the *Titanic* held a kind of quiet grace.

"I don't think I've ever seen something this big built just to move people," Madeleine said. "The biggest ship in the world, and unsinkable, they say."

"It's both," I said. "Sanctuary and machine."

She let out a breathy laugh. "You're a poet now?"

I smirked. "No. Just a carpenter pretending to understand the world."

She looked at me sideways. "You understand more than you let on."

I shrugged. "I understand wood. Structure. What holds weight, and what doesn't."

"And this ship?" she asked. "Do you think it's truly unsinkable?"

I hesitated, then ran my hand along the wall beside us.

"Oh yes," I said. "But even perfect things have seams. Joints. Weak points."

She nodded slowly. "Maybe it's the same with people.

We build ourselves up, polish everything until it shines ... but there's always something soft beneath. Something that creaks when the pressure's too much."

I gave her a long look, my chest tightening. "Yeah," I said. "Exactly like that."

We paused at the top of a stairwell, letting others pass. She looked down the long flight of stairs with a sigh.

"I'm not used to sharing space with so many strangers," she said at last.

"You will be. Give it a day or two. You'll know who snores."

She smirked, playfully slapping my arm away. "And who doesn't bathe."

I rolled my eyes before I held out my hand once more. She took it without hesitation.

"Ready?" I asked.

She nodded. "Let's find our rooms."

But just as we turned toward the stairs, we stopped in unison. A horn sounded outside, deep and distant. The final call.

Madeleine turned to me, eyes bright again. "Do you want to go up? Just for a minute?"

"To the deck?"

She nodded. "I want to see it. I want to wave."

I smiled. "Then let's go."

And so we turned back the way we'd come, arm in arm, leaving the low ceilings and close air behind us as we climbed. The corridors brightened as we went, lamps giving way to daylight that spilled down the stairwells in pale bands. Our footsteps rang sharper on the metal treads, the sounds of the ship changing with every level—less muffled now, more open, threaded with voices and the distant call of whistles.

We passed stewards moving briskly in pressed uniforms, ladies gripping hats and gloves, children darting ahead only to be pulled back by anxious hands. I caught glimpses through portholes of gray water sliding past the hull, the harbor slowly loosening its grip on us. Everything seemed in motion, even the walls, as if the ship herself were stretching awake.

By the time we reached the final stairs, my lungs filled with cooler air, sharp and clean after the warmth below. When we stepped out onto the deck, the light struck all at once—wide sky, open water, the rail gleaming beneath our hands. The harbor spread before us, crowded with faces and waving arms, reduced already to a blur of color and movement as the distance grew.

The deck felt different this time. Not just the height—though we stood far above the third-class corridors now—but the air itself. It was brisk and salted, edged with wind and coal smoke, alive with the thrill of departure. Gulls cried overhead, circling as if reluctant to let us go, and from somewhere deep within the ship came the steady, powerful rumble of machinery, pulling us forward whether we were ready or not.

Madeleine squeezed my arm as the strangers on shore waved and faded, and I stood there at the rail, heart pounding, knowing we had crossed something invisible and irrevocable the moment the harbor began to slip away.

The *Titanic* stood like a cathedral on the water. Beneath our feet, her steel bones stretched the length of a city street. Her four towering funnels cut through the gray sky, and from this height, the crowd on the docks looked tiny. People still waved. Women in hats, children on their fathers' shoulders, porters and stewards, and bystanders clung to the last few seconds of spectacle. Handkerchiefs fluttered like white petals in the wind.

Madeleine stepped to the railing and leaned over, her curls dancing wildly around her cheeks. "It's really happening," she said, her voice caught between laughter and disbelief. "We're actually moving."

I stood beside her, bracing myself against the wind. "No turning back now."

The horn bellowed again, trembling through our ribs. Beneath us, the deck vibrated with life. The mooring ropes were being cast off, pulled in like threads unwinding from a spool. I looked down as a great tugboat passed alongside, its smokestack billowing. The *Titanic* responded, slowly, majestically, easing from the quay like a living thing.

Madeleine gripped the rail tighter. "So this is what leaving feels like. I never thought I'd experience this, you know."

I nodded, though I wasn't sure she meant Southampton.

The crowd on the dock grew smaller with every churning sweep of the *Titanic's* propellers. The warehouses blurred first, then the cranes, then the thin line of waving arms. The cobblestones glistened from an earlier drizzle, fading into a soft smear of motion. A handful of men on bicycles pedaled along the pier as far as they could go, ringing their bells and waving their caps.

Around us, the third-class deck teemed with life. The trembling hush of people leaving home for the first time mixed with the rowdy excitement of those treating this like the grandest adventure of their lives. A stout elderly woman crossed herself dramatically every thirty seconds, muttering a prayer each time, as if she were worried God might forget she'd boarded a ship this large. A cluster of boys pressed their faces to the railing, pointing to a tugboat struggling to pivot in the ship's wake.

"It's going to flip!" one of the boys insisted.

"It is absolutely not going to flip," his friend argued.

"It *should*, though," a third added. "For the drama."

They all nodded solemnly. *For the drama, indeed.*

Madeleine slid in beside me, adjusting the brim of her hat as a gust of wind attempted to steal it. "Do you think this is it?" she asked softly.

I turned toward her. "What do you mean?"

"This feeling." She gestured at everything—the ship, the water, the disappearing shore, and the vibrant chaos of passengers around us. "As though we've stepped out of our old lives and into something … bigger. I can't tell if I'm exhilarated or terrified."

"Both," I said. "Definitely both."

She let out a small laugh. "That follows. My mother always said I had a talent for doing two contradictory things at once. Like being well-bred and hopelessly inconvenient."

I snorted. "I like you inconvenient."

"I know," she said smugly, looking away once more.

The horizon unfurled ahead of us—a silver-blue line where sky and sea blended as if unsure who was leading whom. The channel stretched forward like a promise, curving out of sight, daring us to follow. I looked around us. Families around us gripped hands too tightly, young men grinned with reckless hope, and children pointed at everything, even things they'd already pointed at. I looked at the wide, shimmering water and the disappearing world behind us. And then I looked at Madeleine, and felt the last thread of hesitation snap loose.

The upper decks still echoed in our minds as Madeleine and I descended the narrow stairwell back toward our section of the ship. With each step down, the gleam of polished brass and paneled oak softened into bare steel and practical wood, but even here, there was a sense of newness, fresh paint, clean light bulbs, that proved this was a ship not yet touched by time.

"Let's go," I nudged her at last, "and find our cabins now." She nodded, and then we moved with the flow of other third-class passengers: families, single men with wool caps and suitcases, and young mothers clutching sleeping babies against their chests. The deeper we went, the more languages we heard: Irish, Norwegian, Italian, and Polish. It was like walking through the spine of the world, everyone bound for the same dream.

Signs posted at each stairwell marked our descent. C Deck. Then D. Then E. The air grew warmer as we dropped further into the ship's belly, the hum of the engines growing louder, vibrating faintly through the floor.

"I feel like we've stepped into the ship's bones," Madeleine said as the gleam of polished brass faded into plain metal piping.

I nodded, glancing down the narrow passage. "Now I just want to see the rest of it."

"Me too. Every corner." She looped her arm through mine, her eyes bright with curiosity. "Let's find out, then."

We'd already been wandering along E Deck, passing doors that led to the third-class cabins we were meant to claim, but neither of us was ready to stop yet. The ship felt too vast, too new. When we spotted the stairs down, we exchanged a quick look—just a short detour, we decided, a little exploring on F Deck before we turned back.

That was how we found ourselves paused outside the third-class dining saloon on F Deck, marked by a sign painted in plain black lettering. Through the open doorway, we caught a glimpse of the room beyond: long communal tables, whitewashed walls, and rows of benches already being prepped for the evening meal. A steward in shirtsleeves moved past with a stack of chipped plates, and the scent of potatoes and onions lingered faintly in the air.

"It's no Paris café," Madeleine murmured.

"No, but I bet the food's hot and the bread's thick."

She grinned. "I can live with that."

Farther down the hall, we passed the entrance to the general room, our true destination after dinner. Laughter spilled into the hallway, even this early in the evening.

Inside, a few men were already gathered at a corner table, shuffling cards. A woman played a slow tune on a fiddle in the corner. The room was plain, with bare walls, wooden benches, and low ceilings, but it buzzed with something human and warm. It was the kind of comfort you only find in shared spaces.

"We're definitely coming back here tonight," Madeleine said.

"You read my mind," I replied. "Cards and drinks on the first night at sea."

We finally turned back and climbed up to E Deck, leaving the hum of F Deck behind us, and found the narrow passage that led to the third-class staterooms. The hallway smelled faintly of soap and wood oil, and the floor beneath our feet dipped and swayed almost imperceptibly as the ship moved through open water.

A steward passed us with a clipboard and a polite nod. He glanced down at our tickets and directed us to a split in the corridor, women to the left, men to the right.

Madeleine gave me a look, half amusement, half resignation. "Separated already," she said. "Third class doesn't believe in coed living, I suppose."

"Only for the married," I said with a shrug. "They think they're protecting us."

"From what? Conversation?"

"Sure. *Conversation*." I shrugged with a smirk, and she chuckled at the motion. "I'll meet you at dinner."

"Don't be late," she replied, and disappeared down the left corridor.

I found my room just around the bend, cabin E-88. The door creaked slightly as I pushed it open.

The room was tiny, but clean. Two sets of bunk beds lined the walls, the iron frames freshly painted, and the white sheets crisp and tucked with precision. Each berth had its own wall hook and a single drawer tucked beneath the mattress for belongings. My ticket number was printed on the card taped beside the top bunk on the far side.

There was no carpet, just wooden planks scrubbed smooth, and a small ceiling light that flickered slightly when I turned it on.

A rucksack was already tossed on the bunk across from mine. Someone had arrived ahead of me, though I didn't see them yet. I sat down on the edge of the bed. It creaked slightly. The mattress was thin but not awful, better than a warehouse floor or dock crate by a long shot. A knock on the doorframe made me turn.

"Bathroom's down the hall, third door on the left," said a young man in a cap, his accent Irish. "And don't wait too long. The sinks only run hot water for about fifteen minutes before it goes cold again."

"Got it," I said, nodding my thanks.

He vanished, boots echoing down the corridor.

I stood and poked my head out, following the flow of passengers toward the shared lavatories. The bathroom was surprisingly bright, tiled in white with brass fixtures and small, round basins spaced along one wall. A single metal mirror hung above them, slightly warped. The scent of soap and bleaching powder lingered in the air.

There were a few narrow private stalls set along the wall, their metal doors cool beneath my fingers. A long bench near the back served for changing, and beyond it stretched a narrow room lined with doors that led to the toilets. I washed my hands at the sink, splashing my face with cool water. I caught my reflection in the fogged mirror—cheeks flushed, hair wind-tossed from the deck.

And underneath it all, there was a look in my eyes I didn't recognize at first. Excitement. Anticipation. The kind that came when you didn't know what was ahead, but for once, you were ready to walk toward it.

I dried my hands, smoothed my shirt, and made my way back to my cabin to wait for the dinner bell. Tonight, there would be cards. Laughter. Madeleine. And a ship unlike anything the world had ever seen.

I slipped back to my stateroom not long after, finally giving in to the ache in my feet. I unpacked just enough to feel settled—folding shirts away, tucking my spare boots out of the way—then stretched out for a moment that turned into a short, much-needed nap, the gentle thrum of the engines rocking me under.

The dinner bell jolted me awake, its sharp clang carrying through the ship. Almost at once, the corridors outside my cabin burst into motion—boots striking tile, doors creaking open, voices in a dozen different accents calling to one another. The smell of boiled potatoes, beef stew, and fresh bread drifted through the vents like a promise.

I made my way toward the third-class dining saloon with the rest of the men from my corridor, shoulders brushing in the narrow hallway. The entrance opened just ahead of us, and as I stepped inside, I stopped short. It was far grander than I expected—not chandeliers or velvet wallpaper, but a sense of care, design, and thought put into every surface.

The room was vast—stretching nearly the entire width of the ship, with long pine tables arranged in orderly rows, each one flanked by narrow benches polished smooth by use. The walls were whitewashed and paneled in simple, clean wood, and electric lamps hung evenly along the ceiling, casting a soft golden glow across the room. Their light flickered slightly, but it was steady enough to feel warm, even welcoming.

The air buzzed with conversation as people filed in, seats being claimed and scraped backward. Laughter rolled down the rows in soft waves. Children bounced on benches. Old men set down flat caps beside their bowls and nodded to strangers like they were neighbors back home.

Stewards moved quickly between the tables, carrying trays of soup, tins of butter, baskets of bread, and tall pitchers of water and tea. They didn't linger, but they were kind. A few jokes cracked as they passed, and one ruffled a young boy's hair before moving on.

Madeleine waved from the far end of the saloon. She sat at the single women's section, near the wall, separate, as regulations demanded, but close enough that I could see the glow in her cheeks and the way she leaned toward a young girl beside her, whispering something that made them both laugh.

I, on the other hand, found a space near the center of

the room, across from a Welsh teenager with soot-smudged fingers and a broad grin. Next to him, an older Norwegian man was already ladling soup into his mouth.

"First trip across?" the Welsh boy asked, offering me a crust of bread.

"Oh no," I said, accepting it. "I'm just heading back home. You?"

"Going to join my brother in Chicago," he said, mouth half full. "He says they've got trains out there so long you can sleep on them."

"That sounds about right."

The food was simple but hearty: thick beef stew with carrots and barley, boiled potatoes, brown bread still warm from the oven, and rice pudding for dessert. It was better than I expected. Better than most meals I'd had back in New York. The hum of conversation never really stopped. A toddler let out a triumphant shriek from across the room after taking a bite of pudding. Two Swedish brothers argued playfully over the last roll. A pair of Englishmen debated football near the far bench, voices rising with each point made.

Madeleine caught my eye again as the stewards began clearing trays. She mouthed something.

Cards?

I nodded. *Meet you soon*, I mouthed back.

She stood slowly, smoothing her skirts, and made her way out with the other women, laughing quietly as one of them tried to balance her tray on one hand and a biscuit in the other.

I lingered a moment longer, sipping the last of my tea. The warm clink of tinware, the scrape of benches, the subtle thrum of the engines below—it was all so ordinary, and yet somehow, extraordinary too.

CHAPTER 2

Before the Guests Arrive

OLIVER

I boarded the ship before dawn, through a door most passengers would never notice. The crew entrance sat low along the hull, tucked beneath the grand sweep of first class and far from the noise and spectacle of the main gangways. There were no reporters here, no hats waved in farewell, no music. Just the echo of boots on steel, the smell of fresh paint and coal smoke, and the quiet urgency of men who knew exactly where they were meant to be.

I handed over my papers, nodded to the officer on duty, and stepped inside the *Titanic*. The officer's eyes flicked over me in the way they always did—not looking for who I was, but looking for what I might be. A crease out of place. A button undone. A hint of hesitation that suggested I didn't belong.

His gaze paused on my face for a fraction too long.

"Keep your chin up," he said, quiet enough that only I could hear. Not an order, exactly. A correction. A reminder that even the smallest thing—posture, expression, the way you held your mouth—could be interpreted as defiance.

"Yes, sir," I answered automatically.

I adjusted without thinking: shoulders back, jaw set, eyes steady. The version of myself that belonged to this ship slid into place like a practiced disguise. There was comfort in the ritual of it, in the certainty of rules. Rules were easier than people. Rules didn't change their minds because they disliked the way you laughed, or because you looked at someone a moment too long.

Behind me, another steward entered, younger, nervous in the way new men always were. He fumbled with his papers, dropping one sheet to the floor. The officer didn't raise his voice, didn't need to. A single look did it. The boy went red as he crouched to retrieve the paper, hands shaking slightly.

I watched him, felt a tightness in my chest—not sympathy exactly. Recognition.

When you worked in service, you learned quickly that humiliation didn't have to be loud. It could be delivered in silence. It could be delivered with a raised brow. It could be delivered with a pause that made you feel your own existence as a problem to be solved.

The boy straightened and hurried on, moving too fast, eager to vanish into the corridors before anyone could decide he'd taken up too much time. I wanted to tell him to slow down. To breathe. But advice was dangerous. Attachment was dangerous. On ships like this, you survived by remaining useful and forgettable.

So I did what I always did. I swallowed whatever

softness tried to rise in me and walked forward, letting the ship take me in.

Even after a week of drills and whispered talk, the scale of her still made me pause. Not just her size, but her intention. Every corridor, every stairwell, every polished surface existed to impress someone—to reassure them they were safe, superior, and chosen.

I followed the crew passage forward, the narrow corridor set apart from the passenger spaces, pipes running overhead and bulkheads close on either side. The hum of the ship was already alive beneath my boots as I made my way toward D Deck, where many of the crew were quartered. Somewhere above, engineers were bringing systems online; far below, stokers were already sweating in the bowels of the ship, feeding the fires that would carry us onward.

Before reporting to my post, I stopped at the purser's office. The door stood open, clerks already bent over ledgers and manifests, the air thick with ink, paper, and quiet authority. The purser himself stood near the desk, glasses perched low on his nose, reviewing last-minute arrivals.

"Morning," he said without looking up.

"Morning, sir," I replied, stepping inside.

A steward who learned when to look and when to listen could pick up more than gossip. My eyes drifted, carefully, to the guest list laid open on the desk—names inked in precise columns, stateroom numbers assigned beside them.

The Astors. The Wideners. Several titled Englishmen and wealthy Americans. But there were gaps. Empty lines. Unassigned suites.

I leaned closer, keeping my posture casual. "Not a full house after all?"

The purser snorted softly. "Hardly. Biggest ship in the world, and still a few missing names. Last-minute cancellations. A handful of suites being held, just in case."

"How many?" I asked.

"More than you'd think," he replied, tapping the page with his pen. "First class never fills the way people imagine. They like knowing there's space to spare."

I nodded, committing the information to memory.

Space meant quieter corridors. Fewer eyes. Rooms that would remain untouched for the entire crossing.

"Your assignment's A Deck," the purser added. "Several American families, a few Europeans, and a pair of adjoining suites near the staircase. Expect discretion."

"Yes, sir."

I left the office and continued forward. The Turkish baths came first—arched ceilings tiled in blue and cream, marble benches cool beneath my fingertips, brass fixtures gleaming under electric light. Steam drifted lazily through the air, carrying the faint scent of soap and heated stone. Beyond them lay the swimming pool, its pale green water perfectly still, like a secret waiting to be discovered.

I lingered longer than necessary. Not many people would ever truly *see* this place. They would swim, laugh, and remark upon it over dinner, then forget it existed. I saw the labor behind it—the hands that polished every tile, the effort hidden beneath the illusion of ease.

I moved on. As I climbed toward first class, the corridors

widened, oak-paneled and softly lit, carpets thick enough to swallow sound. Brass numbers gleamed on polished doors, each one a promise of privacy and comfort.

And now that I knew what to look for, I saw them clearly. Doors that would not be opened. Suites left untouched, their locks untested, their flower vases empty. No luggage carts paused outside them. No stewards hovered nearby, waiting for instructions. They existed in a strange limbo—prepared, immaculate, and entirely unused.

I slowed near one such door without realizing I'd done so. It was on B Deck, just off the main staircase—close enough to the heart of first class to feel important, yet set back enough to escape notice. The brass number read B-62, polished but dull with disuse. Whoever had been meant to claim it never arrived. Inside, I knew the bed would remain perfectly made. The sitting room untouched. The air still, unclaimed by breath or movement. A room no one would think to check.

I moved on quickly after that, scolding myself for lingering. First-class stewards weren't meant to imagine spaces as *theirs*, even temporarily. We maintained the illusion of luxury, not the luxury itself. Still, as I walked away, the knowledge stayed with me. The *Titanic* was vast. And not every door had a witness.

I reported for duty just before eight bells. The officers stood near the forward corridor, crisp and composed, clipboards already in hand. I joined the other first-class stewards as assignments were read aloud.

"You'll be assigned forward on A Deck," the chief

steward said. "Mostly families—and a couple of larger rooms near the main stairway. Keep things running smoothly. No delays."

That was code for *be invisible unless summoned.*

"Yes, sir."

I changed in the crew quarters, pulling on my pressed jacket, fastening each button with care. The mirror bolted to the wall reflected a version of me that belonged here—controlled, polished, ready.

By midmorning, the ship was alive. Passengers arrived in waves. I escorted a silver-haired American couple to their suite, carrying nothing myself but directing porters with small, precise gestures. The woman glanced at the room, nodded once, and said, "Acceptable," as though she were approving a purchase rather than a space meant to carry her across an ocean.

Another guest stopped me near the stairwell.

"Is the promenade enclosed?"

"Yes, sir."

"And the sea?"

"Exceptionally calm today, sir."

A man complained his trunk had been placed on the wrong side of the room. I apologized and fixed it. A woman asked if the electric light could be dimmed further. I showed her the switch. A child asked if the ship could really sink. His mother laughed before I could answer.

I unpacked nothing myself—that was not my role—but I supervised quietly, ensuring gloves were laid correctly, shoes aligned, collars brushed. I remembered preferences.

I noted habits. I learned who rang too often and who never rang at all. Most smiled politely. Some barely looked at me. A few spoke as if I were part of the architecture—necessary, but forgettable. I answered every question the same way.

"Yes, the baths are open daily."

"No, the ship doesn't roll much at sea."

"Yes, the crossing should be quite smooth."

When the rush finally eased, I leaned briefly against the wall near the first-class stairwell. Thomas, another steward, joined me, loosening his collar slightly.

"Quiet so far," he said. "Feels strange."

"It does," I replied. "Too much space."

He chuckled. "People pay for space as much as anything else."

I glanced down the corridor toward the grand spaces waiting to be filled with music and voices later that night. "Can't wait for this evening," I said. "Once the guests settle in."

Thomas smirked. "Planning to unwind?"

"Just … look around," I said lightly. "There's a lot of ship we never see while working."

He gave me a knowing look. "Careful. This ship has a way of pulling people into places they're not meant to be."

"Maybe," I said. "But it also feels like a place where anything could happen."

Later, when the final first-class passengers boarded and the doors were secured, I took one last walk through the corridor. Every door was closed now. The ship hummed beneath my feet—steady, powerful, alive. The *Titanic* was underway.

CHAPTER 3

A New World
Below Deck

HENRY

W e left the dining salon together, winding our way through the narrow corridors, buoyed by the warmth of dinner and the energy in the air. There was a lightness to our steps, part nerves, part anticipation, as we climbed the stairs down to F Deck, where the general room was located.

The moment we entered, the atmosphere hit us like a wave. The room was alive. Madeleine took it in all at once. Not just the noise—the laughter, the music, the scrape of benches—but the people themselves. She settled into a chair across from me and rested her elbows lightly on the table, eyes moving from face to face like she was sketching without pencil or paper. She had always watched people this way. Not judgmental. Intent. As if she believed there was something to be learned simply by paying attention.

"You're doing it again," I said, shuffling the cards.

"Doing what?"

"Studying everyone like they're about to sit for a portrait." She smiled faintly.

"People show you who they are when they think no one important is watching."

"That sounds ominous."

"It's practical," she replied. "Look—see how that man leans in when he laughs? He wants to be liked. And that woman there—she keeps her bag on her lap. She doesn't trust anyone yet."

I followed her gaze and realized she was right. Madeleine didn't rush to fill silence. She let it exist, observed what rose to the surface, and only then spoke. It was how she survived rooms that expected her to be smaller.

"Are you excited for New York?" I asked.

Her face lit up at once. "I am. Truly."

I raised an eyebrow.

She laughed, leaning forward. "I've been dreaming about it—the noise, the crowds, the way the city never seems to sleep. It feels like the kind of place where everything is just beginning."

That was when she noticed him—before I did, truly. Her gaze paused, sharpened, then flicked back to me as if to confirm something.

"There's someone here who doesn't belong," she murmured.

I frowned. "That's half the room."

She shook her head. "No. I mean someone who's learned how to disappear."

I followed her gaze then—and felt something stir that I didn't yet have language for.

I nudged her arm. "Don't stare," I said quietly.

She caught herself, lips curving in apology, and let her eyes drift away. We moved on with the crowd, but the feeling lingered with me, unsettled and strangely warm.

Laughter echoed off the walls, mingling with the low strum of a fiddle in the corner. Children sat cross-legged near the door, whispering secrets. Men smoked pipes, trading stories in a dozen languages. Young women chatted at long wooden benches, while older couples played quiet rounds of dominoes. The walls were bare, the furniture simple, but none of that mattered. The room was full of life, louder and brighter than any drawing room in Paris.

There were no barriers here. It was the kind of noise that made you forget yourself. Not because it drowned you out, but because it invited you in. A man near the center of the room was telling a story with his whole body, arms sweeping wide as if he could pull the ocean itself into his point. His companions roared with laughter at the punch-line—even the ones who clearly hadn't understood every word. Laughter didn't require translation. Neither did the way people leaned toward each other, hungry for company, hungry for proof that the world was larger than the one they'd left behind.

Someone began to sing—soft at first, a tentative melody that might have died if the room hadn't welcomed it. But it didn't die. Another voice joined, then another, and soon the song filled the space, not polished, not perfect, but real.

The kind of song you sang when you wanted to remember who you were. The kind you sang when you were trying not to be afraid. Madeleine's eyes shone as she listened. She had that look she got sometimes—the one that made her seem younger, less guarded. She belonged in places like this, where people didn't ask permission to feel things. I didn't belong anywhere, not fully. But in that room, with the song rising and falling like breath, I felt something loosen in me.

A child darted between tables, chased by a sister only a few years older, both of them laughing so hard they could barely run. The girl nearly collided with a broad-shouldered Irishman, who caught her gently by the elbow and set her upright again as if she were made of glass. He winked at her, and she giggled and sprinted away, ponytail flying. There was kindness here. Casual, unremarked. The kind of kindness that didn't demand anything in return.

Madeleine nudged me. "Come on," she said, already pulling a worn deck of cards from her satchel. "Let's see how your American luck holds up."

I shook my head and smiled. "Don't say I didn't warn you. I grew up with five brothers. Cards were a matter of survival."

She grinned. "So is everything when you're a girl in Montmartre."

Madeleine shuffled the deck, her fingers moving like a magician's, deft and deliberate. Her eyes never left mine.

"Let's make this interesting," she said, her tone light but laced with challenge. "Winner buys the next round."

I raised a brow. "You're on."

We eased into the game, the crisp snap of the cards sharp against the smooth tabletop. The wood beneath our elbows was newly polished, still faintly scented with varnish, and it caught the light as we leaned in.

"I think you're bluffing," I said, narrowing my eyes as Madeleine calmly laid down a pair of queens.

"You always think I'm bluffing." She leaned in just enough to smirk. "And yet, I keep winning."

"You cheat."

"I'm French," she replied with a shrug. "We don't cheat. We charm."

I laughed, raking a hand through my hair. "That's one word for it."

I reached for the deck again, letting the familiar motion steady me. Shuffle. Cut. Deal. It was a rhythm I'd carried through years of cramped apartments and noisy gatherings—something you could do with your hands when your mind didn't know where to go. Madeleine watched me with that sly, knowing expression of hers, as if she could read the shape of every thought before I spoke it. I stuck my tongue out at her like a child, and she laughed, delighted, the sound bright enough to make a few people nearby glance over and smile. That was the thing about her. She drew people in. She made strangers feel like friends. She made rooms feel less sharp.

I dealt the next hand and tried to focus on the cards, on the little war between us, on the harmless victory of a well-played trick. But something kept tugging at the edge of my attention. Not a sound. Not a movement I could name.

Just … the sense of being observed. The hair on my arms lifted slightly, the way it did when you stepped into a draft you hadn't expected. I told myself it was nothing—just the crowded room, just my nerves, just my mind inventing ghosts because it didn't know how to relax. Still, I found myself pausing mid-deal, fingers hovering over the next card. And then, almost against my will, my eyes lifted from the table.

Madeleine followed my line of sight and gave a quiet laugh.

"You know," she said, "now you're the one staring."

I tore my eyes away, heat rising to my face. "I wasn't."

She smiled, amused. "Of course not. Still, he does have a way of drawing attention."

I hesitated, then said softly, "He doesn't seem like he belongs down here."

"I don't think he does," I murmured. "Maybe crew, first-class staff, maybe. I imagine they take breaks down here. They're not supposed to mix with passengers on the upper deck. From what I've heard, it makes the rich nervous."

She studied me for a second, then smiled slyly. "You just dealt me a five and a two, you know. You're completely distracted."

I looked down at the cards, groaned, and began to re-shuffle, though my hands moved more slowly now. When I glanced up again, his gaze had finally found its way to ours—or to me. For a brief, weightless moment, the room seemed to fall away.

I didn't know what possessed me, but I let out a small, instinctive smile.

He smiled back—quick, restrained, as if it were a secret meant only for us—before looking away.

The game continued, the room alive with noise once more, but the evening had already shifted. Some people announced themselves loudly. Others did it with silence. And without a word exchanged, he had tilted the night just enough to leave everything feeling different.

CHAPTER 4

The Man
Playing Cards

OLIVER

B y the time the last oyster plates had been cleared from the first-class dining saloon, the room had taken on its evening rhythm: Conversations were low, forks tinkled against porcelain, and stewards moved like shadows between tables. The passengers had all sat down in their tailored suits and silk gloves. Their expectations were set. And for the next few hours, they wouldn't need me.

I passed the service duties to Renshaw, nodded to the assistant purser, and slipped out through the side corridor. My uniform was crisp, collar loosened, and coat folded neatly over my arm. Once I cleared the first-class promenade, I moved quickly. Down the crew stairs, past the service pantry, down again through the guts of the ship where the hallways narrowed, and the walls breathed with steam and distant engine hum.

The further down I went, the less watched I became. I

didn't go to the crew quarters. I didn't want quiet. I wanted something else.

The third-class general room on the *Titanic* sat tucked behind a wide corridor off F Deck, a place I'd only heard about through whispers and boiler-room gossip. Sure, I'd go there every now and then during my other jobs, but this was a first on this ship. It wasn't somewhere I was meant to be. White Star Line policy was clear: First-class stewards didn't linger in steerage. You served the rich, then vanished into the walls.

But I wasn't on duty anymore. And tonight, I wanted to remember what people looked like when they weren't pretending. I slipped through the open door and let the sound wash over me. The room was warm and loud in a way first class never was. Wooden benches packed tight, elbows pressed together, and the air was thick with accents, laughter, and smoke from a pipe in the corner. A boy played a fiddle, his foot tapping out a rhythm faster than the music.

And then I saw him.

He was seated near the back of the room at a small table, a deck of cards in hand. His coat looked a size too small, the cuffs worn thin from work, and his sleeves were rolled to the elbow. He leaned forward in conversation with a girl with dark curls and Parisian sharpness in her eyes. Even as she spoke, though, his gaze drifted up. Right to me. And I stopped walking.

Dirty blond curls, soft and unkempt, like he hadn't decided if he wanted to tame them. Blue eyes, wide and open and startling in their clarity. He was tall, that much was obvious; his frame folded slightly to fit at the table. Broad shoulders, strong wrists, and skillful hands, from what I could tell. Something in the tilt of his mouth told me he laughed easily, even when he didn't mean to.

But it wasn't his posture or his looks that caught me. It was the way he smiled at me.

And I—*God help me*—smiled back.

It was small, just a flicker. Not something I'd practiced in the mirror—the polite nod I gave to passengers. This was mine. I didn't break stride. I walked the room's edge like I belonged to the walls, not to the people in them. But as I passed, I let myself glance again. He was still watching.

The girl leaned in to speak, and he turned away briefly, laughing at whatever joke she made. But it was different now. We'd seen each other. I moved slowly, weaving between tables until I found a seat near the edge of the room, close enough to the stove to feel the warmth on my legs. I draped my coat over the back of the chair and sat down, my posture relaxing inch by inch as the weight of the upper decks finally slid from my shoulders.

A fiddle picked up again in the corner, faster now, jaunty. A few men clapped along while a girl tapped the toe of her boot against the bench leg. Laughter rippled from one table to another. Someone passed a chipped tin cup of something dark and bitter down the line. I accepted it with a nod, letting the warmth coat my throat.

Across the room, he was still there, still playing cards and stealing glances when he thought I wasn't looking. And every time our eyes met, that smile crept back, like we were sharing something already.

It unsettled me how easy it felt. I'd spent my life learning how to fold myself away—how to let glances slide past without catching, how to laugh at the right moments and keep my hands still. But with him, something in me loosened without permission. I didn't feel watched. I felt … seen. He shifted in his chair, stretching his long legs beneath the table. The movement was casual, unguarded, and I noticed it far more than I should have. I noticed everything: the way his sleeves were rolled just enough to expose his wrists, the faint crease between his brows when he concentrated, the way his mouth curved when he smiled—not wide, but deliberate, like he meant it. I sat there, letting the music wash over me with the noise, the heat, and the mess of it all. And for once, I wasn't a steward on duty. I was just a man with a drink and a heartbeat, eyeing a boy across the room who smiled when he saw me.

CHAPTER 5

A Game of Cards and Something More

I tried to keep playing cards, but every time I looked down at my hand, the numbers blurred because he was still there.

He'd taken a seat near the stove, tucked half in shadow like he'd meant to disappear, but didn't want to just yet. His coat was draped over the back of the chair, his sleeves rolled casually, and he held a tin cup in one hand as he watched the fiddle player with quiet interest.

And once—maybe twice—his gaze slipped back toward me.

I must've been staring.

Madeleine didn't even look up from her cards. "You should go talk to him."

My chest tightened. "What? *No.*"

She arched an eyebrow. "Henry."

I kept my eyes on the game. "It'd be weird. He doesn't know me."

She laid down a jack of spades, victorious. "Neither did I when you walked into my father's workshop smelling like varnish and nerves. And that didn't stop you from approaching me."

"That was different. You were being paid to tolerate me."

"And yet, here I am," she said, eyes twinkling. "Cards in hand, about to move to the other side of the world with you by my side, still tolerating you. You're welcome."

I grinned despite myself.

"He's looking at you, you know," she added, almost offhand.

My stomach flipped. "He is *not*."

She leaned in, voice low and smug. "He is. And he's sitting alone. With a drink. Looking very bored."

I glanced up quickly and caught him watching me again, like he was wondering the same thing I was. *Should I?*

Madeleine nudged the deck toward me. "One more hand. Then you go." We played. She won. *Again.*

I sighed, set down my cards, and wiped my hands on my coat like I was prepping for something more dangerous than conversation. "Wish me luck."

Madeleine raised her glass. "*Bonne chance, mon cher.*"

I stood, crossed the room slowly, heart hammering like it thought we were back in New York, outrunning a streetcar.

The man looked up when I got close. A flicker of recognition passed through his expression, like he'd expected this, but wasn't going to be the first to speak.

"Hey," I said, awkward already. "Mind if I join you for a minute?"

He gestured to the empty chair across from him. "Not at all."

His voice was low, English and smooth, suggesting restraint more than ease. I sat, suddenly aware of everything I was doing, how I folded my hands and how I leaned in.

"I'm Henry," I offered.

A pause. "Oliver."

We shook. His hand was warm, callused like mine, but his grip was gentle.

"You don't exactly look like you belong down here," I said, eyeing the crisp collar of his shirt, the tailored cut of his coat. "Not many people in steerage dress like they're on their way to serve oysters to the Astors."

"I work in first class. Tonight was … quiet," he said.

"Your secret's safe with me," I said, grinning. "Though the crowd might notice you don't blend in."

He chuckled. "I suppose I'm a bit overdressed for steerage."

I tilted my head. "You make it work."

His smile pulled to one side.

"I was wondering," I said, shifting slightly, "if you wanted to come play a few hands. I'm losing terribly, and Madeleine—she's the one I'm traveling with—would probably enjoy beating both of us."

He studied me for a breath, then looked past me toward our table.

"She's the one with the sharp eyes," he said.

"That's her."

He considered, then nodded once. "I'd like that."

I stood, trying not to look too pleased. "We're right this way."

He rose and followed, and our night began.

Oliver followed me back to the table with the easy confidence of someone used to being welcomed. His presence drew a few curious glances as we passed, and I couldn't blame them; he looked entirely out of place here among the coal-dusted sleeves and worn boots of steerage.

Madeleine's brows arched the moment she saw us.

"Oliver," I said, gesturing between them. "This is Madeleine. Madeleine, this is … well, the distraction that cost me two rounds."

She stood and extended her hand with a slight, curious smile. "*Enchantée.*"

Oliver bowed slightly as he took it. "The pleasure is mine."

"You're not from around here, are you?" she asked, slipping back into her seat and motioning for him to join us.

"I'm not even sure where 'here' is anymore," he replied, settling into the chair beside me. "But no. Not recently."

I dealt a fresh hand as we all settled, silence wrapping around us. "So, Oliver, what brings someone dressed like you into a third-class card game?"

He chuckled under his breath, accepting his cards without hesitation. "Curiosity. And decent company."

"You work on the ship?" Madeleine asked, clearly intrigued.

"Yes, I do," Oliver said, glancing at her over his cards. "I work in first class."

That piqued her interest immediately—and mine again.

"Doing what, exactly?" I prompted, casually setting down a pair of tens.

He smiled, a faint curve of his mouth that seemed half amusement, half evasion. "I'm a steward."

I blinked. That explained the tailoring, the clean hands, the unruffled posture, and the way he moved through the room without stumbling over anything or anyone. First-class staff were expected to be invisible, efficient, and polished to a shine.

"But … aren't you supposed to be above deck?" Madeleine asked, genuinely curious. "You know, tending to the needs of the rich and oblivious?"

Oliver chuckled. "We do get breaks, you know. Even the gilded elite need time to powder their noses without us hovering." He took a sip from a dented tin cup. "When I'm off-duty, I like to wander—see parts of the ship I don't usually get time for."

"To third class?" I said, raising a brow.

He nodded, resting his cards in a neat fan against the table. "First class is a performance. Always. The posture, the smiles, and the 'yes, sir,' and 'right away, madam.' Up there, you're not a person; you're part of the furniture, polished and positioned. Down here, it's different. No one looks twice at me. I'm not the steward. I'm just another body in the room. I can breathe. Relax. Even lose a game of cards without someone assuming it was for their amusement."

Madeleine looked at him with fresh eyes now—more curious, less enchanted. "So, you intend to hide here."

He didn't flinch. "Wouldn't you?"

I studied him carefully. He wasn't ashamed. He was honest about it, disarmingly so. Most men in his shoes would boast about brushing elbows with the Astors and Rothschilds. Oliver was choosing to spend his limited freedom somewhere with chipped mugs and coal grit in the corners. That said something.

"Don't you worry you'll get caught?" I asked. "Isn't mixing with passengers against the rules?"

He shrugged. "Technically, yes. But I'm not causing trouble. And no one in first class is going to follow me down five decks to the general room to make sure I'm staying in character. They don't know me. They don't care to." He paused for a moment. "Besides, where else on this ship can you find card players willing to bluff with a pair of twos and call it art?"

Madeleine laughed and nudged me beneath the table. "He's talking about you."

"I know," I muttered, pretending to examine my hand, though I could still feel Oliver's presence like static on my skin.

"Maybe we should be charging him," she said. "Entertainment fee."

"Oh, I'm paying," Oliver said. "I just don't know it yet."

The banter continued. Oliver, it turned out, wasn't who he first appeared to be. He wasn't a passenger. He wasn't running away or sailing toward a dream like the rest of us.

He was a man suspended between worlds, slipping between roles like coats hung on a rail.

∾

As the night wore on, the din of the general room began to mellow. The music slowed, voices dropped to murmurs, and a few stewards started stacking stray cups and straightening benches. The warm glow of the lanterns cast long shadows across the floor, flickering softly like the embers of a fire burning low. Madeleine let out a yawn, stifling it behind her hand.

"That's my cue," she said, standing and brushing off her skirts. "I've been up since dawn, and I'm starting to see double."

"You sure you're not just afraid to lose again?" I teased, stacking the cards.

She rolled her eyes. "You wish." Then she turned to Oliver, more warmly now. "It was lovely to meet you, Oliver. I hope we see you again."

"I'm sure you will," he said, rising slightly from his seat as she gathered her things. He gave her a polite nod, gentlemanly without being performative. "Sleep well, Madeleine."

"You too," Madeleine said with a sleepy smile, gathering her things.

"Good night, Madeleine," I called after her.

The door swung shut behind her with a soft click. The room didn't fall silent, but without her brightness, the noise of the general room softened to a distant rhythm beneath the steady thump of cards and the faint creak of the ship's bones.

Oliver leaned back in his chair, stretching slightly, his expression unreadable but at ease. "She's sharp," he said. "I like her."

"She is," I agreed. "Tough as nails, smarter than me, and kind enough not to say it out loud."

He gave a faint smile, the kind that lingered in the eyes longer than on the lips. Then he tapped the top of the deck. "Another round?"

I nodded. "Deal me in."

We fell into an easy rhythm—shuffling, drawing, folding, and playing out each hand. Around us, the room had thinned. A few tired passengers dozed with heads on crossed arms. A lullaby hummed in Norwegian drifted from the corner. Someone's light snoring punctuated the stillness.

I glanced at Oliver as he dealt, noticing again how precise his hands were, like he was born to handle delicate things.

"You're good at this," I said.

"I've spent a lot of time waiting," he replied without looking up, "and cards help pass it quietly."

I considered that, watching the way he held himself—relaxed but always aware, like a man whose instincts never fully shut off. He didn't have the guarded tension of someone hiding something, but there was distance in him, like he'd spent a long time being a version of himself for other people. I wondered what the real version looked like.

Curiosity finally got the better of me.

"So," I said casually, setting down my hand, "what's it like up there? First class?"

Oliver looked up, eyes catching the low light. "You mean when I'm not sneaking down here pretending to be one of you?"

I smirked. "Something like that."

He leaned back, folded his arms, and thought for a moment. "It's orderly. Impeccably clean. Quiet. You don't shout in first class. You request. You don't eat. You dine. Every movement has a purpose, and every smile is rehearsed."

"So not much card playing, then?"

"Only if the stakes are high," he said with a wry twist of his mouth. "And even then, it's about the appearance more than the thrill. A gentleman never sweats, even when he's losing."

I leaned forward. "What about the passengers? Are they as grand as they say?"

Oliver considered that. "Some are kind. Some are cruel. But all of them believe the walls between us mean something." He met my eyes. "Sometimes I think they forget the ocean doesn't care what deck you boarded on."

"Sounds suffocating," I said.

He gave a slight nod. "That's why I came down here. No one notices me. No one expects anything."

"And if they did?"

He smiled again. "Then I'd have to go be someone else for a while."

We sat with that for a moment, and then I looked down at the deck of cards in my hands, the backs worn smooth.

"I don't usually open up and talk to people like this," I said, surprising myself with the admission.

Oliver said nothing, just looked at me, as if he were listening and not waiting to speak.

"I don't know," I added, turning a card in my fingers. "Maybe it's the ship. The sea. Knowing everything's about to change. It makes things feel … clearer, like they matter more. Or maybe less."

He tilted his head slightly. "I feel the same way. Out here," he said, "no one's watching. The stories we tell about ourselves … they're easier to believe."

I met his eyes. "Then let's make up a good one."

He smiled at that, and I began to shuffle again, this time slower, savoring the quiet between us.

So we played on. We were just two strangers on borrowed time, sharing a table in the dim, humming belly of the *Titanic*. The engines thrummed beneath us like a heartbeat, steady and strong. Above us, a black sky stretched out in every direction, endless and unknowable. And somehow, in all that vastness, I felt seen.

I dealt another hand, slower now, more for the rhythm than the competition. The general room was quieting down to a hum, the kind of hush that only came late, when the day's edge had softened, and people began surrendering to sleep.

"So," I said, glancing at Oliver. The silence snuck its way back to us every so often, and I desperately fought to keep it away. "Tell me something else."

He raised an eyebrow. "That's a broad request."

"Something about first class," I clarified. "Something I'd never get to see."

He considered that as he sorted his cards idly. "There's a lounge with a fireplace," he said. "Real marble. Oak-paneled walls. They serve tea with sugar cubes stacked like little pyramids. And there's a reading room that smells like leather and lemon oil."

I gave a low whistle. "Sounds like a palace."

"It's designed to be," he said. "Illusions help people forget they're in a metal box floating in the middle of the ocean."

I chuckled. "What about the pool? I heard there's a swimming pool. Below decks, but heated."

"There is," Oliver confirmed. "Turkish baths too, a place where the wealthy go to sweat out their indulgences. All tiled in white and blue. Feels like something from a Roman bathhouse."

"That's wild," I said, half laughing, half awed. "I can't even imagine what it must be like."

Oliver glanced at me, and for the first time that night, his expression shifted into something close to mischief. "If you're curious," he said, lowering his voice a little, "I could show you tomorrow. During one of my breaks."

I looked up, surprised. "Seriously?"

"I know how to get around without being seen," he said. "There are stairwells the passengers don't use. Service corridors. If we time it right, we won't be noticed."

I raised an eyebrow. "You do this sort of thing often?"

He gave a small, crooked smile. "Not often. But …

sometimes. On special occasions, I suppose." My cheeks burned as he continued, "There are places on this ship where the walls between classes are thin. If you know where to look."

There was something thrilling about the idea. The forbidden edges of a world I'd only heard about in rumors and overheard scraps. First class had always felt like another country, but Oliver wasn't just offering a glimpse. He was offering passage.

"But," he added, tone more measured now, "I'd have to be careful. I can get away with things, but not everything. If I'm caught bringing a third-class passenger into the first-class Turkish baths …"

"You'd lose your job," I finished quietly.

He nodded. "Discipline on board is strict. Especially for the crew."

That grounded the moment. The stakes weren't nothing.

"You don't have to," I said, meaning it. The last thing I wanted was for him to get in trouble because of me.

He looked at me, his green eyes steady. "I wouldn't offer if I didn't want to."

I cleared my throat and glanced down at my cards. "Well then," I said, voice lighter, "guess I'd better win a few more rounds before I bathe like royalty."

Oliver smiled, shaking his head. "You'll need more than a winning streak to pass for one of them."

"I'll practice my posture."

"And your arrogance."

We both laughed, low and tired and genuine. The last of

the other passengers filtered out of the room, leaving just the two of us and the muffled groan of the sea pressing against the hull. Somewhere far above us, people in tuxedos and silk gloves must have also been retiring to staterooms the size of small houses. But down here, in this dim corner of the ship, with worn cards between us and promises passed like secrets, I felt like I'd been given something even better than that.

Oliver glanced down at the small watch chained to his waistcoat. The silver caught the light as he flipped it open. His expression shifted, just slightly. Duty called him back.

"I should get going," he said, rising slowly. "I'm back on shift in a few hours, and if I turn up late, someone will notice."

I stood too, not wanting to stretch the moment but not quite ready to let it go, either. "Right. You probably have to go fold napkins or polish a doorknob until it reflects your soul."

He smirked. "Something like that."

For a moment, we just stood there. Neither of us moved to leave.

"I'd like to see you again," he said finally, his voice quieter now. "If you're free tomorrow."

I nodded, heart skipping in that small, uncertain way it did when something real began to form.

"Yeah. I'd like that."

"My shift starts at seven," he said. "But I get a short break around noon. If you're near the third-class stairwell off D Deck, I can find you."

"I'll be there."

He held my gaze a second longer, then gave a slight, almost reluctant nod and turned to go. His footsteps were soundless as he crossed the room, his coat catching briefly on the back of a chair before he slipped through the door and vanished into the corridor. And just like that, he was gone.

CHAPTER 6

A Steward's Heart

OLIVER

The game had ended an hour ago, but my heart hadn't caught up. I could still see Henry's grin as the Irishman raked in his winnings—three pennies and a button—and how the lamplight had caught on his cheek when he laughed. It was the kind of laugh that made me forget, for a fleeting moment, who I was supposed to be—a steward, a servant, and a man who knew better than to linger too long over anyone, let alone another man.

But Henry made it feel simple.

Now, as I stepped out of the third-class general room, the air seemed different—lighter, even though it smelled faintly of coal and salt. The corridor curved gently with the ship's hull, lanterns swinging slightly with the motion of the sea. My shoes clicked softly against the linoleum floor, echoing in the empty space. The *Titanic* hummed around me as I walked with my hands in my pockets, whistling low, still smiling to myself like a fool.

Every corner I turned carried the warmth of what had

just been—the sight of Henry leaning back in his chair, sleeves rolled up, and the quick gleam in his eye when I teased him over a bad hand. The way Henry's fingers had brushed mine, quick and accidental, yet leaving behind something that pulsed and refused to fade.

I touched his fingertips without thinking, as though the ghost of that touch might still linger as I passed through a narrow stairwell meant for crew use, the metal cool beneath my hand as I climbed. The sounds changed as I rose. Music drifted faintly from above decks, laughter muffled from a parlor somewhere far away, and dishes clanked from the pantry two levels up. The ship never truly slept. It was its own small city, alive even in the middle of the night. I rounded another corner and nearly walked straight into someone.

"Evenin', Oliver," a voice echoed. It was Miller, a senior steward from the à la carte restaurant—round-faced, sharp-eyed, carrying a rag and a metal bucket that smelled faintly of polish. He raised an eyebrow at my grin. "You look far too pleased with yourself for someone on duty after midnight. What are you smiling about?"

"Just finished up below," I said.

Miller's eyes narrowed, amused. "Uh-huh. Well, you might want to fix that collar of yours before Chief Stewart spots you. Looks like you've been wrestling ghosts, or worse."

I straightened, tugging at my collar, feeling the heat rise in my cheeks. "Right you are. I'll be heading in."

"Good lad," Miller said, still grinning as he passed. "Best not to let the ship see you that happy. It'll start askin' questions."

I chuckled under my breath and kept walking. The corridor tightened as I descended back toward the crew quarters, passing a few more stewards—half asleep, half drunk—muttering greetings as they made their way toward bunks or duty posts.

When I reached my cabin door, I paused for a moment before pushing it open. Inside, the room was dim, just the glow of a single bulb casting soft light on the narrow bunks. Two of the other stewards were already asleep, breathing in unison. The space smelled of starch, wool, and the faint, salty damp that never quite left the air at sea.

I moved quietly. I hung my uniform jacket neatly on its peg, smoothed the fabric, and removed my tie. I could still feel the weight of Henry's gaze when he'd said goodnight. It was a memory I thought would linger long after the *Titanic* reached her destination.

I caught my reflection in the small mirror above the washbasin, staring at my flushed face, hair mussed from the long day, and that same irrepressible smile still tugging at my mouth.

"*Fool*," I whispered to myself, though the word carried no shame, only a kind of wonder.

I washed my hands in cold water and then climbed into my bunk. The mattress creaked softly under me. From the other side of the room, someone shifted in their sleep, muttering a name I didn't catch.

I lay there staring at the ceiling, hands folded behind my head. Henry's voice returned to my mind. And so did his smile when it spread slowly, like sunlight breaking through clouds. And his hands, rough and honest, and how they'd felt when they brushed against my own.

It was madness, I knew that. I'd seen men punished for less. They were mocked, sent off the ship, and whispered about, but the thought didn't frighten me the way it should have. Not tonight. I smiled into the dark, wondering if Henry was still awake, somewhere below, lying on his own bunk and thinking the same thing.

The *Titanic* creaked softly, settling into the rhythm of the Atlantic. I let my eyes close, the hum of the engines rocking me gently toward dreams. But even as sleep began to pull at me, my thoughts refused to quiet. I told Henry I'd be off duty by midday tomorrow, and Henry had promised to meet me, too.

Tomorrow, at noon.

CHAPTER 7

The First Morning at Sea

HENRY

I woke before the ship's bells rang, stirred not by sound but by a strange sense of anticipation that pulsed beneath my skin. The bunk above me creaked faintly with the weight of a snoring man. Around the room, the other men were still asleep, breaths slow and heavy in the close, shared air. One stirred in his sleep. Another muttered something in a language I didn't understand. I was already wide awake.

It was my first morning waking aboard the *Titanic*, and despite the thin mattress and the distant and constant hum of the engines, I felt like I'd slept in silk. For the first time in what felt like years, I hadn't woken up with dread in my stomach.

I dressed quickly in the dim light, careful not to disturb the others. The floor was cold under my boots, but I didn't mind. There was something about walking the corridors of a ship this massive that made you feel part of something vast, like being inside a machine built to hold stories.

Madeleine was waiting for me outside her cabin, her hair hastily pinned, her coat already buttoned. She looked bleary-eyed but bright, like someone trying to pretend she hadn't woken up just five minutes earlier.

"I'm not a morning person," she mumbled as we fell in step, "but the thought of hot tea and a roll with real butter is enough to drag me from the grave."

"High praise," I said, grinning.

We were halfway down the corridor when Madeleine stopped short, put a hand on each of our shoulders, and hissed, "Listen to me. Let's sit together. And if anyone asks, we're married."

I blinked. "Married?"

"Yes," she said, already shooing us forward. "We just need to act like we adore each other. That part shouldn't be difficult."

And so, rehearsing our lie with exchanged glances and poorly suppressed smiles, we made our way down to the third-class dining saloon.

The room was already buzzing by the time we arrived. It was a warm, chaotic hive of clattering cutlery, shouted greetings, and children sliding back and forth on the benches as if the place were a playground disguised as a dining room. The air smelled of fried eggs, strong tea, stewed tomatoes, and fresh, still-steaming bread. For a moment, I just stood there and let it all wash over me. The stewards moved between tables, serving plates stacked with porridge and rashers of bacon. We found seats beside a quiet couple and a young boy eating an entire apple like it was the last food he'd ever see.

Madeleine sipped her tea and sighed contentedly. "I could get used to this."

I could, too.

After breakfast, we decided to head topside. The sun had broken through the morning haze, pouring down in clean streaks across the ship's decks. We climbed the stairs to the poop deck, our designated slice of fresh air, and stepped out into a crisp breeze that smelled of salt and iron and somewhere far away. The Atlantic stretched in every direction, blue-gray and endless.

Madeleine tipped her face up toward the light. "This," she said softly, "is the best part."

And I agreed.

We stood at the railing, side by side, letting the wind pull at our coats, and the sun warm our cheeks. The ship glided forward so smoothly that it was hard to believe we were moving at all. Just the soft churn of white water below, the gulls long gone behind us, and a horizon that promised something new. I glanced at the clock tower above the deck—almost noon. Soon, I'd see Oliver again.

The sun had risen higher by the time we settled on a wooden bench near the stern, just out of the wind. The hum of the engines vibrated softly beneath our feet, and the deck around us had begun to stir with passengers, families bundled against the breeze, and children chasing each other with the wild energy only the open sea could inspire.

Madeleine sat beside me, legs tucked beneath her, sipping slowly from a tin cup of weak coffee she'd brought up from the galley. Her dark curls were still escaping their pins, and her cheeks had taken on a pink flush from the cold.

"You're distracted," she said without looking at me.

"I'm enjoying the view," I replied.

"You haven't looked at the ocean in ten minutes," she said, turning toward me with a knowing smile. "You've looked at the clock five times."

I rolled my eyes, trying to hide my grin. "It's only four."

Madeleine smirked. "So. *Noon?*"

I glanced at her, cautious. "What about it?"

"I'm guessing that's what you're waiting for. If it were any later, you'd seem more relaxed. We don't have anything planned then, so I'm guessing it has something to do with your mysterious friend. And I have a strong feeling it won't involve the third-class section this time. I don't think he'd risk being seen here during the day."

I blinked once. "How … did you figure that out?"

She shrugged. "I know you. So that's when you're meeting, correct?" she asked, leaning her elbow on the back of the bench. "So he can sneak you into the forbidden world of champagne and gold-plated bathtubs?"

I laughed. "I don't think they bathe in champagne, Madeleine."

"Of course not," she said. "That's for brushing their teeth."

I shook my head, but the warmth between us made me

smile. "Yes, Oliver's meeting me at twelve. He gets a break from his duties and said he could show me the swimming pool. And the Turkish baths."

Her eyebrows shot up. "The ones with marble floors and hot steam and towels warmed by servants?"

"Probably less glamorous than that," I said, but I couldn't deny the flutter in my chest. "Still … he said he knows the corridors. How to avoid the stewards on duty and the stair-cases no one uses. It's risky, but—"

"But you're going," she finished for me, eyes twinkling.

I nodded slowly. "Yeah. I'm going."

She didn't say anything right away. The breeze picked up a little, tugging at the hem of her coat, and the ship groaned softly beneath us. Then she turned toward me fully, expression more thoughtful now.

"You fancy him, don't you?" she asked.

I hesitated. "I don't even know him."

"That's not a yes."

"It's not a no either."

She studied me. "Well, he did sneak into third class just to play cards and stayed to talk to you."

I gave a dry laugh. "You're not helping."

"I'm just saying … he doesn't seem like someone who does things by accident." Her voice softened. "And neither do you."

I looked out across the sea. The light shimmered against the surface like hammered metal, all motion and mystery. Somewhere below that same horizon, New York waited. And now, so did Oliver.

"I don't know what this is," I admitted. "But I want to find out."

Madeleine nudged me gently with her shoulder. "Then go find out. I'll be here if you get arrested."

"Appreciated."

She smiled, leaned back, and closed her eyes to the sun. "Just promise me one thing."

"What?"

"If they do have champagne bathtubs, steal a bottle."

CHAPTER 8

The Secrets Beneath the Surface

HENRY

By the time the clock neared noon, I was pacing near the third-class stairwell off D Deck, heart pounding a little harder than I'd expected. My palms were damp despite the chill. I had no idea what I was doing, only that I didn't want to miss it.

Then, from the far end of the corridor, Oliver appeared. He moved like a shadow, perfectly at ease in a place most passengers never even noticed. He wore a clean black waistcoat over his crisp shirt, with sleeves rolled neatly to the elbows, and a narrow steward's cap perched just right on his head. If I hadn't known better, I'd have thought he was still on duty.

He gave me a nod. "Ready?"

"As I'll ever be."

He didn't smile, but something flickered in his expression—approval, maybe. Then he turned and gestured for me to follow. We slipped into a narrow crew stairwell, dimly lit and echoing slightly with the thrum of machinery somewhere deep below. Pipes ran along the walls like veins, some hissing quietly.

"You know your way around," I whispered as we climbed.

"I've memorized every inch of this place since I first arrived," he replied softly. "Knowing where not to be seen is half the job."

Every time we heard footsteps, Oliver would motion for me to duck into a side corridor or behind a stack of linen carts. At last, we slipped into a small service pantry, pressed shoulder to shoulder between rows of gleaming silver teapots. I tried not to laugh, breath caught in my throat.

"This is ridiculous," I murmured.

"Would you rather be on deck?" he whispered back.

I shook my head. My breath caught with the sudden awareness of just how close to me he was, before it was time to move again.

We emerged on E Deck, only to descend again via a narrow flight of service stairs. The further we went, the more the air changed, becoming warmer and more humid. And then, suddenly, the corridor opened up.

Oliver led me down a wide, tiled hallway where the walls gleamed white and blue beneath the lamps. Brass fittings lined the walls, polished to a shine. A sign etched in ornate lettering read: First Class Turkish Baths & Swimming Pool.

I stared at it, stunned. "You weren't joking."

Oliver smirked and pushed open a side door. Inside was another world. The first-class swimming pool stretched out before us, long, narrow, and filled with shimmering, green-blue water. Soft steam rose from the surface, catching the light from small glass windows high above. The walls were tiled with elegant Romanesque patterns, and bronze railings framed the pool's edge like something from a cathedral. I stepped closer, awe sinking deep in my chest.

"No one's here," I said.

"They swim early," Oliver replied. "Most of them are at lunch now, or reading in the lounge. This is the quietest it'll be."

We stood there for a moment, silent. I tried to imagine what it must be like to live in that world above, where things like this weren't wonders, but expectations.

Oliver nodded to a hallway on the far side. "Come on. The baths are through there."

I followed him through another doorway, and the air grew hotter. We passed through a steam room, the fog curling around us in thick, fragrant waves, and into a domed space with mosaic tiles that glittered under soft lanterns. A cold plunge pool rested in the center, circular and deep, beside a wall of small changing booths and a bench stacked with clean linen towels.

"This is beautiful," I said, my voice echoing slightly in the heat. "I'm half expecting Cleopatra to step out of one of those rooms."

Oliver chuckled. "I thought the same my first time." I turned to him, still catching my breath.

"Why show me this?"

He met my gaze evenly. "Because most people will

never see it. And because … I wanted to see your face when you did."

I felt my heart stutter, just for a second. The room's heat had nothing to do with it. We stepped into one of the curtained changing booths tucked along the tiled wall. It was barely wide enough for two sets of shoulders, and we didn't speak as we turned our backs to undress, aware of everything that wasn't being said. The curtain swayed behind us, rustling faintly as we changed out of our shirts, boots, and socks. I caught a glimpse of Oliver's bare back in the reflection of a small bronze wall plate polished enough to shimmer. His frame was lean, built from motion and muscle, with pale skin marked here and there by faded lines, scars from trays, and burns from tea kettles.

He folded his uniform neatly, set it aside, and passed me a towel from the stack. "Ready?"

"Just about."

We stepped out into the bathing chamber, both wrapped in linen, bare feet echoing softly on the patterned tile. The Turkish baths weren't just impressive; they were breathtaking. A wide marble platform sat at the center of the room, surrounded by a low mosaic-tiled bench that curved like the edge of a sunken temple. Lanterns hung from domed alcoves above, casting golden light that danced across the steam curling along the ceiling. The walls were covered in geometric tilework, deep indigo and green against cream, and every corner gleamed with brass fixtures or marble spouts dripping warm water into shallow basins. It didn't feel like a ship. It felt like somewhere ancient, stolen from Cairo or

Constantinople, buried beneath the surface of the Atlantic in secret.

Oliver sat at the edge of the hot slab, legs outstretched, towel slung loosely over his waist. I joined him, lowering myself beside him, my skin already flushed from the heat and humidity. For a moment, neither of us spoke. I couldn't quite read his expression, but something in his eyes had shifted.

It was a pause that wasn't just silence, but a space waiting to be crossed. I leaned back, resting on my elbows, letting the warmth sink into my muscles, drawing out the aches I hadn't even noticed.

"How many people know about this?" I asked.

He shook his head. "Not many. You'd be surprised how much of the ship is designed to be unseen. This is for the richest of the rich … and those who come around to maintain it and spread the word amongst us."

"I'm starting to believe that."

We sat in silence again. The hush of steam and dripping water filled the space like music.

"I keep thinking a place like this shouldn't exist," I said quietly. "Not on a ship. It feels like a dream."

Oliver glanced at me, his profile soft in the glow. "That's the point. First-class passengers want to forget they're at sea. They want a palace that floats."

"And do you?" I asked.

He gave a small smile, not quite bitter. "Sometimes. But I work behind the curtain. People like me don't forget where we are."

He looked down at the mosaic beneath our feet, tracing a line of blue tile with his toe.

"I grew up in Whitechapel," he said after a moment. "Two rooms. Four brothers. No baths. No quiet. The idea of something like this might as well have been the moon."

I turned to study him, watching the way the steam curled around his jawline and softened the lines of his throat and shoulders. "And now you have the keys to the moon."

"Only on break, when no one is watching, and I can pretend it's there for me, too," he said, but the corner of his mouth twitched upward. I didn't know what to say. So I looked back at the tiles and the gold band running along the arching walls like sunlight frozen in stone.

"You ever wonder," I said slowly, "what would it be like to stop pretending completely? Just … for a while?"

He didn't answer right away.

Instead, he reached down to the brass fixture beside him, twisted the valve, and scooped up a shallow bowl of warm water. Without a word, he poured it gently over the marble near my feet. The water pooled and shimmered, gliding over the pattern as if to reveal something beneath.

"I wonder about that all the time, actually," he said.

I shifted slightly closer, my thigh brushing his just for a second. He didn't pull away. And we stayed like that. Two men on borrowed time, wrapped in linen, in a hidden palace built for someone else. Letting the heat and the hush strip the world away. Before I could reply, voices echoed in the corridor beyond, drawing closer.

Oliver's expression sharpened. "Time to go."

He took my arm and guided me back to the changing rooms to grab our clothes and then through the doorway. We slipped behind a curtained alcove as the footsteps passed. They belonged to two stewards speaking in hushed, clipped tones about linen delivery and afternoon duties. Oliver waited, absolutely still, his breath steady. I stood beside him, trying to do the same.

The voices drifted down the tiled corridor, fading with each step. Oliver tilted his head, listening until he was sure the danger had passed. Then he turned to me, his voice low and sure.

"They're heading to the service lockers. We've got time."

My heart was still pounding, but I nodded. "You sure?"

He didn't answer. He just smiled.

We slipped back out into the corridor and returned to the pool room like thieves sneaking back to admire stolen treasure. This time, we didn't just stand at the edge; we stepped inside.

The room was hushed, the sound of water lapping gently against the pool's tiled walls like a whisper. Soft light filtered through arched glass panels set high in the walls, diffusing through the steam and casting faint ripples across the polished white tiles. The pool itself stretched forty feet long and twenty feet wide, the water a pale, aquamarine green. It shimmered under the light, clean and almost glowing.

The floor surrounding the pool was lined with ivory and cobalt tiles in intricate geometric patterns, bordered in gold-flecked accents that glinted when the light hit them just right. Sturdy handrails ran down each end of the pool, dipping into the warm water, and a ladder at the far corner disappeared into the depths like a promise.

"They'll be gone for thirty minutes. Maybe more," Oliver said. "If we're quick, no one will miss us."

I stared at the glowing pool, the light from beneath the surface turning the water into something alive. "You're serious?"

He smirked, stepping barefoot across the tile. "I didn't bring you all this way just to look at it."

He plucked a towel from a small linen stack, turned, and held it out to me, an invitation more than a command. A trace of challenge lingered in his expression, but something softer, too. Something that made the heat in the room feel more like anticipation than steam.

There was a beat of hesitation in me, not out of fear, but disbelief. Still, I hung up my clothes and followed him to the pool's edge. The air was warm, thick with steam and the faint scent of chlorine. When I dipped a toe into the water, I was surprised; it wasn't cold at all. It was heated. We looked at each other, grinning like boys up to no good.

"On three?" Oliver asked.

"Three," I agreed.

We dove. The water enveloped me in a rush of warmth and weightlessness. It was the cleanest thing I'd ever felt.

Oliver surfaced beside me, slicking his hair back with one hand.

"This is incredible," I said, treading water, my voice echoing across the tiles.

"I know," he said, eyes bright.

We floated there for a while, the two of us alone in the heart of a ship built for royalty, drifting in a pool we were never supposed to touch. Somewhere, far above, the rich sipped wine and read newspapers under chandeliers. But down here, beneath all their luxury, two strangers shared something better than privilege: a secret.

We floated in silence for a few minutes, our breaths slowing, the water rocking gently around us like a lullaby. The hush in the room felt almost sacred. It was our own stolen sanctuary far below the gilded distractions of the upper decks.

I finally broke the silence. "So … how long have you been with White Star?"

Oliver didn't answer right away. He tilted his head back, eyes closed, hair slicked flat against his scalp. "Almost four years," he said eventually. "Started in the engine crew on the *Arabic.* Barely saw daylight for six months. Then worked my way up, mess steward, then second-class, now here."

"First-class steward," I said, a note of awe in my voice.

He shrugged. "It sounds more glamorous than it is. I make beds. I polish boots. I pretend to know which wines go with which meats and keep a straight face when someone complains their champagne is too cold."

I laughed softly.

"But …" He glanced over at me, expression softening. "It's a step. Every ship and every promotion, it's another inch forward."

"Toward what?"

"A better life," he said, no hesitation this time. "I don't

want to serve forever. I want something that's mine. A shop, maybe. Somewhere no one tells me who I'm allowed to be."

The words hung between us. I wanted to ask more, but I also didn't. I already knew what he meant. I knew the weight of pretending and playing a part because stepping outside it might mean losing everything.

He floated closer, arms stretched wide across the water. "What about you?" he asked.

I hesitated, treading water slowly in place.

"I'm going back to New York," I said finally. "My mother's ill. I got a telegram just over a week ago. My brother said she's taken a bad turn … I'd better come home."

Oliver's face softened. "I'm sorry."

I nodded. "Thanks. I haven't seen her in a few years. Not since I left to find work abroad. I was chasing … I don't know. Something bigger. I thought if I could just learn a trade and earn a proper living, I could send something home. I thought it would mean something."

"Did it?"

"Some of it, yeah," I said. "I sent what I could. I learned a lot. But now …" I trailed off and looked up at the vaulted ceiling. The soft steam curled toward the overhead glass panels. "Now I don't know. I don't know what I'm walking back into. If my brother's even telling the truth. He was always better at guilt than details."

Oliver was quiet, listening the way few people do.

"And I don't know what I'll do once I'm there," I admitted. "I don't have a plan. Just a ticket, a ship, and the words I haven't said to her."

"That's something," he said. "Most people don't even have that."

I gave him a tired smile. "You make it sound noble."

He shook his head. "It's the truth."

The water rippled gently between us, and I let myself float backward until I was staring straight up at the ceiling again. I didn't know why it felt easier to talk here, in the quiet steam of a first-class pool we had no business being in. Maybe it was because no one could hear us. Or maybe it was because he asked.

"Sometimes," I said, "I think if I just disappear into the crowd when we dock, I won't have to face any of it. I could vanish and start over."

Oliver drifted beside me again, his voice low. "And would that make you happy?"

I thought about that for a moment, then shook my head. "No. But it might make things easier."

He didn't argue. He just floated beside me, both of us suspended in that strange warmth between sea and steel and sky, not quite knowing who we'd be when the ship reached land, but knowing, somehow, we weren't alone in the uncertainty.

I turned my head and found him already watching me, his green eyes soft under the golden light filtering through the steam. There was something unspoken in his gaze, something that asked permission and offered it in the same breath. The air between us thickened, charged in a way I couldn't quite name. My pulse beat in my throat, not from nerves, but from how suddenly aware I was of every inch between us, and how much I wanted to close them.

Oliver drifted closer, slow and unhurried. The water barely rippled around him, like it was even holding its breath.

"You're not what I expected, you know," he said quietly.

"Neither are you."

He smiled, small and real. "Is that a good thing?"

"Actually, it's the only thing keeping me sane right now."

He was inches from me now. I could see the droplets on his lashes, the slight flush on his cheek from the heat, and the way his breath hitched when I didn't look away. My heart felt like it was climbing out of my chest. I didn't know what would happen after this, but right now, in this stolen, silent place, all I knew was that I wanted to kiss him.

It was a ridiculous thought I shouldn't even have, but it popped into my mind anyway, refusing to leave. He leaned in. So did I. Our foreheads nearly touched. I could feel the warmth of his skin, the rise and fall of his chest. My eyes fluttered shut.

And then, *click*. The sound of a door latch turning shattered the stillness like a dropped glass.

We broke apart, fast, pushing back through the water, hearts pounding for a different reason now. From the far end of the pool, a first-class passenger, a middle-aged man in a striped robe and slippers squeaking on the tile, entered the room holding a towel and humming to himself.

He didn't see us at first. We stayed low in the water, the steam working in our favor. Oliver gave me a sharp glance and started swimming toward the shallow end with smooth, silent strokes. I followed, blood roaring in my ears.

We climbed out quickly but quietly, grabbed our towels and clothes, and slipped back into our undershirts. Oliver reached for the door, opening it just wide enough for us to slip through. As soon as we were in the hallway, he exhaled sharply, pressing his back to the cool tile wall. His wet hair clung to his forehead, his chest rising and falling beneath his damp shirt. We headed back to get dressed again, lost in silence for what seemed like forever, before I finally broke it.

"That was close," I whispered.

He looked at me, eyes still dark. "Too close."

Neither of us moved.

"I wanted to," I said softly. "Just so you know."

"I know," he replied. "Me too." We stared at each other in the quiet, the corridor empty now, nothing but the drip of water echoing down the steel walls. "But not here," he added, voice lower now. "Not yet."

I nodded. It wasn't fear that held us back; it was the world outside.

He reached for my hand for the briefest moment, fingers brushing mine, and then we were moving again, like two shadows slipping back into the heart of the ship. We didn't say a word as we darted through the corridor, still damp, still breathless, hearts racing like we'd just outrun a storm.

Oliver led the way through a tight utility passage, where the walls were slick with condensation, and the air was thick with heat from the ship's inner workings. I followed, trying not to laugh, but failing miserably. Each time our boots squeaked against the tile, we had to stifle our giggles like two boys sneaking out past curfew.

"That was—"

"Absolutely insane," Oliver finished, grinning.

We turned a corner and burst through a service door that led back into the quieter halls near third class. The lighting was dimmer here, the ship's pulse a little slower, but the giddy buzz between us hadn't settled.

"I thought that man saw us," I whispered.

Oliver laughed under his breath, one hand braced against the wall. "He didn't see a thing. He was too busy adjusting his robe."

I pressed a hand to my chest, trying to slow my heart. "I haven't run that fast since I was caught stealing bread from a bakery window when I was ten."

"Oh, so you're a criminal," he said with a grin, nudging me with his elbow. "Explains everything."

"You're the one dragging third-class passengers into forbidden bathhouses."

He laughed again. It echoed softly in the narrow corridor, but then, as quickly as it had come, the laughter faded. Not all at once; instead, it just … quieted. I saw it shift in his face before he even spoke. He glanced down the hallway behind us, made sure it was empty, then turned to me.

"Listen," he said, voice lower now, still catching his breath. "That was fun. I don't regret doing it the slightest bit." He stepped in closer, his body shielding the space between us like we were in a bubble only the two of us could enter. "I've never done it for anyone before, but I realize now that what we did back there was risky."

My heart momentarily dropped to my stomach. "I know, but—"

"I could've lost everything. My job. My record—"

"I don't want that to happen," I interrupted him, looking at his soaked curls clinging to his forehead, and the intensity in his eyes that stole my breath. "I don't want you to risk anything."

"I've worked too hard to climb this far. Years of polishing brass and swallowing pride just to get a chance in first class. I can't even afford a rumor."

This is it, I thought to myself, *the moment where our chance is snatched away before it was even given.*

"I want to keep seeing you, Henry, but while we're here, as much as I dislike it, it will have to be in secret. In the in-between spaces, when no one's looking."

This was the price of that freedom—this was the cost of what we were choosing. And still, I found myself smiling.

"We'll be careful," I said. "But I'm not sorry."

He held my gaze. "Neither am I."

Then, after a pause, he reached out and gently touched the back of my hand—just for a second.

"Get dry," he murmured. "And don't look so guilty when you walk back in."

"I'll try."

He smirked. "You're terrible at lying."

He started to turn away again, then hesitated. Something in his eyes shifted—still warm, but brighter now, a flicker of daring behind it.

"Actually," he said, stepping back toward me, "before we settle to keep this a secret, I've got one more surprise."

I raised an eyebrow, still catching my breath. "More sneaking around?"

"Of course," he said, grinning. "But this one's better."

"I'm listening."

"I think I can get you and Madeleine into the à la carte restaurant. Tonight."

I blinked. "Tonight? Are you serious? But you just said—"

"I know what I said, but this is one more thing I want you to see. And I'm confident we can get this done," he said. "Second dinner seating starts soon. That's when it's busiest—guests are preoccupied, and stewards are stretched thin. And there's a back corridor that leads to the service entrance. If you're dressed right and don't draw attention, no one will blink."

"And you'll just … waltz us in?"

He shook his head. "Not me. I'll be working the starboard suites by then. But Jules is covering the restaurant shift tonight. He owes me a favor, and he likes showing off. I already asked him. He said he can hold the side entrance for five minutes. Long enough to let you and Madeleine slip in."

My heart kicked up again, same as it had in the pool. "Is this actually going to work?"

Oliver nodded. "I wouldn't have offered it if I wasn't sure. You'll get maybe an hour before someone starts asking questions, but that's enough to see the lighting, the murals, and the chandeliers. It's like walking into another world."

I stared at him, stunned. "Why are you doing this?"

His eyes met mine, steady now, no trace of mischief. "Because I want you to see the things they say aren't meant for people like us. I can do this one more thing for you."

I opened my mouth, but nothing came out.

He took a step back, slipping into the corridor shadows like he had so many times before. "Tell Madeleine. Come near the portside stairwell at half past six. Jules will be waiting. And wear something decent. You're going to dinner in first class."

CHAPTER 9

A Steward's Silence

I left him at the pool without looking back. Not because I didn't want to—but because if I did, I wouldn't have walked away at all. The air changed the moment I stepped out of the tiled warmth and into the service corridor. Steam gave way to cool metal and the low, constant thrum of the ship. The sounds of the pool—the gentle lap of water, the echo of Henry's breath when he laughed—fell away as if someone had shut a door in my chest.

I adjusted my jacket. Smoothed my cuffs. Pulled the mask back on. First-class steward. Invisible. Composed. Useful. That was the role that kept me employed, fed, and unseen. And right now, it was the only thing standing between what I wanted and what the world allowed.

I took the service stairs two at a time, heart still racing in a way no amount of discipline could slow. My skin remembered the heat of the baths, the brush of Henry's thigh, the way he'd looked at me—open, unguarded, like he hadn't learned yet how dangerous that could be. I envied him for it.

By the time I reached A Deck, my breathing had evened out. The corridors here were quiet in that particular first-class way—thick carpet swallowing sound, polished wood catching the light just enough to reassure without inviting attention. A lady's laughter drifted faintly from behind a stateroom door. Somewhere ahead, a steward knocked softly and murmured an apology.

I slipped back into the rhythm of duty. A coat retrieved. A message delivered. A tray removed without comment. Every task felt slightly unreal, as though my body had returned but some essential part of me was still standing barefoot beside a forbidden pool, watching a man who shouldn't exist in my life smile like he already did. It was dangerous to think that way. So I didn't—until I reached the à la carte restaurant.

The doors were open now, the room alive with quiet luxury. Linen gleamed beneath the chandeliers. Crystal caught the light. The low murmur of conversation drifted across the tables like music you didn't have to listen to. And there, near the service station, was Jules. He stood with one hip leaned casually against the sideboard, jacket unbuttoned, posture relaxed in the way only someone very good at his job could afford. His dark curls were neatly combed, his expression alert and amused as he scanned the room. Jules always looked like he knew something you didn't—and enjoyed it.

"Oliver," he said when he saw me, lips curving. "You look flushed."

"Steam rooms will do that," I replied evenly with a wink.

His eyes flicked to mine, sharp and knowing. He didn't

ask where I'd been. Jules was excellent at not asking questions that already had answers.

"Walk with me," he said, turning toward the side corridor that led behind the kitchen doors.

I followed. The noise shifted immediately—china clinking, copper pans hissing, cooks calling orders in rapid French and English. Heat rolled out from the galley, sharp with butter and wine reduction. Jules stopped near a stack of folded linens, far enough from the bustle to speak without being overheard.

"So," he said, arms folding loosely. "Your friends."

I exhaled through my nose. "You can do it?"

He tilted his head. "I can. The question is whether I should."

I met his gaze. "I wouldn't ask if it weren't worth the risk."

Jules studied me for a moment longer than was comfortable. Then he smiled—not teasing this time, but thoughtful.

"You're careful," he said. "That's why this surprises me."

"It shouldn't," I replied quietly. "You know what it's like to live between the lines."

He laughed softly. "Ah. So that's it." He leaned closer, lowering his voice. "Tonight, second seating. The room will be half full. If two extra guests slip in through the service entrance wearing their confidence properly, no one will notice for at least an hour. Maybe longer."

"That's enough," I said.

"For dessert and champagne," he added. "Not for loitering."

"I understand."

Jules's smile sharpened. "Do you?"

I didn't answer immediately. Because understanding meant acknowledging what I was risking. Not just my position, but the fragile order I'd built my life on. It meant admitting that somewhere between duty and desire, I'd already chosen a side.

"Yes," I said at last. "I do."

He nodded once. "Then I'll hold the door. Five minutes, no more. Port side corridor. If they're not there on time, I shut it."

"They'll be there," I said.

"I assumed." He straightened his jacket and clapped me once on the shoulder. "Try not to look like you care too much, Oliver. That's how people get noticed."

I turned to leave, then hesitated. "Jules."

"Yes?"

"Thank you."

His expression softened, just slightly. "Be careful."

I returned to the first-class staterooms. The corridors were hushed, doors stood closed and immaculate, each one guarding a private world I was trained never to enter unless summoned. As I resumed my duties—delivering folded linens, collecting trays left just outside the thresholds, adjusting lamps and straightening gloves laid carefully on bedside tables—I felt the familiar duality settle back into place. Up here, I was precise and unobtrusive. A presence meant to be forgotten the moment I stepped away. Below decks, there was a man with blue eyes who looked at me like I was something worth seeing. Tonight, if everything went exactly right, those two worlds would brush against one another— only briefly—through starched linen, muted footsteps, and time stolen between doors that were never meant to open for men like us. I paused outside a stateroom to smooth my cuffs and caught my reflection in the polished brass of the doorplate. Perfect posture. Neutral expression. And beneath it all, my heart was already counting minutes.

CHAPTER 10

A Taste of First Class

HENRY

I didn't walk. I ran down the third-class corridor, with my boots echoing on the narrow metal floor, dodging stewards, sleepy passengers, and a boy dragging a wooden toy duck by a string. I skidded around the corner, nearly took out a laundry cart, and stopped outside Madeleine's cabin, breathless.

I knocked twice, quickly, then once more for urgency.

"Madeleine!" I hissed through the door. "It's me—open up!"

The door creaked open an inch, and one of her wide brown eyes peered out. "Henry, what—did something happen?"

I grinned, still catching my breath. "We're going to dinner. In first class. Tonight."

The door flew open. She stood there in her stocking feet, her hair half pinned and her blouse half buttoned, blinking at me like I'd grown a second head.

"You're delirious," she said flatly. "Have you had sunstroke?"

"Oliver," I said, barely able to contain myself. "He's sneaking us into the à la carte restaurant."

Madeleine blinked again. "*The* à la carte restaurant?"

"With the gilded chairs and real crystal and the Parisian silverware, yes."

Her mouth fell open slightly, then shut again. "You're not joking."

"Dead serious. We're to meet one of the stewards at half past six by the portside stairwell. We'll go through the service corridor."

A pause. And then she squealed. "We're going to first class?"

"I know!"

She yanked me into the room and slammed the door behind us. "What are we going to wear?"

"I have my dark coat," I said, brushing off my sleeves as if that could make them look newer. "And I think my collar will survive a quick starch. You?"

She was already rifling through the trunk under her bunk, tossing aside sketches and bits of ribbon. "There's a dress. It's not much, but it's clean. Navy blue. I wore it in Paris to that little gallery opening."

"That'll work," I said. "You'll look like you belong there."

She looked up at me, breathless and glowing. "You think so?"

"I *know* so."

We moved fast, spinning around each other in the cramped cabin like dancers in a frantic waltz. She pinned her hair back into something elegant, slipping in one of the small enamel clips her mother had given her. I pressed my shirt with shaking hands, fingers fumbling with buttons that never seemed so small before.

Madeleine emerged in her dress a few minutes later, brushing imaginary dust from the sleeves. It was modest but graceful, with a high waist and delicate embroidery around the collar. She looked at me, brow raised, eyes sparkling. "How do I look?"

"Like trouble," I said, grinning.

She grinned back. "And you look like a boy who just conned his way into Versailles."

I straightened my collar and tried to smooth the creases from my coat. "Let's just hope no one asks for our names on the guest list."

Madeleine grabbed her shawl and looped it around her arms. "We could always say we're nouveau riche and terribly shy."

"Perfect," I said, pushing the door open. "Come on. We've got a staircase to find, and a table in first class with our name on it."

We slipped into the corridor like we'd done it a hundred times before. But tonight, we weren't passengers in third class. We were guests of the impossible.

The corridor hummed with quiet life as we crept along D Deck, our footsteps muffled by worn soles and adrenaline. Madeleine clutched her shawl tight around her arms, her eyes wide with nervous excitement. I kept checking behind us, half expecting a steward to step out and demand to know what two third-class passengers were doing dressed for the Ritz.

The portside stairwell loomed ahead, dark and narrow. Standing beside it, perfectly at ease, was a tall man in a pressed steward's uniform with a head of dark, curling hair and the sharpest cheekbones I'd ever seen. He leaned against the wall, twirling a silver pocket watch between two fingers.

"You must be Henry," he said in a smooth, lightly accented voice. "And this"—he smiled at Madeleine—"must be the lovely friend Oliver warned me about."

"I warned him about you," came a voice from behind.

Oliver emerged from a side corridor, already dressed for duty, but he looked like he'd stepped out of a photograph too perfect to be real. His coat was immaculate, deep black, and pressed so sharply it caught the low light of the corridor with every movement. His shoes gleamed like polished glass, the laces crisp, not a scuff in sight. Every line of his was deliberate. His collar was straight, his shoulders squared, his dark hair neatly parted and tucked just so beneath his steward's cap.

He was handsome in a way that made you look twice, not just because of the uniform, but because of the man inside it. There was something about the line of his jaw, the set of his mouth, and the confidence in how he carried himself that made the air feel heavier when he walked into a room.

And yet, when he saw me, when his eyes met mine, that perfect exterior softened—just slightly, barely a crack in the mask.

"This is Jules," he said. "He's risking a lot, so stay close and don't speak unless spoken to."

Jules winked. "Don't worry. No one ever notices a Frenchman with a tray, especially when the rich are drunk on claret and compliments."

He checked his watch, then glanced toward the hall. "Timing is perfect. Dinner's well underway."

Without another word, he turned and led us into the service corridor behind the à la carte restaurant. The walls were lined with stacked silver trays, folded napkins, wine crates, and polished carts loaded with untouched dessert. Voices rang through the walls, along with delicate laughter, the scrape of silverware, and music as faint as perfume.

Jules stopped at a discreet, half-open side door. "Ready?"

Madeleine grabbed my hand. I squeezed once, then nodded.

He pushed it open, and the world changed. We stepped out of steel and steam and into opulence.

The à la carte restaurant glowed like a dream. The light was warm and gold-toned, filtered through delicate wall sconces and crystal chandeliers that shimmered like glass stars. The ceiling was painted with floral flourishes and soft pastel hues, bordered with fine gilt moldings. Everything gleamed, from the polished mahogany wainscoting to the white linen tablecloths that fell in elegant folds to the floor.

Servers moved like choreography, gliding between tables in pristine uniforms and carrying trays of glistening meats and sauces poured from silver vessels. The tables were small and intimate, each one dressed with crystal stemware, monogrammed flatware, and china so fine you could see the flicker of candlelight through it.

Men in black tailcoats and starched white ties and women in silks and beaded gowns spoke in murmurs, their voices soft with wealth. There was no shouting here and no haste, only the slow indulgence of luxury drawn out like a note of music. There weren't many of them, perhaps a dozen, scattered across the room in pairs or trios, each tucked into a table as if the space had been designed only for them. They sipped from crystal glasses without urgency, pausing between bites to lean in with quiet laughter or the gentle clink of silver. Their jewels caught the light like constellations. Their lives, it seemed, moved at a different tempo, measured not by time, but by taste.

Madeleine inhaled sharply beside me. "I ...," she whispered. "Henry, I've never seen anything like this."

Neither had I. For once, I found myself at a loss for words.

Jules led us along the back wall like ghosts, invisible in the periphery.

We passed a dessert station where a waiter was shaving chocolate curls onto a cream torte. At another table, a sommelier gently uncorked a bottle of champagne with the reverence of a priest preparing for mass.

Madeleine brushed my arm. "Are we dreaming?"

"If we are," I murmured, "don't wake me up."

Jules stopped at a narrow alcove near the windowed end of the restaurant, beside a brass-paneled column. "You can watch from here until I seat you," he whispered.

We stood there, half in shadow, and drank it in. After ten minutes, Jules guided us along the perimeter toward our table, invisible in the background. Or so we thought. When we slid into our seats behind the lacquered column, I felt it. *Eyes*.

At first, I ignored it. We were so close to getting away with it that I didn't want to ruin it with worry. But then Madeleine shifted in her chair, leaned toward me, and whispered without turning her head. "We're being watched."

I glanced up casually and caught it, too.

At a table across the room, a couple, maybe in their late fifties, sat upright, stiff-backed and quiet. The man wore a monocle, of all things, and the woman's beaded gown glimmered under the chandelier light like frost. Her lips pursed the moment our eyes met. No smile. No nod. Just observation.

"They know we don't belong here," I murmured.

Madeleine didn't flinch. She picked up her dessert fork with perfect poise. "Then let's give them a show."

I almost laughed, but she wasn't joking. She sat straighter, lifted her chin, and relaxed her shoulders, like someone who lived this life would do. For a moment, I even believed we belonged here.

I tried to match her grace, smoothing the napkin across my lap. I could feel the weight of that couple's stare like a second coat on my shoulders, but I didn't care.

"Let them look," I whispered. "We've come further than they ever will."

Madeleine smiled then. "For a moment, I thought they were going to summon the captain to have us tossed out."

"If they do, I'll toss my champagne in his face."

She snorted, laughing under her breath. "You wouldn't."

"I absolutely would, even if it's the last thing I do. That bottle probably costs more than my apprenticeship."

A waiter passed again, setting down a small dish of sugared almonds with a bow so subtle it felt like a secret. He didn't look twice at us.

"That's the thing," Madeleine said softly, looking around. "They all pretend not to watch. But they do. They always do."

I watched her observe the people in gowns and gloves who'd never spent a day sanding wood or nursing sore hands after a day in the cold.

"What would you make of this," I asked, "if you painted it?"

She didn't hesitate. "A room full of mirrors. Crystal surfaces and polite shadows. And in the corner, two thieves with hearts too full to fit in their pockets."

I blinked.

She looked at me. "Too much?"

I shook my head. "Just enough."

We sat there for another minute, half in shadow, breathing it all in, the music, the warmth, the quiet weight of stolen belongings. Even the scrutiny from the other diners began to fade, replaced by something calmer. We weren't welcome, but we were present. And for tonight, that was a kind of victory.

"I don't think I ever want to eat downstairs again," Madeleine said dreamily.

"Then let's never go back," I said.

She laughed. "You always did have an appetite for fantasy."

"And you always did know how to dress the part."

Her eyes softened, and for the first time that night, I saw the girl from Montmartre, standing in sawdust and sunlight, dreaming with a pencil in her hand.

"Thank you," she said quietly.

"For what?"

"For bringing me with you."

I started to answer, but that was when I saw Oliver. He caught a glimpse of me, too. We exchanged a smile that lasted barely for a second before he was back to his duty, and my attention turned back to Madeleine.

Jules approached us then, offering a polite smile he would give to any other guest. He paused behind my chair. "One hour," he murmured, eyes flicking between us. "If anyone asks, you're guests of Mr. Lafitte. Say it with confidence, and no one will question it."

Madeleine and I looked at each other with a slight nod. That was a good plan, indeed. The tablecloth was soft as silk beneath my fingers, and the napkins pressed into perfect folds. A small silver vase in the center held two ivory roses and a sprig of lavender, the scent just strong enough to notice. Light from the chandelier above us cast soft ripples across the crystal glasses like water under moonlight.

Like a miracle, a waiter passed by and, without so much as blinking, placed two crystal flutes before us, filled with champagne. Behind him, another steward approached with a silver platter bearing two delicate dessert plates.

The plates were set down before us. On mine was a slice of gâteau aux fraises, layered sponge and cream, topped with ripe strawberries so perfect they looked painted. Madeleine's was something darker and richer: a square of chocolate mousse with curls of candied orange rind resting like ribbon on top.

We stared at our plates.

"I feel like I should apologize to the bread we had this morning," Madeleine whispered.

"I think the bread would understand," I said, lifting my fork. "And encourage us to go for it, even."

We ate slowly, as if each bite were a secret and the flavors might vanish if we didn't savor them fully. The champagne tickled the back of my throat and sent a warmth through my chest that had nothing to do with the alcohol.

Madeleine closed her eyes on a bite of mousse and let out the quietest sigh. "This is what the other side of the world tastes like."

I smiled. "And for a little while, it's ours."

For a moment, everything faded—the boundaries between decks, the weight of class, and the fear of being caught. Here, in this small pocket of gold and linen, we were no longer passengers stashed in the ship's belly.

The hush of the restaurant carried on around us, murmurs in French and English, the clink of silver, and the soft uncorking of another bottle nearby. But no one noticed us. Or maybe they saw what we wanted them to see: a pair of late-seated guests, perfectly composed, dressed just well enough to pass.

We raised our glasses.

"To Oliver," Madeleine said softly.

I smiled, raising mine. "To all the doors he opens."

The champagne was half gone. The dessert plates, barely touched, sat like fragile artwork between us. Madeleine rested her chin in her hand, watching the room with a dreamy smile, her eyes drifting across the chandeliers, the gowns, and the servers moving like dancers.

"This," she said, "is the part I'll remember forever."

I nodded, but my eyes weren't on the room anymore. They were on him.

Across the restaurant, just beyond the polished mahogany archway that framed the service entrance, Oliver emerged through the golden haze in his crisp steward's coat. Then his eyes found mine once more, and for just a flicker of a second, the formality slipped again. His gaze softened, the corners of his mouth lifting into a smile that I had grown to adore. It was quick, gone almost as soon as it appeared, but it settled in my chest like an ember. And everything in the room felt different after that.

I sat up a little straighter. He was coming toward us.

Madeleine noticed too. "Is that—?"

Before she could finish, a man stepped in front of Oliver. It wasn't another steward, but an officer. He wore the navy uniform of *Titanic's* command crew, with brass buttons and white gloves. His face was unreadable, and when he leaned in, he didn't raise his voice. Instead, he whispered into Oliver's ear. The color drained slightly from Oliver's face.

He blinked, startled, then nodded once.

The officer placed a hand firmly on Oliver's shoulder and turned away. Oliver stood still for a breath, eyes flicking toward our table again, as if he wanted to say something, but he didn't. He turned and followed the officer out of the restaurant. Just like that, he was gone.

Madeleine lowered her glass. "What was that?"

"I don't know," I said. My voice sounded too calm, even to my own ears.

We stared at the archway, waiting for him to return. A minute passed. Then two.

The restaurant's golden glow felt dimmer now. The chandeliers still sparkled, but the magic had cracked like a porcelain dish with a hairline fracture you couldn't ignore.

Then Jules appeared at our side, all charming smile and cool confidence, though his eyes flicked toward the empty service archway.

"It's time to go," he said softly.

Madeleine stood, adjusting her shawl. "Are we in trouble?"

"No," Jules said, giving her a quick shake of his head. Then he glanced at me, voice dropping even lower. "Oliver asked me to tell you he'll meet you in the crew passage. Just past the pantry corridor. He said you'd know the one."

I blinked. "He did?"

Jules gave me a pointed look. "Don't be long. And walk like you're meant to be there."

We followed him out the side corridor, slipping past trays of silverware, down tiled halls, and into the soft hum of steel and steam and hidden things.

When we reached the stairwell that would take us back to third class, I touched Madeleine's arm.

"Go ahead," I said quietly. "I'll meet you in a bit."

She didn't ask or tease me this time. Instead, she gave me a knowing look and nodded once before disappearing down the stairs. I waited in the shadow of the junction, heart in my throat.

The corridor was dim, lit by a single gas lamp flickering weakly above a narrow crew way lined with stacked linen carts and silent doors. Footsteps echoed down the passage. And then, there he was. Oliver moved toward me through the half-light like he'd stepped out of the quiet heart of the ship itself.

"Hey," I said.

Oliver glanced over his shoulder to make sure we were alone. Then he faced me fully, jaw tight, voice low. "Sorry, I disappeared. The officer has been watching me since yesterday. I didn't want to make things worse."

"I get it," I said. "It just … felt sudden."

"It was." He looked away, then back again. "I didn't know he'd pull me aside. Something about a linen rotation that didn't match the log. He's suspicious of everyone lately."

"But everything is well?" I eyed him softly. "And you're safe?"

"Yeah … I think so," Oliver murmured, tension still visible in his shoulders.

"Can I see you later? If you can come to the third class—"

Oliver exhaled through his nose, the faintest shake of his head. "It's going to be a full night. I'm covering two cabins and then the Palm Court. I might not get another break."

I blinked. "Oh."

"If I can get away, I will," he added quickly. "I'll find you."

"But you don't know if you'll be able to."

"No," he said. "I don't."

I nodded, swallowing down the sting before it could rise in my throat. This hardly made any sense. I barely knew the man, but something had already sprouted from my heart—affection, unlike any other I had ever experienced before. "Right. Of course."

Oliver stepped forward. "This is the job. This ship. Everything we are … we're already pushing our luck."

"I know," I said, maybe too fast. "I'm not asking for anything. I just …" I trailed off for a moment. "I enjoy spending time with you. I know we've just met, and I shouldn't care this much, but … I do."

Oliver's jaw tightened. "I care too. I promise you, if I can come, I will. And if I can't, then I'll make it up to you," he said. "Somehow."

I gave him a small, tight smile. "I should go."

He didn't stop me. So I turned, one foot in front of the other, every step back to third class heavier than the last.

CHAPTER 11

After the Magic Breaks

HENRY

Madeleine was waiting for me just past the bend in the corridor, leaning casually against the wall, arms crossed and one eyebrow arched in that way she had when she knew something and was waiting for me to say it first.

"There you are," she said as I approached. "I was starting to think you'd gotten yourself in trouble."

I gave her a tired smile, the weight of the evening still lingering in my chest. "Not quite."

She studied me for a moment, then looped her arm through mine without asking. "Well, did he say anything?"

"Yeah," I murmured. "Just not what I hoped."

She didn't press. She never did when it mattered.

We walked the quiet third-class corridor side by side, her hand resting lightly on my arm. She looked content, and for that, I was eternally grateful to Oliver. We were still wrapped in the shimmer of first class, even as we descended back into the steel bones of the ship that belonged to us.

Neither of us spoke. The night was already becoming a memory, soft and shining and bittersweet around the edges.

And we carried it with us, both the glow and the ache.

"I'm going to lie down," she said as we reached her cabin door. "My feet still think they're walking on velvet."

I managed a small smile. "You looked like you belonged there. Perhaps, someday, you will."

"Nonsense." She glanced at me with a small smile. "So did you, by the way."

But the compliment didn't land as it should have. Other thoughts roamed inside my mind, all revolving around Oliver.

Madeleine lingered. "You alright?"

"Just need some air," I said. "I'll go up on deck for a bit, and then head to bed."

She nodded, kissed my cheek, and slipped inside her room. I turned and walked toward the aft stairs, boots quiet on the steel floor.

The deck was nearly deserted at this hour, wrapped in moonlight, fog, and the soft hush of the Atlantic surrounding everything. A single lantern burned near the rail, casting a golden halo on the boards. The stars above were crisp and endless, brighter than anything I'd seen in years.

I leaned against the railing, hands gripping the cold iron, eyes on the long trail of wake behind the ship—white foam fading into black sea. Silence was paranoia's best friend, it seemed, because more thoughts snuck into my mind. What had the officer said to Oliver? Was it really about linens? And what could have possibly made him look so shaken?

The wind tugged at my collar, and the cold settled into my sleeves. I didn't move. I didn't want to. Something in me hoped he might come looking. A few hours had passed. And then I heard the door open behind me. I didn't turn around until a figure stopped beside me.

"Hey," Oliver said, voice low, rougher than usual. "You're out late."

"So are you."

He didn't answer right away. I glanced over. He looked tired. His hair was still neatly combed, but there were shadows under his eyes and that same tightness in his jaw I'd seen just before he disappeared.

"I wanted to find you," he said. A silence settled between us. Not tense, but heavy with everything left unsaid since the restaurant. Then he took a breath and said, "I'm sorry. About tonight. I wanted you to have fun, but I know I must have stressed you out with the whole officer thing."

I looked at him fully now. "Are you going to tell me what really happened?" I arched my brow. "Because I have a feeling that it wasn't just about linens."

"It wasn't. A passenger reported me," he said, jaw tightening. "For being in the first-class pool. With company." My stomach turned. "They didn't see us clearly," he added. "And they didn't get names. Just reported that a steward was 'fraternizing inappropriately' and 'behaving in a way not befitting his position.'" He gave a bitter little smile. "Which means I was seen, and that's enough."

"What will they do?"

He exhaled slowly, watching the stars. "Nothing yet. But I was questioned and warned. Told to 'be mindful of my boundaries' and 'remember my station.' I said I was assisting a guest and that it was a misunderstanding. For now, they're buying it."

I looked back at the sea, trying to quiet the storm in my chest. We stood there for a while, letting the waves speak for us.

"I hate that just being near me can put everything you've worked for in jeopardy," I said.

He turned to me. "I knew the risk. I still know it."

"And it doesn't scare you?"

He was quiet for a moment. "It does. But not enough to stop."

The cold wind cut between us, but I felt warmer with him standing there. Like maybe the danger wasn't in being close—it was in pretending it didn't matter.

"I don't want you to get hurt because of me," I said.

He looked at me, eyes steady. "Then let's not give them a reason. What happens in private stays there. They don't have to know about it."

The ship groaned softly beneath us, deep and low like a sleeping animal, and the sea stretched dark and endless in every direction. Oliver stood beside me, close enough that I could feel the warmth of him, even in the wind.

Neither of us spoke for a long time. The silence wasn't uncomfortable; it had weight, like something just beneath the surface, waiting. Then Oliver exhaled, slow and steady, like a man reaching the end of something he couldn't carry anymore.

"I didn't expect this," he said.

I turned slightly toward him. "What do you mean?"

"You," he said, eyes still fixed on the water. "Us. Any of it. I came on this ship thinking I'd keep my head down and do my job. I didn't think there'd be … this. Especially not so soon. So suddenly. So all-consumingly." The way he said this made my chest tighten. "I've met all kinds of people on these ships. Some kind. Some cruel. Some who forget your name the moment they hand you a coat. But you …" He looked at me now. "You saw me. Not the uniform, or the tray in my hand. *Me*. And that's not something I'm used to."

I swallowed, unsure what to say. The wind picked up, tugging at our sleeves, the cold biting our fingers. But we still didn't move.

He rubbed his palms together and glanced at the stars. "I have to get back to my shift. The night steward's already covering for me longer than he should." Oliver took a step away before stopping again. His breath misted in the cold air, disappearing almost as quickly as he spoke. I looked up. He was in front of me, closer than he'd dared to stand all night. His hand brushed mine before settling against my wrist.

"I shouldn't," he murmured.

"I know," I whispered back.

"But I want to."

My heart thudded once, like the ship itself had struck something deep beneath the surface. "And so do I."

I didn't move. I didn't breathe. I let him close the last inch between us.

He kissed me.

Not cautiously, not fleetingly, but with all the pent-up fear and longing and relief he'd been carrying since the first moment we'd seen each other. His lips were warm despite the cold. His hand rose from my wrist to the side of my neck, fingers curling as if anchoring himself to me before the world could take it away.

The Atlantic wind howled around us, the ship groaning and creaking beneath our feet, but all I felt was him. His breath. His warmth. His choice.

When he finally broke the kiss, he lingered there—forehead against mine, breathing as though he'd run the length of the promenade.

"I have to go," he said, voice rough, barely a whisper. "They'll notice if I'm gone any longer. But I just wanted to find you and tell you everything I've been thinking about since I met you."

I nodded, though I didn't let go of him right away. Neither did he.

His fingers brushed mine, and still it sent that same bright, aching jolt through me. "Tonight. At two. Meet me in the third-class general room. I should be done by then."

The words were soft, but there was nothing uncertain about them. His eyes held mine—steady and sure, lit with something that felt dangerously close to hope.

I swallowed, breath catching in my throat. "I'll be there."

He pulled back slowly, as if leaving took effort and space

between us resisted being opened again. At the doorway, he looked over his shoulder, but that single glance felt like a hand closing around my heart. Then he disappeared down the stairs, swallowed by the dim corridor and the low, steady heartbeat of the ship. I stayed at the rail long after he'd gone, the Atlantic wind biting through my coat, my pulse still shaped by the warmth of his kiss.

Tonight. *Two o'clock*.

CHAPTER 12

Midnight Promises

OLIVER

I stood waiting just outside the general room, leaning against the wall with my arms crossed, the light flickering across the sharp edge of my cheekbone. I'd been listening for every footstep between decks.

I had no idea what had come over me. For years, I'd been driven by the need to build a better life for myself. This was one way to do that, and I'd already come a long way. Still, for reasons I couldn't explain, I couldn't stop myself.

Henry was unlike anyone I'd ever met. He reached me in ways I hadn't thought possible. I believed affection and love—or anything close to it—were out of reach while I was here … but that was before he came into my life.

At last, there he was, with that boyish smile and dreamy eyes that made my breath hitch.

"You came," I said, voice low.

"Of course."

I reached for his hand. "Come on. We don't have much time."

We moved quickly, quietly. I led the way through another crew passage. With each step, I was aware of how dangerous this was—for me *and* my job. Still, the urge to show him everything this world had to offer was stronger than reason.

We passed the narrow stairs and brass pipes lining the walls, bare bulbs casting weak yellow light. The ship was a maze, but I'd learned my way around it.

"Most passengers are asleep," I whispered over my shoulder. "First class is dead silent this time of night. Stewards are off-duty. Officers rotate shifts. It's the perfect window."

"And if we get caught?" Henry whispered back. "I don't want you to risk—"

"We won't," I promised. We passed through one last service door, and suddenly, the air changed. It smelled like polished oak and lemon oil. I turned, reached for another set of doors, and pushed them open with care.

And there it was. *The Grand Staircase.*

We stepped into a world of carved wood and golden light. Even in the dim glow from the high overhead dome, the staircase shimmered. Ornate wrought iron railings curled like vines, their edges gilded. The dark oak gleamed under layers of polish, smooth and flawless. Each balustrade was carved in perfect symmetry. The steps themselves were wide and sweeping, tapering outward as they descended in a graceful arc. The ceiling soared overhead, crowned by a glass dome that allowed just the faintest trace of starlight to bleed through.

At the base of the staircase stood the clock flanked by

two carved cherubs. Above it, golden script read: *Honor and Glory Crowning Time.*

I looked back at Henry, who looked as if he had suffered a heart attack. "You alright?"

"I …" Henry swallowed. "I've seen sketches and read about it. But this …"

"I know," I said. "It does that to people."

The silence in the space was unlike any I'd known. It wasn't empty; it was reverent, like the whole ship had stopped just for us. No footsteps. No orders barked down the hall—just the hush of midnight wealth, and two shadows who didn't belong.

"How many people actually get to see this like this?" Henry asked.

I shrugged. "Maybe a handful. Stewards who clean it in the early morning. A few officers who like to walk it during rounds. No passengers. Never like this."

"And now me."

I nodded. "And now you."

Henry turned slowly in place, taking it all in. His face was unguarded, mouth slightly parted, breath shallow with wonder. His eyes reflected the light from the chandelier overhead, like he was holding a piece of the room inside him. And his expression … God, his expression. It was the kind of reverence you couldn't fake. The kind of awe that made a thing sacred just by being seen.

His coat was worn. His boots scuffed. And yet, at that moment, he looked more beautiful than any of the gowns or tuxedos I'd seen pass through this staircase. More breathtaking than any glittering heiress or finely dressed gentleman who'd ever glided down those steps.

And he didn't even know it.

He didn't know how handsome he looked standing there, with his shoulders slightly turned, his profile catching the lantern glow. There was something in the way he tilted his head up to take in the clock—something that made me want to reach for him, not out of want, but out of need.

I didn't, though. Instead, I let myself memorize him— the line of his jaw, the quiet strength in how he held himself, and the softness around his eyes when he forgot I was watching.

I'd brought him here thinking I was giving him a glimpse behind the curtain. But standing there, he was the most extraordinary thing in the room, and I wasn't sure how long I could keep pretending otherwise.

We stood there for what felt like forever, side by side, not speaking. There were no champagne flutes, no music, and no chandeliers blazing. Just wood and brass and stars above us, and a ship built to make gods out of men.

"I wanted you to see it," I said finally. "Not the noise of first class. Not the dining rooms or the salons. This. The heart of the ship. I figured you'd like it." I looked at him, the light from the dome catching the edge of his smile.

"Thank you," he whispered.

I glanced at his watch. "We have some time. Let's make it count."

We walked the landing slowly, as if each step would

echo through time. The silence in the Grand Staircase was cathedral-like. Every polished surface caught the faintest trace of moonlight spilling through the stained glass dome above us.

Henry moved to the center of the landing, just below the clock. The cherubs above it watched, frozen in their carved grace, holding the weight of history between them. He looked up at the words, then turned slowly to me. "You'd think they carved it just to mock people like us."

I shook my head. "There's nothing to mock. In fact, I think they'd envy us and how we feel." Henry parted his lips, as if he wanted to say something, but no words left them as I stepped toward him. "You've undone me from the moment I saw you."

Henry swallowed slightly. "Then we're both undone."

I reached for his hand—slowly, giving him time to pull away, but he didn't. His fingers laced with mine as we stood there, beneath the great clock that crowned the staircase. And there, in the quiet heart of the *Titanic*, I kissed him once more.

I didn't pull away right away. I rested my forehead against his and let my breath catch up with my body. My hands hovered at his sides, not quite touching, as if I were reminding myself that this—him—was real, and not something the ship had invented to test me.

"This is reckless," I said quietly.

Henry didn't move. "Yes." The simplicity of it made my chest tighten.

"If anyone sees us here—if someone so much as pauses

and looks too closely—everything unravels. My position, my references, every ship that would ever take me again." I let out a shaky breath, half laugh, half warning. "I don't get dismissed. I disappear. And the terrifying part is ... knowing that, and still standing here with you."

Henry lifted his head just enough to look at me. His eyes were steady. Not naive. Not careless. "And if we don't do this," he said, "what do you lose?"

I swallowed. I had an answer. That frightened me more than the risk. "I lose the part of myself that noticed you," I admitted. "The part that didn't look away."

He reached for my sleeve then, fingers brushing the cuff of my coat. The touch was light, almost cautious, like he was offering me the chance to step back. I didn't.

"I've spent years learning how to be unremarkable," I said. "How to stand where I'm told. How to want only what doesn't leave marks." I let out a breath that felt like it had been waiting. "And you walk into a room like you don't know how to make yourself smaller."

Henry smiled faintly. "I learned that from people who tried."

That—that—was the moment it stopped being just attraction. I stepped closer, close enough that the edge of the clock shadow cut across both of us. "If this becomes something," I said carefully, "it won't be easy. There are rules. Eyes. Consequences."

"I know," he said. "You might have to pretend you don't know me in public."

"I already pretend worse things." I laughed softly despite

myself, then sobered. "And if I tell you to stop—if I need to stop—"

Henry didn't hesitate. "Then we stop."

No bargaining. No persuasion. Consent, spoken plainly. I nodded once, letting that settle into my bones.

"Then stay," I said. "Just for now."

He did. We didn't kiss again immediately. Instead, we stood there in the heart of the ship—two men beneath a grand clock meant to measure time—and let the moment exist without rushing it into something it wasn't ready to become. That restraint was its own intimacy. When I finally leaned in again, it wasn't hunger that drove me. It was choice. It was a truth spoken without words, tender and deliberate. His lips were soft, and the press of his body against mine was as gentle as it was certain. I closed my eyes.

For once, I wasn't afraid of being seen. For once, the world outside the moment didn't exist. Not the fear. Not the consequences. Not the weight of everything that waited at port.

Just him. Just us.

I pulled back slowly, our foreheads brushing, breath mingling.

"It feels like the first time all over again," I murmured. I wanted to do it again and again. And I did. Without a word, I leaned in again. This time, the kiss was different, filled with more hunger, like I needed him more than I needed air. A small, muffled moan escaped his lips and blended into the kiss, and, at that moment, I knew I did need more of him. He did, too. I could see it in his eyes.

"Come with me," I murmured, barely audible. His breath brushed my lips as he nodded. I had no time to think clearly—all I knew was that I wanted to be alone with him, somewhere secluded and private, where I could touch him like I wanted to.

We moved through the narrow passageways until we reached a quiet corner of one of the reading rooms, where beautiful paintings lined the walls, and statues stood scattered in soft shadows. I paid them no mind, though. Every bit of my attention was on him. This was far less romantic than where I wanted us to be, but also the only thing I could think of right now.

The moment the door closed behind us, my hand slipped to his waist, fingers brushing the edge of his shirt, hesitating there for only a heartbeat before moving lower. Henry's breath hitched as my knuckles grazed the waistband of his trousers, and then, slowly, carefully, I began to undo the first button.

Without a word, I turned him gently, guiding me to the polished wall. My heart thundered. My hand rested at the small of his back, grounding him.

I leaned in, lips brushing the shell of his ear. "Tell me to stop, and I will."

He didn't. Instead, he reached back for me, finding my hand with his and holding it tight. My other hand slid around his waist, slow and certain. Then lower.

I undid the buttons at his waistband one by one, each movement deliberate, like I was unwrapping something I'd ached for, not just something I wanted. My fingers brushed his skin, and my breath hitched, catching in my throat. Henry closed his eyes, while a slow heat bloomed beneath my ribs, low and insistent.

All I could feel was him. My chest pressed against his back, solid and sure. My breath was at his neck, warm and uneven. And God—it felt good. Not just the touch, but the knowing, that he wanted me, here, like this. That we'd stolen this moment out from under the weight of the world and made it ours. The ship groaned softly around us like it was reminding us of how close we always were to being caught.

My lips crashed into his, soft yet insistent, his hair falling into his eyes as he pressed closer. I closed my eyes, savoring the warmth of his mouth, the sweetness of his breath, and the closeness in this moment. My hands slid down his bare chest, gentle but purposeful, tracing the contours of his body. I wanted to memorize every inch.

Henry shivered, his fingers tangling in my hair, pulling me closer, needing more. Our kiss deepened, his tongue brushing against mine, slow and tender, as if we had all the time in the world.

My hands moved lower, resting on the waistband of his trousers, and he mirrored my touch, his fingers brushing the band of my pants. We were both trembling, nervous and eager, as we unbuttoned and unzipped our clothes, our breaths mingling in the air between us.

My cock sprang free first, thick and flushed, the head already glistening with arousal. Henry swallowed hard. "You're beautiful," was all he whispered, reaching out to stroke me gently, his thumb brushing my sensitive tip.

I gasped, my head falling back, hair cascading over my shoulders. Henry grinned, and then it was his turn as we freed him from the confines of his trousers. My eyes widened, my lips parting in a silent moan as I took him in.

"God, Henry," I breathed, my hand wrapping around him. He groaned, his head tipping back as I stroked him slowly. We were both hard, both needy, but we were taking our time, savoring every moment, every touch, and every gasp.

Henry guided my hand, showing me the rhythm he liked, and I nodded, my movements becoming more confident, more sure. He did the same for me, his fingers sliding up and down my length, his thumb pressing into the vein that throbbed along my shaft.

I leaned in, my lips brushing his ear, my breath hot against his skin. "I want to taste you," I murmured, and he shuddered, his hands tightening on my hips. I dropped to my knees, my hair falling around my face, and he watched as I took him into my mouth.

My lips wrapped around him, warm and wet, my tongue swirling around the sensitive crown. Henry groaned, his hands tangling in my hair, holding me close but not too tight. I hummed, and, in turn, he thrust gently, just a little, testing the waters. I moaned around him, my hands gripping his thighs, encouraging him to go deeper. He did, just a fraction more, and I took him again, my mouth stretching around him, my throat closing in.

"Oliver," he gasped, his hips bucking involuntarily, and I pulled back, my eyes meeting his, full of desire and devotion.

"More," he pleaded, and I nodded, taking him in again, my pace slow and deliberate. My tongue flicked at the sensitive spot just under the head, and Henry cried out, his fingers digging into my scalp. I was gentle but thorough, my mouth working him with a rhythm that had him teetering on the edge of release, I could tell.

He pulled me off with a whimper, his breath coming in ragged gasps. "Not yet," he managed, and I smiled, a wicked glint in my eye. "Your turn," he added, and I chuckled. He knelt before me, his hands resting on my hips, and I mirrored his earlier actions, guiding him to me. He licked his lips, his mouth watering, and I shivered, my hands threading through his hair.

Time passed, and I was lost in utter bliss, as was he. We took turns, each of us exploring the other with our mouths, our hands, and our bodies as we ended up on the sofa in one of the corners. We were both moaning, both trembling, both on the edge, but we were holding back, savoring the buildup and the anticipation. Both of us just wanted this moment to last forever.

Finally, Henry pulled away, his lips swollen, body throbbing with need. We stood, our bodies flush against each other, pressing together, hot and heavy. He reached for me, my hands gripping his hips, and he did the same, our fingers intertwining as we pressed closer.

"I want you," I whispered, my lips brushing his, and he nodded, his eyes dark with desire.

"I want you too." As simple as that.

CHAPTER 13

Young and In Love

HENRY

"Henry," Oliver panted, "I need more."

I did, too. I needed so much more. I nodded, and he reached for the oil lamp nearby. He poured a small amount onto his palm, the oil glistening in the soft light. I shivered with anticipation coiling in my gut. He coated his fingers, and then he reached between us, pressing against me.

Spread out on one of the sofas, I gasped, gripping his shoulders, my body tensing as he pushed inside. He was gentle, slow, and careful as he stretched me open with his fingers. I whimpered, and he kissed me, his lips soft and soothing against mine.

"Relax," he murmured, his voice a low rumble against my lips, and I tried, my body loosening as he worked me open. He added another finger, then another, his touch sending sparks of pleasure through me. I moaned, my hips rocking into his hand, as I throbbed with need.

"Oh, God," I gasped, "please." A moment later, he

positioned himself at my opening, and I nodded, my breath coming in short, sharp gasps. Oliver pushed in, slow and steady, and the sensation of him filling me was all-consuming. I cried out, my hands digging into his shoulders. My body stretched to accommodate him, wanting to take every single inch. He was bigger than I expected, but we were taking our time, savoring every moment and every sensation.

His hips pressed against mine, and he was buried deep inside me. We stayed like that for a moment, our breaths mingling, our hearts pounding in our chests. Then he pulled back, slow and steady, and I whimpered, my body aching for more.

We quickly found a rhythm, his hips snapping into mine, pounding into me with a steady, relentless pace. His hands roamed over me. His touch was confident now as his fingers traced the lines of my muscles and the curves of my body.

I wrapped my legs around his waist, my heels digging into his back. He groaned as his thrusts became more urgent. I was tight around him, my walls clenching with every movement.

"Oliver," I gasped, my voice hoarse with need, "I'm close. Oh, God, I'm so close …"

He reached between us, his fingers wrapping around me, stroking me in time with his thrusts. I cried out, and he quickened his pace. His movements were frantic now, pounding into me with abandon.

"Come for me," he groaned, his voice rough with desire.

I didn't need to be told twice. My body was already on the edge, and my orgasm crashed over me like a wave. I cried out as I pulsed in his hand, my release spilling over his fingers. He followed soon after, his hips snapping into mine, him twitching inside me as he found his own release.

We stayed like that for a moment. His lips were all over me, wherever they could reach, and his hands caressed my body before he finally gathered the strength to pull out. He slipped free with a soft sigh, and I whimpered, my body aching with the loss. He caught me as I slid down the sofa, my legs like jelly, and he smiled. It was a soft, loving curve of his lips that sent warmth spreading through my chest.

"That was—," I started, but he cut me off with a kiss, his lips soft and tender against mine.

"I know," he murmured. "I loved every second of it."

His eyes held mine, and for a moment, my stomach flipped. Love was something I'd always thought out of the question—at least for now. When I left, my focus had been on work. Now that I'd returned, it would be on my mother. Yet, amid it all, perhaps there was room for love, too.

I wasn't sure how it would work … only that I wanted to find a way to make it happen.

"Thank you for bringing me here. It means more than you know. Without you, none of this would be possible, and I just—"

He leaned in, silencing my words with his lips once more. The kiss was demanding in a way that stole my breath and made me feel alive all at once. I loved every second of it, finding myself surrendering without a second thought.

"You deserve all of it … and more." Oliver stepped back just enough to look at me, not with hesitation, but with something soft and unguarded. His eyes met mine as he straightened the collar of his shirt, his fingers moving slowly, like he didn't want to rush the moment back into reality.

I buttoned my trousers, stealing a glance at him as I did.

He caught it, smirked, and then reached out, tugging me gently toward him by the edge of my coat.

"You're trouble," he whispered.

"You started it," I murmured back, and kissed him again.

It was slower this time, and deeper. Not frantic, not hurried—just us, mouths meeting in the quiet aftermath, the kind of kiss that lingered even after it ended. We didn't have to speak. The warmth between us said everything.

Then, a door creaked open somewhere down the corridor. A faint voice followed, along with the low thud of footsteps.

Oliver pulled back, eyes wide.

We froze.

For a second, we just stared at each other—then, without a word, we bolted. We ran out of the reading room and for the nearest crew door, ducking through the shadows of the staircase. Our shoulders knocked together, boots echoing off the marble, our muffled laughter chasing us into the dark.

We didn't stop until we were halfway down the service passage, lungs burning, faces aching from smiling too hard. He reached for my hand, and I gave it to him, without hesitation or fear. And for once, we weren't running away.

We were running together.

CHAPTER 14

The Heart of
the Ship

HENRY

The hush of the hour wrapped around us. There were no footsteps and no voices, only the occasional low hum of distant machinery and the whisper of our breath.

Oliver walked ahead of me, his steps soft and precise. We passed through another velvet-curtained archway, and the corridor opened up into a wide, gently curving hallway lit by wall sconces that glowed like captured candlelight. The floor beneath us was thick with carpet, deep green with a gold woven border, soft enough to muffle every step. The walls were paneled in dark walnut, polished so finely they reflected our movements in faint, ghostlike shapes.

I'd never seen a hallway so wide and so still.

Each door we passed was numbered in gold, inset with dark wood plaques and brass fittings gleaming under the lights. Some doors bore wreaths of carved roses, others an elegant scroll design. A few had trays placed neatly outside with the remains of late-night tea or brandy service. There were no stewards now, and watchful eyes—just us.

Oliver slowed near the far end, then stopped in front of a door marked B-62.

"This one's unoccupied," he said quietly, glancing over his shoulder to be sure the corridor was empty. "First class was never fully booked. A few of the larger suites stayed empty from the start—reserved, held, or simply never claimed." His hand lingered on the key a moment before he added, lower now, "We should stay here tonight. No one will come looking."

"You want me to sleep here?" I asked, half stunned, half breathless.

His voice was low and steady. "Just tonight. It's late. Safer. And you won't exactly be comfortable in steerage after this."

He pushed the door open, and I stepped inside a world I hadn't imagined, even in dreams. The room wasn't just large; it was grand. A sitting parlor and a sleeping chamber were joined by an arched doorway, bathed in amber light from an electric chandelier overhead. The walls were dressed in cream-and-gold damask wallpaper, trimmed with crown molding. A velvet settee sat beneath a wide porthole, its curtains drawn open to reveal a starlit sea.

There was a writing desk with brass fixtures and a blotter laid perfectly square. An armchair upholstered in dark plum velvet stood beside a low marble-topped table with a crystal decanter still half full of untouched brandy.

Through the arch, the bedroom revealed itself in quiet opulence: a large canopied bed, layered in crisp white linens and embroidered pillows. At its foot stood a polished, elegant cedar chest. The walls here were a muted sage, hung with framed etchings of English countryside estates—someone's idea of comfort and pedigree.

The air didn't smell like metal or steam or sweat. It carried clean linen, warm wood, and the faint trace of citrus polish.

I turned to Oliver, still standing in the doorway. "I don't know what to say."

"You don't have to say anything." He stepped inside, shutting the door gently behind him. "No one will be checking it tonight. If you leave by six, no one will know you were ever here."

I looked around again. "This is the kind of room people write about."

He smiled faintly. "People die saving for a glimpse of this."

"And you …" I turned back to him. "You just … gave it to me."

He met my eyes, quiet and sure. "I wanted you to know what it feels like to take up space like this. To rest like this. I don't think I can give you much in this world, but I wanted you to have this."

The words landed in my chest and stayed there. I crossed to the settee, running a hand over the velvet, then to the bed, brushing my fingertips across the coverlet.

"It's beautiful," I said.

He stepped closer. "So are you."

I looked at him, the dim light catching in his eyes.

He didn't move to kiss me again. He just stood there, watching me and waiting, not for permission, but for understanding. And I gave it with a single nod.

Oliver closed the distance slowly, quietly turning the lock behind him with a soft click. The room fell into stillness, the world outside sealed off like a bad dream. Here, for one night, there were no corridors to sneak down, no officers to avoid, and no names to fake.

"I'll stay, too," he said softly, almost like he was asking.

I looked up at him, heart full. "I'd like that."

The room fell into a hush that felt different from the quiet outside. It was layered and rich, the kind of stillness that belonged to wealth.

Instead of turning toward the bed, Oliver walked to the marble-topped table in the sitting room and pulled open a cabinet just beneath it. From inside, he withdrew a dark green bottle nestled in a shallow crate of straw—champagne with a gold-embossed foreign label. A pair of slender crystal flutes rested beside it.

"You're full of surprises," I said, smiling as he placed the bottle on the table.

"I found it yesterday," he said, uncorking it with a soft pop. "This suite was meant for someone important. Whoever they were, they never came aboard." He poured, the bubbles rising in a fine stream. "Their loss. Our win."

He handed me a glass and raised his own. "To borrowed nights."

I clinked his gently. "And stolen mornings." We drank.

The champagne was drier than I expected, with the crisp bite of something expensive. I sank into the velvet settee, and the cushion swallowed me in comfort. Oliver joined me a moment later, shoulders relaxed, one foot tucked beneath him as he turned slightly to face me.

We didn't rush the conversation. The quiet between us wasn't awkward—it was full of flickering glances, the soft crinkle of linen, and the steady thrum of the ship somewhere far beneath us.

"What were you like before the ship?" I asked, twirling the stem of my glass.

He gave a small, self-deprecating laugh. "Quieter. Angrier. A bit of both, I suppose."

"You don't seem angry now."

"That's because I'm here. With you."

The words hit me in that soft, vulnerable place I'd tried to protect all voyage.

I leaned back against the armrest, watching him in the golden light. His sleeves were rolled up again, forearms bare, and a sliver of collar undone. He looked almost undone himself—no longer the steward gliding through first-class cabins, but just a man brimming with thoughts and stories he didn't usually tell.

"What about you?" he asked.

"I think I've always been looking for a way out," I said. "I just didn't know what I was trying to escape."

His gaze softened. "And do you think you've found it?"

"Maybe," I said, and then quieter, "Maybe it's not about

escape. Maybe it's about who you get to be when you stop running."

Oliver nodded slowly. "That's why I brought you here. I wanted to show you the version of you that doesn't have to hide. Even if it's just for tonight."

I set my empty glass down. "Then I'm glad it's with you."

He reached over, brushing his fingers against my wrist, light at first, then more deliberate. I leaned in. The kiss came slowly, like we knew the world wouldn't always give us this much space to feel it.

We sat like that for a while longer, talking in the hush, with our knees touching and heads bowed close. I told him about my mother, about Madeleine, and about the weight I carried without knowing how to name it. He told me about Whitechapel and his brothers, and about long winters with no fire and dreams too fragile to speak aloud.

And when the bottle was empty, and our words had softened to whispers, he took my hand and led me to the bed. There was no rush. He stepped toward me, not with urgency, but with calm—the way someone walked into a room they'd been missing all their life. He shed his coat and draped it gently over the back of the velvet armchair. His waistcoat followed.

We undressed slowly, side by side, in the hush of linen and flickering lamplight, as if it were sacred, not lustful or rushed. We were just two people unburdening ourselves of layers, of roles, and every version of ourselves we'd had to play.

When we slipped beneath the crisp sheets, we didn't

reach for each other like strangers chasing hunger. We moved as if the ship had stopped, the world stilled, and this bed in this room was the only place left to land. He lay beside me, his arm sliding under my neck as he pulled me close. I tucked my head against his chest and felt the steady rhythm of his heartbeat. He smelled like steam and soap and the lingering echo of the lavender air in the room. We didn't speak much. Just the occasional whisper in the dark. A soft laugh. A brush of lips against a forehead. The trace of fingertips along a shoulder. Each moment was a question answered in warmth and breath and quiet touch.

Outside, the sea stretched black and endless, carrying the ship and every secret inside it, into the cold Atlantic night. But here, in that gilded room no one had claimed, two men made a claim of their own. Not forever, just for now. And it was enough.

CHAPTER 15

Borrowed Mornings

HENRY

The room was still dim when I opened my eyes, the first pale hints of morning pressing at the edges of the curtains. The air smelled faintly of lavender and linen, and beside me, I could feel the slow, steady rise and fall of Oliver's breathing. He was already half awake, his arm resting loosely around my waist, his forehead tucked gently against my shoulder. Neither of us moved at first. The weight of sleep still clung to our limbs, and for a few stolen minutes, we let it.

Then came the low groan of the ship shifting beneath us, along with a distant clang of metal and the ordinary sounds of the day starting to stir.

Oliver exhaled slowly, his voice low and rough with sleep. "We should go."

I turned to look at him. His eyes were open now, hazy with rest but clear with knowing. The world was waking up, which meant we couldn't stay.

He sat up, reaching for his shirt, which was draped

across the chair. "Give me ten minutes, and I'll get you back without being seen."

We dressed quietly, side by side with no urgency and no words. It was a slow return to the uniforms we wore for the world, he in his crisp steward's coat, I in the same clothes I'd boarded with, now touched by a night I'd never forget.

Before we left, he looked back at the room, at the bed we'd shared. The windows still cast soft morning light across the velvet cushions.

"I wish I could give you this every night," he said.

I shook my head. "You already gave me more than I ever expected."

He smiled, just a little, and opened the door. We moved through the hallways like smoke, silent and invisible. The first-class corridors were mostly empty, with only a few stewards quietly arranging breakfast trays or adjusting flower vases on sideboards. Oliver led me back through the staff stairwells, pausing at every corner.

Finally, just before the final stair down to third class, he turned to me. "I'll find you later," he said.

I nodded. "I know."

Then, with one last look, no kiss and no words, he disappeared up the stairs, and I slipped back into the humbler heart of the ship. By the time I made it to the general room, the day had started. Third-class passengers were stirring, washing up, and greeting the light with tired smiles and hopeful chatter.

I found Madeleine sitting at our usual table, brushing

crumbs from a crust of bread onto a plate, still in her night robe, hair pinned in loose curls.

She looked up and blinked. "You look like someone who hasn't slept."

I slid into the seat across from her and gave her a crooked smile. "That's because I haven't. For the most part."

Her eyes narrowed. "*Oh?*"

I didn't say anything right away. I just stared down at the table, still feeling the phantom warmth of fine linen on my skin. Then I looked up at her, and for once, didn't try to deflect.

"I spent the night in a first-class stateroom," I said.

Madeleine blinked. "*What?*"

"With Oliver."

She stared at me, wide-eyed, mouth parting as if to ask a hundred questions at once.

I shrugged, still unsure how to describe the quiet, golden world we'd stepped into together. "He wanted me to know what it felt like," I said. "To belong somewhere like that, even just once."

Madeleine's expression softened. She reached across the table and took my hand. "You did," she said. "And you do. I'm so happy for you, Henry. You deserve someone like this ... to give you the world."

I swallowed the lump that had formed in my throat. "I just wish I could give him the world in return."

She shook her head softly. "Don't be ridiculous. Of course you do. You have so much more to offer than you realize. And it doesn't all have to be money." She squeezed my hand, warm and reassuring. "You are special. Don't ever forget that."

I nodded, unable to find the right words, and soon the conversation drifted away, breaking into chatter about everything and nothing all at once.

After Madeleine left to wash up, I stayed behind in the general room, cradling a half-cold cup of tea between my palms, the chipped rim pressing lightly into my fingers. The room had mostly emptied now, aside from a few scattered passengers murmuring over cards or folded newspapers, the soft clink of tin cups being stacked in the corner. But I didn't notice any of it.

My eyes were fixed on the narrow porthole above the bench across from me. The ocean beyond was calm and glass-like, and it did that thing it always did, where it made everything inside feel small and quiet. Like it was trying to remind me how big the world truly was, and how little control I actually had.

My thoughts had nowhere to go but inward. *I was falling for him.*

There. I said it, even just to myself. Even if the words didn't quite fit in my chest yet, the truth of it was like the sea outside: undeniable, vast, and strangely still. I was falling for Oliver.

Everything about him defied the lines the world tried to draw. He didn't just move through the ship; he navigated it like a secret language. He slipped past locked doors and sharp glances, not because he didn't care about the rules, but because he knew exactly how they worked, and when they deserved to be broken. He used charm where force would've failed. He found corners no one looked in and made them into doorways.

And somehow, impossibly, he'd *really* seen me.

I'd been invisible for so long I forgot what it felt like to be looked at without being dismissed, without being flattened into something useful or ornamental. He looked at me like I was worth the risk—like I was a secret worth learning. That alone undid me.

But now that it had happened and now that I'd shared a bed with him, now that I'd watched him, asleep and soft in lamplight, one hand curled near his chest like a boy dreaming, I didn't know what to do with it. Because how could this work? That thought circled back to the front of my mind. He was a steward for the White Star Line. A man with a reputation to protect. A future to build. A uniform that came with more rules than buttons. One wrong move, and everything he'd scraped together could vanish. He'd told me as much. And I was going back to New York to a sick mother I hadn't seen in years, and to tenement windows and sleepless nights. I didn't have a job waiting for me. I didn't even know what street I'd land on. I just knew that the moment we docked, the current would pull us in different directions. Different oceans. Different destinations.

I pressed my forehead against the cool rim of the cup and closed my eyes. The metal was cold, but my thoughts were fevered. It wasn't just the risk. It was the shape of our lives. He lived in motion—ship to ship, face to face, constantly wearing someone else's expectations. And I'd been running for so long that stillness felt dangerous. Going home was supposed to mean grounding. Some version of normal, whatever that meant.

And yet …

I could still feel his hand on my back, the way his forehead had rested against mine beneath that carved wooden clock like a benediction. I wanted it to matter. I wanted more. I wanted the version of him who laughed with me in stolen stairwells and the version of me who smiled without bracing first. I wanted to wake up with him in a world that didn't require an exit plan.

But I didn't know what that looked like. And worse, I didn't know if Oliver did either. Would he leave the White Star Line? Would he even want to? Could we ever build something real while still hiding in the shadows?

When Madeleine returned, she didn't say anything at first. She sat across from me and wrapped her shawl around her shoulders, her long braid damp and dark down her back. Her cheeks were still rosy from warm water and soap, but her eyes were sharp, clear, fixed on me like she already knew every thought running through my head.

"You're thinking yourself in circles," she said. "I can tell."

"Yeah," I murmured. "I am."

She reached across the table and gently pried the cup from my hands. Her fingers lingered against mine, warm. Steady. "Then stop thinking. Start figuring it out. You're not alone. Whatever happens, you'll have me by your side. You know that, right?"

I gave her a half-hearted smile as I nodded slightly.

"You ever feel like love's something you're supposed to sneak around with?" I asked. "Like it's this secret too sharp to hold?"

She tilted her head slightly, lips twitching. "All the time."

I looked at her. "You're braver than me."

"No," she said gently. "I'm just tired of waiting for permission." There was a pause. "And you should be, too. You should decide what you want, and go for it."

"I want him," I said. "And not just for a night. I want to know what it means to have mornings. to argue over toast, and to touch his hand in a crowd and not have to flinch."

Madeleine didn't look surprised. She looked … proud. "Then build the life where that's allowed."

"I don't even know how."

"Start with him," she said. "Start by telling him what you just told me. Have you done that?"

I stared at her. "And if he doesn't want it? If he's not ready?"

She gave a slight shrug. "Then at least you'll know. At least you'll have spoken it out loud. That's all you can do, isn't it?"

I nodded, my throat tight. I looked at her and remembered why she was here. It wasn't just about a boy who painted her portrait under Paris skies. It was about chasing a life she'd never been allowed to imagine until now. Maybe I needed to do the same.

Love, I realized, wasn't something you could figure out in a world like this, not when everything beautiful had to be kept quiet. And still … I couldn't stop wanting it. And that had to mean something.

CHAPTER 16

Between Duty and Desire

T he moment Henry disappeared into the stairwell, the hush of the first-class corridor pressed in around me like a held breath. The silence that had carried us through the night felt suddenly fragile, like crystal cracked at the rim or lace unraveling. I stood there a moment longer, listening to the echo of his steps fade downward, swallowed by the ship's inner machinery and the distant murmur of waking passengers.

Then I turned, straightened my coat, and headed toward the stewards' passageway.

The shift was immediate. The walnut paneling gave way to plain white bulkheads, and the plush carpet thinned to a hard, narrow runner. The sconces lost their golden glow and became small bulbs that buzzed faintly, flickering with the ship's pulse. I walked faster, shoulders squared. Every step tightened the distance between the world I'd just been allowed into and the one that owned me.

My heart was still somewhere in that unclaimed first-class suite, in the shape of Henry's sleeping breath and in the warmth of his body against mine. In the soft, astonished way he had looked at me under the lamplight, like I was something more than a uniform and a name sewn into a ledger.

But here, in these corridors, I was only a steward again.

I slipped into the small service room assigned to the bedroom stewards on duty. It was barely larger than a closet: a bench, a thin mirror, a pair of hooks on the wall, and a washbasin with a cracked rim. My reflection looked strange in the dim light—hair mussed, collar crooked, and cheeks warmed with something that didn't belong to the morning or the ship. I looked like a man who'd been kissed all night.

For a long moment, I just stood there, gripping the edges of the basin until my knuckles blanched, trying to steady the trembling in my chest. Last night had been … impossible. It was a stolen universe tucked into silk sheets. A place where Henry and I weren't divided by class or convention or the watchful eyes of the world. A place where I wasn't invisible. And I so selfishly wanted all of it to become a reality.

I splashed cold water on my face. It didn't help. I could still feel the heat of his skin against mine. I dried off, then reached for my uniform. The fabric felt heavier than usual, like chain mail I'd forgotten how to wear. I buttoned the vest, smoothing the lapels the way I always did, but the gesture felt foreign, as if I were dressing someone else.

I tightened my tie, straightened my collar, and pinned back the loose strand of hair Henry had tucked behind my ear hours before. Then I looked into the mirror again. There, I saw him. Oliver the steward. Efficient, polite, and silent when spoken to. Indentured to the RMS with no room left for dreams that didn't fit inside his assigned cabin trunk. But beneath all that … there was still the boy from last night who had kissed Henry in the glow of the Grand Staircase. The boy who had slipped between crisp sheets and let himself love, just once, without shame.

I breathed out, long and slow. "I can't lose him," I whispered to no one. With those words on my lips, I stepped into the passageway and returned to first class. I moved with the familiar rhythm—quiet footsteps, efficient posture, and eyes forward—but inside, nothing felt familiar at all.

Every hallway reminded me of him now. The soft amber lighting. The hush of carpet underfoot. The echo of our laughter in that suite. The memory of his hand resting in mine.

I reached the Grand Staircase before I meant to. The early morning emptiness made it look almost unreal. The dome overhead glowed like a pale sunrise trapped in glass. The carved wood gleamed softly, still warm with the memory of our bodies leaning close, lips brushing, and breath shared in the quietest hours of the night. I gripped the polished railing, feeling the smoothness under my palm. This place, meant for the rich and confident, was claimed secretly by two men who had no right to such extravagance. What happened now? What *could* happen?

I descended to the first-class landing, forcing myself onward. Duty didn't pause for love—not the kind I had, tucked away behind locked doors and stolen hours. I had cabins to check and passengers to greet with a smile that meant everything and nothing all at once.

But Henry—God, Henry … His eyes last night, full of awe and fear and something so tender it had nearly undone me. The way he'd whispered my name like it anchored him. The way he'd looked at me afterward, half asleep, half astonished, curled against my chest like he belonged there. He loved me. I *knew* it. The realization struck like sunlight in a dark room.

And I loved him enough to risk everything and enough to imagine a world past these corridors, past the RMS and the rules written by men who didn't know us. I loved him enough to believe that maybe the night we shared wasn't an ending.

But the thought twisted in my gut. What if last night made everything harder? What if it was just one night for him, and everything for me? What if the world on the other side of the gangway had no place for men like us? What if his mother disapproved, or his family forbade it? What if he woke up this morning, back in steerage, and realized it had all been a mistake?

I swallowed hard and forced myself to keep moving. I had to enter suite B-14 and begin the morning fire, arrange the flowers with steady hands, and make beds that hadn't known breath or warmth since yesterday.

All the while, last night pulsed beneath my ribs. His laugh. His kiss. His weight against mine. His whisper as he said, "*Stay.*"

By the time my shift settled into its routine, my thoughts were spinning, and I leaned against the service trolley, gripping its handle.

The White Star Line owned my contract—my life and my time. Men like me didn't just walk away. Running wasn't impossible, but it was dangerous and illegal. If they found me, they'd drag me back, strip me of pay, and ruin any chance of respectable work afterward.

A knock at the cabin door jolted me back. Soon, a passenger wanted hot tea. A child asked where the promenade deck was. A gentleman requested breakfast early. It all felt distant, like I was living two lives at once—one before the Grand Staircase, and one after.

By the time I slipped into the pantry to fetch linens, my throat was tight, and my eyes were stinging. I pressed a hand to my chest where Henry had rested his head the night before. "I'll find him later," I promised the quiet room. "And whatever happens next … I'll face it."

The ship moved beneath my feet. My pulse steadied. And I knew, tonight, or tomorrow, or somewhere between here and New York, I would have to choose—duty or him.

CHAPTER 17

Ice in the Air

HENRY

By midmorning, I couldn't sit in the general room any longer. The air inside felt too heavy, thick with questions I couldn't answer, glances that meant nothing, and the static buzz of waiting for something that never came. I'd hoped Oliver would find a way to slip me a note, a glance, or a moment. But the hours kept passing, and all I had was silence. So, instead, I found Madeleine on the deck.

She was sitting on a bench near the railing, bundled in two scarves and her heaviest shawl, cupping her hands around a tin mug of tea that had long since gone cold. The sky above was a washed-out blue, with the sun shining weakly through a thin layer of cloud, casting everything in a pale, colorless light.

I slid onto the bench beside her and tugged my coat tighter around me. I'd layered a sweater underneath, but even with the sun overhead, the air had an edge. It wasn't the usual kind of cold. This was sharper and more precise, like a blade that hadn't yet touched skin, but was hovering just close enough to feel.

"You feel that?" Madeleine asked, her breath rising in a pale cloud between us.

I nodded. "Yeah."

She tilted her head back to study the sky, her eyes squinting against the brightness. "It's different today. Like the cold's not just in the air; it's in the bones of the ship."

The ocean behind us was unnaturally still. It was flat and blue, with only the churn of the *Titanic's* wake to remind us we were moving. There wasn't even enough wind to ripple the surface. It looked like glass, untouched, endless, and waiting.

"You ever smell ice before?" she asked suddenly.

I turned to her. "Smell it?"

She nodded, tugging her scarf higher. "You can, you know, when it's close. It has this bitter, metallic scent—dry and clean. It cuts through everything else."

I breathed in, slowly. Beneath the tang of salt and faint coal smoke, I could feel that strange sharpness in the air, something hollow and cold and far older than the ship we stood on.

"I think I can smell it," I said quietly.

She didn't say anything after that. Instead, she just tucked her hands into her sleeves and leaned against me, shoulder to shoulder. We sat there, staring out over the railing, the light reflecting off the water like broken glass. I wasn't looking for ice, though. I was looking for him.

I wondered where Oliver was and whether he felt the

cold too. If it reached him between shifts and silver trays, between rooms where his name was never spoken, only summoned. If he paused for a moment in some corridor and thought of me the way I kept thinking of him.

Madeleine shifted slightly beside me. "Do you think the ship ever sleeps?"

"No," I said. "I think it just waits."

She let out a quiet breath.

"Like you are?" She turned to look at me. I opened my mouth to answer, but whatever I meant to say never came. "I can tell he's captured your heart," she continued, "but he's a man with responsibilities. He's not just traveling from one place to another." She gave me a gentle nudge. "I can see you're lost in your thoughts, but this is just how things are. And don't forget, you're on the *Titanic*. You should be enjoying every moment of this trip, not sulking."

I laughed at that, rolling my eyes despite myself. "You may be right," I said. "At least a little."

"I always am," she murmured.

We sat there a while longer, neither of us speaking, wrapped in silence and extra layers, beneath a sky that looked too bright for how cold it had become. The wind picked up again, sharp and sudden, and I pulled my coat tighter, not against the air, but against the feeling settling in my chest. A stillness that didn't feel right. A waiting that didn't feel like hope.

I left the deck before noon, hands numb despite my gloves, feet half asleep from sitting so still. The corridor back to E Deck was quiet, echoing with the soft hum of the ship's machinery and the occasional clatter of a tray or a door shutting two decks above.

I walked slowly, head down, not really thinking about where I was going, only that I didn't want to sit still again. Movement felt like purpose, even if I didn't have one. That was when I saw him.

At first, I wasn't sure. He was at the end of the corridor, facing away, coat slightly wrinkled, one hand pressed flat against the wall, as if he were trying to listen for something inside it. Then he turned, and it was him. Oliver.

His eyes caught mine immediately, like he'd been hoping for exactly this. He exhaled, relief rushing into his face. "Thank God."

I froze where I stood, unsure whether to run to him or make him come to me. He chose for me, closing the distance in a few quick strides, stopping just short of touching me.

"I've been looking for you," he said.

My throat felt tight. "I noticed."

He winced, guilt flickering across his features. "I'm sorry. It's been a mess since this morning."

I didn't speak, waiting for more. He ran a hand through his hair.

"First class is panicking over the cold. Suddenly, everyone wants more blankets, extra heaters, and hot drinks delivered every hour. Someone even asked for fur-lined slippers." He scoffed, then softened. "The officers—" He lowered his voice, glancing around. "They're on edge, too. I overheard a conversation this morning. One of the officers mentioned they'd gotten messages from other ships. Ice reported in the area. Not right on top of us, but close enough to take seriously."

That pulled me in a little. "Icebergs?"

He nodded. "And with how calm the water is, they're worried they won't see them until they're right on top of us. No waves to break around them. No moon last night either."

I looked past him, down the corridor. The ship's stillness suddenly felt too quiet, as if it were holding its breath. He must've seen something shift in my face, because his voice gentled again.

"Hey. I'm all right. You're all right. I just didn't want you thinking I'd disappeared."

"I did think that for a moment," I admitted. "I didn't know if it was about … us. Or if it was just the job."

"It's not us. It's the job," he said quietly. "I can't always choose when it pulls me away."

I nodded, the tension loosening in my chest by inches. "I know."

He finally reached out, fingers brushing the sleeve of my coat. It wasn't quite a touch, but just enough to remind me he was still there.

"I hated not being able to find you this morning," he said. "But I've been thinking about that room … and what we did before."

He didn't say anything else right away. Neither did I. The ship hummed around us, steady and deceptive, as if nothing in the world could ever go wrong aboard something this grand. Oliver stepped closer. Not all at once—just enough that I felt the heat of him through my coat. His voice dropped. "Henry," he said, "I need to know something."

I swallowed. "Ask."

"Are you afraid of this?"

He gestured vaguely between us. "Of me."

The honesty of the question startled me more than the closeness. I thought about lying. About deflecting. Instead, I shook my head.

"I'm afraid of wanting it," I said.

"That feels worse." His breath caught—just slightly. "That's exactly how I feel." The space between us closed without either of us consciously choosing it. His hand lifted, paused as if asking permission, then brushed my knuckles. The contact was light, tentative, but it sent a jolt through me that had nothing to do with fear.

"If you tell me to stop," he said quietly, "I will."

I didn't answer with words. I leaned in. The kiss was not urgent. It was careful—soft lips meeting, testing, retreating, then meeting again with more confidence. His mouth was warm, tasting faintly of smoke and tea. I felt him exhale against me, the sound low and almost reverent, like he'd been holding his breath for far too long. My hand found his coat, fingers curling into the fabric like an anchor. He responded instantly, one arm sliding around my waist, pulling me closer. The world narrowed to sensation: the slow press of his body, the brush of his thumb at my jaw, the way my chest rose and fell against his. When he kissed me again, deeper this time, I let myself melt into it. I forgot the rules. I forgot the risks. I forgot where we were. All that existed was the man holding me like I was something precious and breakable. We broke apart only when footsteps echoed faintly down the corridor. Oliver rested his forehead against mine, breath unsteady.

"We shouldn't," he murmured.

"I know."

But neither of us moved away. His thumb traced a small, unconscious circle against my hip, grounding me.

"Just … give me a moment," he said. "I need to remember how to walk away from you."

I laughed softly, despite myself. "Good luck."

"Every time someone handed me a coat or barked an order, I thought about your face in that reading room." That undid something in me.

"I thought about it too," I said.

His eyes searched mine, softer now. "Can we walk?"

I nodded. "Anywhere."

He smiled, and we turned down the corridor together, shoulders just barely brushing as we moved through the quiet. And for the first time all day, I felt warm again.

We didn't walk far. The deck curved gently beneath our feet, the boards slick with frost and salt, the railings rimed white where breath and spray had frozen together. The night air was sharp enough to sting, but neither of us complained. It felt important to stay where the cold could touch us—like proof we were still here. Oliver stopped near the stern, where the noise of the ship softened into something quieter. The lights behind us cast long shadows across the deck, and beyond the rail, the ocean stretched black and endless, broken only by scattered stars and the occasional pale glint of ice far off in the distance. He rested his hands on the railing, shoulders tense, eyes fixed on the water.

"You ever feel like the sea knows something you don't?" he asked quietly.

I nodded. "It doesn't give much away."

"No," he agreed. "But it keeps its secrets well."

We stood there for a moment, the silence settling between us—not awkward, not empty, just heavy with everything we weren't saying. The wind tugged at his coat, and without thinking, I stepped closer, shielding him from it with my body. He noticed. I could tell by the way his breath hitched.

"You don't have to do that," he said softly.

"I know," I replied. "I want to."

That earned me a glance—brief, searching, unguarded. Then he turned back to the sea, but he didn't move away.

"I don't usually let people see me like this," he admitted. "Not when I'm off duty. Not when I don't have somewhere specific I'm supposed to be."

"What does that feel like?" I asked.

He considered it. "Unsteady. Like the floor might disappear if I stop paying attention."

I understood that too well. I leaned my forearms on the rail beside him, close enough that our coats brushed.

"You're allowed to rest," I said. "Even just for a minute."

He exhaled, long and slow, like the suggestion alone had loosened something in him. His shoulders dropped a fraction.

"Henry," he said, my name quieter now. "If this voyage were different—if the world were kinder—this wouldn't feel like something we have to steal."

I turned my head, meeting his gaze fully. "Then let's not treat it like theft."

His brow furrowed. "What do you mean?"

"I mean," I said carefully, "that whatever this is … it doesn't have to be rushed. Or hidden in panic. It can just exist."

The wind gusted, stronger now. Oliver's hand slid along the railing, fingers brushing mine by accident—or not. This time, neither of us moved away.

"You say that like it's easy," he murmured.

"I know it's not," I replied. "But I also know I don't want to pretend this didn't happen."

Something shifted in his expression—fear giving way to resolve. He turned toward me fully then, close enough that I could feel his warmth despite the cold.

"Neither do I," he said.

He reached up slowly, deliberately, and cupped my jaw—not possessive, not rushed. Just steady. Asking. I didn't answer with words. The kiss was brief, restrained by the open night and the risk of being seen, but it carried weight. His lips were cold from the air, warm where they met mine. When he pulled back, his forehead rested against mine for a heartbeat longer than necessary.

"Stay with me," he said, barely audible.

"I am," I replied.

We stood there a while longer, hands brushing, shoulders

touching, the ship moving steadily beneath us—vast and confident and utterly unaware of the quiet promise being forged on its deck. Neither of us noticed how still the water had become.

The quiet felt earned, like something we'd fought our way into without realizing it. We stood shoulder to shoulder at the rail, the night air sharp enough to sting, the ship cutting through the dark with a confidence that felt almost arrogant in retrospect. Oliver leaned forward slightly, resting his forearms on the cold iron. I watched the way his breath fogged and vanished, how he seemed to be measuring himself against the sea.

"Can I tell you something?" he said.

I turned toward him. "You never have to ask."

He let out a slow breath, one that sounded like it had been waiting a long time to be released. "I've been on ships since I was sixteen. Smaller ones. Older ones. Ones that creaked and groaned like they were already tired of carrying people's dreams." He smiled faintly. "I thought this one would be different. Not just because of the size, but because of what it represented."

"And what was that?" I asked.

"A future that didn't require me to disappear into it," he said. "A job where I could finally be … respectable. Invisible, but respectable."

He glanced at me then, something fragile in his eyes. "I told myself that was enough."

I swallowed. "Was it?"

"No," he said simply. "But it felt safer than wanting more."

I nodded. I understood that better than I wanted to admit.

"I spent most of my life convincing myself that if I stayed useful, I wouldn't have to be honest." His mouth curved into a small, knowing smile. "You don't strike me as someone who enjoys lying."

"I don't," I said. "But I'm very good at it."

He laughed quietly at that, then sobered again. "I was always careful. Always watching where I looked, how long I lingered. Ships are full of rules, Henry—spoken and unspoken. And the unspoken ones are the most dangerous."

"I know," I said.

For a moment, neither of us spoke. The water slipped past the hull in complete silence, black and endless. I realized then how strange it was to feel so still on something that was constantly moving.

"I didn't plan for you," Oliver said at last.

I smiled faintly. "I hope that's not a complaint."

"No," he replied quickly. "God, no. Just … a confession." He hesitated, then continued. "I didn't plan to feel seen. Or to want something I couldn't pack away at the end of a shift."

My chest tightened. "And now?"

"And now," he said, "I don't want to pack it away."

The honesty of it landed between us, heavy and warm all at once. I reached out before I could think better of it, my fingers brushing his sleeve, then curling around his wrist. He didn't pull away.

"I don't know what happens after this voyage," I said

quietly. "All I know is that before I met you, I was bracing myself for a life that felt smaller every day."

"And now?" he asked.

"Now it feels like I've already stepped into something I can't pretend doesn't exist."

He turned fully toward me then, the lamplight catching the planes of his face, the fatigue and determination etched side by side.

"I'm afraid," he admitted.

"So am I," I said.

He smiled—not brightly, but honestly.

"Good. That means we're paying attention."

We stood like that, hands loosely joined, the cold forgotten, the ship humming steadily beneath us. If the world had ended right then, it would have felt almost gentle. Neither of us noticed the way the water had gone flat as glass. Neither of us noticed the absence of wind.

We walked together, neither of us saying much at first. The hum of the ship filled the space between our footsteps, soft and rhythmic, as if urging us onward. Oliver's shoulder brushed mine now and then. Whether it was accidental or intentional, I didn't care. It felt good, like something that had been taken away was settling back into place. We passed through one corridor, then another, silent as ghosts, until we reached a darker turn in the hallway where no one lingered. Oliver slowed, then stopped, his back against the paneled wall, eyes glinting in the low light.

"I've got something planned," he said, that familiar flicker of mischief returning to his voice. "If you're up for it."

I raised an eyebrow. "More surprises?"

He grinned. "Just one. Maybe two."

I waited.

He leaned in a little, lowering his voice. "I've got the last shift off tonight. It's rare, but I traded for it; don't ask how. I want to take you somewhere."

I stared at him, curious. "Where?"

"The first-class smoking room."

I blinked. "You're kidding."

He shook his head. "Quiet as a church just before midnight. Everyone'll be asleep or in their suites. I've snuck in once before quickly and have always wanted to go back. Beautiful place, mahogany walls, leather chairs, fireplaces still warm. There's a chessboard set up that no one touches after dark."

"Chess?"

"And whiskey," he added, with a lopsided smile. "If I can charm the bartender's assistant into looking the other way."

I laughed. "You're unbelievable."

"Tell me no," he said, still smiling, but his eyes searching mine for the answer he hoped for.

"Alright," I said. "Eleven?"

"Eleven," he confirmed. "I'll come find you."

He paused, then added more quietly, "And after … we could sneak back to that stateroom. Just for the night. One more time."

I didn't even hesitate. "Yes."

The warmth between us was immediate, like the sun rising under our skin. We didn't need more words. He straightened his coat, eyes sweeping over the corridor. "I have to go. If I'm late for rounds, I'll never hear the end of it."

"Be careful," I said.

He smirked. "You too."

And with that, he slipped back into the shadows—already blending into the bones of the ship like he'd never stopped moving. But I stood still, watching where he'd gone, feeling that now-familiar flutter of anticipation bloom quietly in my chest. Eleven o'clock. Chess. Whiskey. And *him*.

CHAPTER 18

One Last Night of Light

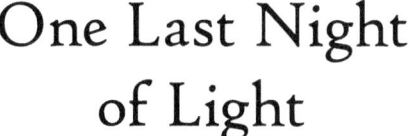

HENRY

Madeleine had just finished pinning up her hair when I stepped into the corridor. We'd spent the evening quietly, reading in the general room, and sharing a cup of tea in silence. She hadn't asked about Oliver anymore, but I knew she was watching me, waiting for the moment I'd disappear into another part of the ship.

"I'm heading to bed," she said now, looping her shawl over her arm. "Try to get some rest tonight, will you?"

I hesitated. "You too."

She paused, studying me with that soft, perceptive gaze that always made me feel seen. "Henry?"

"Yeah?"

"Be careful."

"I will," I said.

She stepped forward once more, cupping my cheeks with her hands. "And stop being so in your head over everything.

This is a big thing we're doing, you and I. A chance for a new beginning. In life *and* in love. Act like it. Embrace it."

I nodded. Somewhere along the way, I must have forgotten that. "Of course."

She smiled faintly, stepped back, and slipped through her cabin door. The latch clicked softly behind her.

I waited a few beats, then turned down the corridor, heart already picking up speed. When I reached the stairwell, Oliver was there, leaning against the frame, coat neatly buttoned, hair combed back. He looked tired, but when he saw me, he straightened with that spark in his eyes.

"You ready?" he asked quietly.

I nodded. "More than."

We moved quickly, weaving through narrow crew passages and staircases meant for invisible people. The ship was quieter than usual, with the soft thrum of the engines, the occasional murmur from behind closed doors, and the distant clink of silver being polished for the next day's breakfast. Every now and then, Oliver would pause, listening for footsteps. At one junction, we ducked behind a trolley stacked with towels as two stewards passed, mid-conversation, oblivious. We waited, breath held, until their voices faded into the hull. It was thrilling, terrifying, and so utterly wonderful.

By the time we reached the door at the edge of A Deck, my heart was beating as loud as the engines. Oliver turned the handle carefully and opened it just wide enough for us to slip through. And suddenly, we were in another world. The first-class smoking room opened before us like something out of a novel, dimly lit, grand, and steeped in the rich scent of old leather, pipe tobacco, and polished wood.

The room was paneled in dark mahogany, every surface gleaming with a soft, amber sheen. The walls rose high, dressed in embossed leather, and lined with carved wooden pilasters. A row of tall windows, now dark and curtained, stretched along one side of the room, while brass sconces flickered gently on the other, their glow casting slow-moving shadows across the floor.

Club chairs upholstered in burgundy leather were arranged in quiet groupings around low tables, many of which held chessboards, books, or half-finished glasses of Scotch left behind by guests who had already turned in. In the corner, a marble fireplace still glowed faintly with the last of the coals, warmth lingering in the air like the echo of conversation.

A long, built-in bar stretched along the far wall, behind which stood shelves of decanters and crystal bottles, each filled with amber and gold and deep red spirits. A single, half-empty bottle stood uncorked beside two etched glasses.

The room wasn't crowded; just a handful of passengers lingered, their voices low and contented. A few older gentlemen played cards near the far window. The soft flutter of shuffling decks was barely audible beneath the crackle of the fire. Another pair sat by the bar, sipping brandy and speaking in the low tones of men in no hurry to return to their cabins. The hush of late evening had settled over everything, the kind of quiet that made the space feel more like a study than a salon.

Oliver motioned toward a corner table where a chess-board waited, its pieces already arranged for a new game.

"Very few people come in here after eleven," he said softly.

I stepped further into the room, letting the luxury wash over me. Everything was intentional and designed not just for comfort, but for power. This was the kind of space where men made decisions, sealed deals, and laughed with their cigars while the rest of the ship slept beneath them. And yet, here I was. Just a boy from Lower Manhattan, standing on thick carpet in first class, about to play chess beneath gilded sconces with a steward who looked at me like I wasn't an accident.

Oliver pulled out a chair for me.

"You know how to play?" he asked.

I smiled, taking the seat. "If you're ready to lose … yes."

He grinned back, sitting across from me. "I've already lost. There's no way I'll be able to focus on the game when you're next to me."

The room wrapped around us like a secret; warm, still, and soaked in the scent of old leather, pipe smoke, and something faintly sweet from the fireplace's glowing coals. No one had entered since we'd arrived. The only sounds were the soft click of chess pieces and the low hum of the ship's engines far below.

Oliver narrowed his eyes at the board, lips pursed in thought. His sleeves were rolled to the elbow, and he tapped his knuckle against a captured bishop as he considered his next move.

"You're not half bad," he murmured.

I grinned. "And here I thought you invited me here just for the view."

"I did," he said without looking up. "But the game's a bonus."

He moved his rook, then sat back with a satisfied smile.

"I knew it," I said. "Trap."

"Not yet. But close."

I stared at the board, my mind already spinning. The silence between us stretched, familiar and comfortable.

Then he said, more quietly, "Can I ask you something?"

I glanced up. "You can ask me anything."

He kept his eyes on the board. "What happens when we dock in New York?"

The question settled heavily between us, like a second board we'd just begun to play.

I took a slow breath. "I've been trying not to think about it."

"But you have," he said. "Haven't you?"

"Of course I have," I said. "I'll go back to the city, check on my mother, and try to get a job. Maybe carpentry, maybe something steadier if I can find it."

"And that's it?" he asked.

I met his eyes. "I don't know what else there can be."

He nodded slowly, then leaned forward, forearms on the table. "I've been thinking, Henry. If I don't sign on to the return voyage … I could stay. In New York. At least for a bit."

My breath caught. "You'd do that?"

He looked down, his voice quieter now. "There's nothing

for me in Southampton but another ship. Another staircase. Another name on a list of passengers I'll never speak to again."

"And in New York?"

"There might be you." I couldn't speak for a moment. "I'm not saying it'd be easy," he continued. "I don't even know what kind of work I'd find. But I want more than this. More than linen gloves and 'yes sir' and sleeping in a cupboard between duties. I want … you."

"Do you mean it?" I asked.

He looked at me then, steady and sure. "I've never meant anything more."

He stood slowly and circled the table, his footsteps soundless on the thick carpet. When he reached me, he paused and looked around the room. His gaze swept across every shadowed corner, the windows, and the bar. He moved to the door and checked the hallway beyond. Only when he was certain the room was empty did he return.

"I hate that I have to do that," he said quietly. "But I'm not going to risk you."

"You're not," I said. "Not anymore."

Then he took my face in both hands gently and leaned in. And when our lips met, the world vanished. It wasn't rushed or shy; it was slow and full and entirely ours. He kissed me like he was memorizing it. Like he wasn't sure if we'd get another chance. I kissed him back like I knew we would.

But just as we leaned into each other, as his hand slid to the back of my neck and our bodies pressed close, everything shifted. A deep, strange vibration rippled through the floor beneath our feet. Then came a low, distant groan, like the ship had bent somewhere deep in its bones. A muted, metallic boom sounded from far forward.

"Do you feel that?" I asked. He did. I knew it from the way his body had gone still.

Oliver pulled back sharply, his brow furrowing. "What was that?"

We both turned toward the far end of the smoking room. The fireplace trembled faintly. A glass at the bar rattled in place. The entire ship seemed to pause for a moment, like it had inhaled and was holding its breath. A chill settled in my spine, and it had nothing to do with the cold.

"I don't know," I said. "But I don't like it."

Oliver looked toward the door, instincts already sharpening. "Something's not right."

And as the warmth of the room gave way to a rising, unfamiliar stillness, I realized the night was no longer ours. The moment the vibration passed, Oliver and I exchanged a glance, no words, just a flicker of understanding. We moved.

He was the first to the door of the smoking room, already halfway into the corridor by the time I caught up. The polished halls of first class, so quiet and still just minutes earlier, now echoed faintly with footsteps, doors creaking open, and hushed voices asking, "*Did you feel that?*"

We turned a corner and passed a steward in half uniform, hair tousled, muttering something under his breath as he headed the opposite direction. We didn't stop to ask.

By the time we reached the Grand Staircase, more

passengers were emerging from their suites in silk robes and quilted dressing gowns, blinking like they'd just woken from a dream they couldn't quite remember. One man in a navy dressing coat was laughing, arm draped over his wife's shoulders.

"Must've scraped a wave," he said confidently. "Nothing to worry about."

But something in Oliver's stride said otherwise.

We pushed through the tall doors to the open deck, and the cold hit us instantly, sharp and dry, cutting deeper than any wind I'd felt since we'd left port. The stars still glittered above in their same impossible clarity. The sea around us looked untouched.

A small crowd had gathered near the starboard railing. Some were leaning over the edge. Others knelt beside something scattered across the deck, crunching under their boots.

It was *ice*. Chunks of it, some the size of fists, others jagged and glittering like broken crystal, strewn across the floorboards like forgotten party favors. A young boy darted past us, laughing, holding a shard the size of a book. "Look, Papa! It's real ice!"

One of the older men looked up from inspecting the deck. He was wrapped in a dark robe, cigarette dangling from his lips.

"Ship hit something," he said casually, as if commenting on the weather. "Starboard bow. Captain hasn't said anything yet, but you can smell it in the air."

Oliver went still beside me. A moment later, a voice called out behind us.

"Mr. Walker." We turned to see a junior officer approaching quickly, his expression tight, his breath puffing in white clouds. "Sir, you're needed forward. First-class passengers are beginning to ask questions. You're assigned to the A Deck suites tonight, correct?"

"Yes," Oliver replied instantly, his tone snapping into formality.

The officer gave him a curt nod. "Good. Escort passengers as needed. We'll be making announcements shortly. There's no cause for alarm, but we're proceeding with caution." Then he turned and disappeared down the deck without waiting for a reply. Oliver stood frozen for a beat, eyes on the trail of ice at our feet, then on the distant curve of the ocean. I could see the shift from the man who had just kissed me, to the steward who had a role to play.

"I have to go," he said quietly.

I nodded. "I figured."

He turned to me, eyes searching mine. "Go find Madeleine. Bring her up here. Dress warm, layers if you can. There might be nothing to worry about, but just in case."

"Where do I meet you?"

"I'll be up here," he said. "Somewhere."

I reached out and briefly touched his hand. "Be safe."

"You too," he said. "And hurry."

CHAPTER 19

Locked Gates

HENRY

I turned from the deck, the cold still burning in my chest, and sprinted for the stairwell. Each step down felt steeper than the last, not just from the tilt of the ship, which hadn't changed, but from the way everything else had. The weight in the air. The hum of unease. The knowledge that something had happened, and that something hadn't stopped happening.

The first-class corridor was busier now. Doors creaked open. Slippers shuffled against the carpet. Men in dressing gowns and women with shawls wrapped tight around their shoulders stepped into the hallways, rubbing sleep from their eyes, asking the same soft question to anyone who passed.

"Did something happen?"

"Why did we stop?"

No one answered with certainty. A steward passed me, jaw tight, telling a couple it was likely "just a precaution." Another insisted the crew was "checking the hull." But their voices were too quick and too flat. They were repeating, not reassuring.

I kept moving, down the crew stairwell, into the narrower passages where the walls were steel and utilitarian, the air colder now than it had been just hours ago. Somewhere between D and E Deck, I stopped short.

The engines had stopped. I hadn't noticed at first, because you couldn't notice a heartbeat until it was gone. But now, it was obvious. The deep thrum that had pulsed beneath our feet since we left Southampton, constant and alive, was gone. The floor was still. The silence pressed into my ears like pressure at the bottom of the sea. I moved faster.

By the time I reached the third-class corridors, the atmosphere had changed completely. The general room was half full, even though it was well past midnight. People sat with their coats thrown over their nightclothes. A few were barefoot, clutching blankets and muttering nervously in their own languages. Children rubbed their eyes while their parents whispered in hushed voices, exchanging rumors. I passed a woman pacing near the stairwell, her hand trembling as she clutched a prayer card.

"Something's wrong," she muttered. "It's not normal for the ship to be this quiet."

I found Madeleine in her cabin, already awake, pulling a second skirt over her nightdress.

She looked up sharply when she saw me. "Henry?"

"We need to go," I said. "*Now.*"

Her eyes swept over my face, and she didn't ask questions. She just nodded and grabbed her coat.

"What's happening?"

"We hit something. Ice, I think. Oliver said to come to the deck. He's working, but he said to dress warm and fast."

She shoved her feet into her boots. "Is it serious?"

"I don't know," I said. "But I don't like the silence."

A deep metallic creak echoed somewhere behind the walls, far away and slow, like the ship was shifting in its sleep. I opened the door and held it for her. She stepped into the corridor and paused, her breath catching in her throat as she looked around.

All down the hallway, third-class passengers were emerging from their rooms. Not in panic, but alert. Faces peeked out behind doors, voices whispering in Norwegian, Italian, and Irish. There was no shouting yet, but the silence of the engines was doing more than any alarm bell could. It was waking them. We stayed in third class, hemmed in by cold steel and confusion.

The air was no longer just tense; it was changing. The corridor outside our cabins was thick with voices, bodies, and the squeal of boots on metal floors. Everywhere, people were gathering in the narrow halls, bundled in coats and blankets, some clutching children, others white-knuckling rosaries. A steward passed through, shouting over the growing noise.

"Everyone, back to your cabins! Get your life jackets on—now!"

The words hit like a slap. Madeleine and I looked at each other, wide-eyed. Neither of us moved for a beat. Then we did. We pushed through the throng, elbows bumping, shoulders pressing, trying to move through bodies that had gone rigid with fear and disbelief. More stewards barked instructions from opposite ends of the passage. Most people didn't know where to go. Some didn't understand English. Others just stared, waiting for someone else to tell them it was all a mistake. We reached my room, and I yanked the door open. My hands were shaking.

"They're under the beds," I said, already dropping to my knees to retrieve the pale cork-and-canvas life jackets. I tossed one to Madeleine, who was tying her boots with trembling fingers.

"You think it's really sinking?" she asked, breathless.

"I don't know," I said. "But I'm not waiting to find out."

We shrugged into the jackets, tightening the straps as best we could. They smelled like dust and seawater, and they creaked when we moved. Mine was too snug around the chest; Madeleine's was a little loose. They weren't made to fit—they were made to float.

The moment we stepped back into the corridor, everything had changed again. The ship was tilting. Subtle at first, just enough to make you shift your balance and to question if your legs were tired. But then the hallway seemed to curve, like gravity had quietly changed its mind. People were moving faster now—no more questions, just footsteps. Children cried, and mothers called names. Doors opened, closed, opened again. Stewards were yelling.

We stopped at the top of a stairwell that led to a lower passageway, one of the arteries beneath even our deck. Soaked passengers were coming up the stairs in clumps,

gasping and dripping. Some were barefoot, trousers clinging to their legs, skirts waterlogged. One man was yelling
in Italian, gesturing frantically behind him. A boy no older
than ten shouted, "It's coming in! It's already flooding!"
A woman sobbed as she climbed, water still spilling from
her hem.

Madeleine clutched my arm. "*Mon Dieu.*"

"The ship is sinking!" someone screamed. The words
rippled through the corridor like fire. Someone else turned
to run. Another slipped and crashed against the wall. A
suitcase burst open. A shoe skidded across the metal floor
and was left behind.

Madeleine's grip tightened. "What do we do?" she whispered. I swallowed hard, steadying her with one hand as the
deck tilted just a little more beneath our boots.

"We find a way up," I said. "We find Oliver. And we
don't stop moving."

The ship had not yet decided how loudly it wanted to
die. That was the most frightening part. People still spoke
in reasonable tones. Stewards still tried to organize lines.
The electric lights still glowed with stubborn brightness, as
if illumination alone might keep the water out. It would have
been easier if there had been screaming already—if terror
had arrived fully formed instead of creeping. Madeleine
noticed it too.

"This is the part I don't like," she murmured. "When
people think there's still time."

The floor beneath our boots felt subtly wrong—not
slanted enough to provoke panic, just enough to require

constant correction. My body kept adjusting before my mind caught up. A man passed us, soaking wet from the waist down, his eyes glassy with shock.

"It's flooding," he said to no one in particular. "Below. It's already—"

A steward cut him off sharply. "Sir, please return to your cabin."

The man stared at him, disbelief written across his face. Then he laughed—a brittle, broken sound—and staggered past us without another word.

"That's not order," Madeleine said quietly. "That's denial."

We turned another corner and heard it clearly for the first time: water. Not a splash. Not a drip. A moving sound. A deliberate one. It slid through the corridors like an animal learning the shape of its cage. My chest tightened.

"Henry," Madeleine said. "Listen to me. If anyone tells us to wait—"

"We don't," I finished.

She nodded once. Approval. Resolve. We moved faster.

The corridors should have led upward. That was the lie of the ship—every staircase promised escape, and every passageway delivered confusion instead. We turned corner after corner only to find ourselves funneled back into the same narrowing arteries of steel, voices ricocheting off the walls, orders contradicting each other faster than anyone could obey them.

"Back to your cabins!" someone shouted from behind us.

"No—up this way!" another voice cried ahead.

A steward stood at an intersection, hands shaking as he pointed in two different directions within the span of seconds. Sweat streaked down his temples despite the cold. He looked at us like we were already ghosts. We followed one set of instructions, then another, then none at all. A woman collapsed against the wall near the base of a stairwell, clutching a child who was screaming for someone named Patrick. Her other children were gone—sent ahead, she said, sent back, she didn't know. She grabbed my coat as we passed.

"They told me to wait," she sobbed. "They said they'd come back."

They hadn't. The floor pitched slightly beneath our feet—not enough to knock us over, but enough to make the lie impossible to ignore. The ship was changing. Gravity itself was being rewritten. Madeleine looked at me then, eyes sharp and frightened and searching.

"Henry," she whispered. "This isn't order. This is delay."

I nodded. The word wait echoed in my skull like a death sentence. I thought of all the times I had waited in my life— waited for permission, for acceptance, for the world to tell me when I was allowed to move. The *Titanic* had been built on waiting: waiting for class, waiting for clearance, waiting for doors to open. Waiting was killing people.

"Don't listen anymore," I said, low and fierce. "We don't wait."

Another shout echoed from somewhere below—cut short by a sound I couldn't mistake for anything but water slamming into metal. The lights flickered. That was when panic finally broke loose. Someone ran past us barefoot, coat flapping open, eyes wild. Another slipped and fell, scrambling to get back up as the deck tilted again, steeper this time. Somewhere behind us, a door burst open and seawater rushed through with terrifying speed. Madeleine grabbed my arm.

"Henry—"

"I know," I said.

My voice sounded strange to my own ears. Steadier than I felt.

"This ship isn't saving anyone. We save ourselves."

I turned us sharply down a narrower passage, one Oliver had shown me days ago—a service corridor meant for invisible people. The walls were bare steel here, the lighting dimmer, the air colder. We ran. Behind us, someone screamed. Ahead of us, the ship groaned like an animal realizing it had been mortally wounded. And for the first time, I understood something with terrifying clarity: Survival wasn't about following rules anymore. It was about refusing them.

CHAPTER 20

The Ship Breaks
Its Silence

OLIVER

For a few seconds, the world seemed to hold still. Then the engines stopped. The steady thrum that had been the heartbeat of the ship ceased. It was so quiet that I could hear my own breathing. The air felt heavier somehow, expectant. I stood motionless, hand on the wall, listening. Somewhere far below, metal echoed. It was a dull clang, like a door slamming in the depths. Then voices.

"Did you feel that?" someone called from down the corridor.

"What happened?" another replied. "Maybe a propeller threw."

I tried to steady my breathing. I'd felt small vibrations on ships before. This one had been different, though, but surely not serious. Still, something in my gut twisted uneasily. I turned and began to climb toward the first-class decks. My mind told me I was following orders. Logically, I knew I should check in with Mr. Hughes, my superior, but my heart was somewhere else, down below in the steerage cabins where Henry would be, frightened.

The corridors grew brighter as I ascended, the plain walls of the crew sections giving way to the opulent warmth of first class. Mahogany paneling gleamed under the electric lights, rich and polished, the smell of fresh varnish and perfume still lingering from earlier in the evening.

When I stepped into the first-class lounge, it was like entering another world. The vast room stretched before me with gilt ceilings, high arched windows, and deep armchairs upholstered in crimson velvet. A clock above the mantel ticked softly, steady as a heartbeat. But the usual hum of voices, the laughter, and the clinking of glasses were all gone.

Now there was only quiet. A few passengers stood in their nightclothes, peering curiously into the corridor. A man in a dressing gown had a newspaper folded under his arm, as though waiting for someone to bring him the morning edition. A young couple whispered by the fireplace, glancing about with wide eyes.

I straightened my waistcoat and moved among them.

"Why have the engines stopped?" a man asked me as I passed by.

"All quite all right, sir," I said gently. "The officers are only running a routine inspection."

The words felt strange on my tongue, hollow and rehearsed, but it was what I was meant to say. I continued through the lounge, past the reading tables and the great clock. Every sound seemed louder now: the faint crackle of the fire, and the rustle of slippers on carpet.

The ship gave a faint lurch, barely perceptible, but enough to make a vase tremble on its pedestal. A single petal fell from the arrangement of roses beside it, drifting soundlessly to the floor. My pulse quickened. I quickened my pace. I found Mr. Hughes near the Grand Staircase, his expression carefully measured, speaking in low tones with two other stewards. His posture was calm, his voice even. He was the very image of authority.

"Sir," I said, bowing my head slightly. "What's happened?"

Hughes looked at me with a faint frown, then gestured for me to step closer. "We've struck ice," he said quietly. "Starboard side, forward compartments. A bit of a scrape, nothing more. The watertight doors are closed."

"Iceberg?" I repeated, my voice lower now.

Hughes nodded once. "Aye. She'll be fine. Mr. Andrews says the pumps can handle the inflow."

The words were calm, but the look in Hughes's eyes wasn't. Beneath that mask of composure, something was flickering—unease, maybe even fear.

"Orders are to wake the passengers," Hughes continued briskly. "Have them put on their life belts and make their way up to the boat deck. Quietly, mind you. No need to startle anyone. Say it's only a precaution."

I swallowed. "Yes, sir."

"Good lad. Keep them calm."

He turned away, already giving the same instructions to another steward. I hesitated only a moment before I started down the corridor again, knocking gently on doors.

"Pardon me, sir. Captain's orders, if you'll kindly dress and put on your life belt. Just a drill."

"Ma'am, please fasten this—yes, that's it. No need for alarm, just to be safe."

The first-class passengers were slow to rouse, their faces pale and puzzled in the lamplight. Some smiled indulgently, as though humoring a child. Others complained about the hour or the cold.

"Really," one gentleman muttered, "waking us up for a bit of ice."

But I saw the uncertainty in their eyes, and the way they moved faster when the floor tilted slightly beneath them. I worked quickly, my voice calm even as my own nerves frayed. The air felt cooler now, the draft stronger as I neared the stairwell. Somewhere far above, a door slammed open and shut with the tilt. By the time I'd finished this section, the hallways were filled with softly murmuring figures: ladies in furs and slippers, and men with half-fastened coats, clutching life belts. I looked toward the staircase, where Mr. Hughes was still directing passengers toward the deck. My duty was done for now, but my thoughts were already far below. *Henry.*

I pictured him down there in the third-class cabins with the narrow bunks, the low ceilings, and the laughter now replaced by confusion. There would be little warning for them, and little help if things worsened. I could see Henry's face so clearly in my mind, along with the soft lines of worry, and the steady strength in his hands. Without another thought, I stepped out of the line of passengers and slipped through the service corridor. The passageway was deserted. The hum of voices from above faded behind me as I descended. The metal stairs vibrated faintly under my shoes from the ship's shifting weight. The air grew colder the lower I went, sharp with the smell of iron and seawater.

When I reached the door to the open deck, I pushed it open, and the cold hit me like a blow. The Atlantic spread around us, black and glinting under the stars. Ice floated on the water in chunks, gleaming like shards of glass. Men in uniforms moved briskly among the lifeboats, their breath misting in the freezing air. There was no shouting yet, no chaos, but something was building. I heard it in the voices around me.

"Mail room's flooding already."

"She's taking on water fast."

"They say an hour. Maybe less."

An hour. I stood still, my breath caught. The wind tore at my hair, and the cold sank into my bones. I looked up at the towering funnels, the gleaming railings, and the shining decks. The ship that had been called unsinkable was now groaning faintly beneath the stars.

An hour.

I turned back toward the stairwell, heart pounding. I could think of nothing now but Henry. He was somewhere below, trusting me, and waiting for news that would never come unless I brought it myself. The night pressed in around me, full of stars and the smell of ice and salt. I clenched my jaw, squared my shoulders, and began to run down the stairs, back into the depths of the ship, and toward the man I loved.

CHAPTER 21

Running Out of Time

T he ship was still tilting, just slightly, but now it was enough to feel in your knees. Every step upward took more effort than the one before. Madeleine and I held on to the railing as we climbed toward the upper deck stairwell, passing more passengers stumbling through the dim corridor. Some were dressed, some still barefoot, clutching coats or bags, eyes wide and searching. The life jackets now creaked around every chest. We were all wearing the same fear.

The passage leading to the stairwell was packed by the time we reached it. A crowd had formed, thirty, maybe forty people, pressed shoulder to shoulder in the narrow space at the base of the next flight of stairs. And at the top of the stairs, between the decks above and us, stood a tall, locked iron gate. The kind that divided us from first and second class. The kind that had always been there. Only now, it wasn't just a formality. It was a wall.

"What's going on?" Madeleine asked, gripping my arm.

We edged forward, trying to see, but it was chaos. Voices rose, languages overlapping. Some were yelling in English, others in Swedish, Irish, and Italian—accents thick with desperation.

"They've locked it!" people shouted. "They won't let us up!"

Madeleine's hand tightened around mine. Not in fear— in focus.

"They're buying time," she said. "For someone else. And if we stand here, we become part of what they're holding back."

Around us, panic surged. People pressed forward, shouting, pleading, pounding on the gate as if noise alone might unlock it. The steward on the other side kept repeating the same phrase, his voice thinning with every repetition.

"Please remain calm."

Madeleine wasn't listening to him. She was scanning the corridor—floor, walls, ceiling—mapping the space the way she did when sketching a room before deciding where the light should fall.

"We don't wait," she said. "Waiting is how you drown."

She tugged my sleeve, just enough to pull my attention fully back to her.

"Henry. Look at me."

I did. Her eyes were bright—not with panic, but with resolve.

"There will be another way," she said. "There always is. But we won't find it standing still."

A scream echoed from below, followed by the unmistakable sound of water hitting metal. Madeleine moved first. She slipped sideways through the crowd—not shoving, not apologizing—just moving with purpose. People followed without realizing why. Fear looks for direction. Madeleine gave it one.

"This way," she said, already halfway down a narrower passage. "The floor slopes less."

"How do you know?" I shouted.

"Because I've been paying attention!"

When the water came later—fast, brutal, unforgiving—she didn't scream. She counted. Steps. Turns. Doors.

"Left," she said once, without hesitation. "The ship lists less here."

I trusted her without question. She wasn't brave because she lacked fear. She was brave because she refused to let fear decide for her. We rounded the next corner at a run and skidded to a stop. Another gate stood across the corridor, iron bars pulled shut and locked fast, cutting the passage in two. On the other side, a stairwell rose upward, empty and brightly lit. Madeleine stared at it for half a second, jaw tightening.

"Of course," she said flatly. "Not this way either."

A young man slammed his shoulder against the bars. "You can't do this!" he shouted.

A steward stood on the other side of the gate, just one man, sweating, pale, trying to hold his ground. He wasn't shouting. He wasn't even answering. He just kept repeating the same phrase like a prayer.

"Please stay calm. Orders are to wait. Someone will come to escort you."

But no one was coming. I looked up. Behind the steward, I could barely make out the white-painted walls and polished wood of the decks above: calmer, quieter, with only a few second-class passengers drifting toward the lifeboat stations, guided by officers and stewards with whistles and white gloves. There was no panic up there. But down here, it was building like pressure behind glass. A child started crying behind me. A woman whispered Hail Marys in Irish under her breath. An older man collapsed onto a bench, chest heaving, face ghost-white. Madeleine turned to me, her voice barely above a whisper.

"They're really keeping us down here."

I nodded, my throat dry. "They're trying to keep order."

"They're locking us in."

She was right. This wasn't about order. This was about control. This was about deciding who would survive first.

Then she looked at me, as if the realization had finally sunk in. She stared for a long moment before shaking her head. "No. This isn't right. They can't keep us here."

Before I even had time to speak, she spun around and pushed her way toward the gate, slipping into the loudest part of the crowd—where people were shouting for freedom. The cold crept in, finding its way through the crush of bodies pressing and colliding around us.

"Madeleine, I—"

She didn't listen. Instead, she forced her way to the

front of the gate and began shouting, "We have to get through! The lower decks are flooding! People are coming up soaked!" The steward's eyes darted to hers, but he didn't unlock the gate.

"I'm sorry," he said again, softer this time. "I'm just following orders."

"Orders?" Madeleine repeated. "You're letting us die here! We won't make it through if—"

Her voice was swallowed by the panic around her, by the desperate cries and fists pounding for freedom. The crowd surged forward, bodies pressing and lunging all at once, and Madeleine stumbled. I reached out, caught her hand, and yanked her back toward me.

Madeleine's grip tightened around my hand as another passenger rattled the gate and shouted in vain. The steward on the other side had stopped responding entirely; he just stood there, unmoving, eyes glassy, like he wasn't really seeing us anymore.

The gate loomed like a mouth that had decided not to open. Iron bars stretched from wall to wall, black paint chipped from years of hands that had never been meant to push against them. On the other side, the stairwell rose— wide, carpeted, calm. Up there, people moved in orderly lines, guided by officers whose voices were firm but not raised. Down here, nothing moved the way it was supposed to. A man pressed his face between the bars, breath fogging the iron.

"My wife is up there," he said hoarsely. "She went ahead to fetch the children. I just need to—"

"Please step back," the steward said, not meeting his eyes.

Someone laughed—sharp, breaking. "Step back where?"

A woman pushed forward and tried to slide folded money through the bars. "Please," she whispered. "Just one person."

The steward didn't take it. He stared straight ahead, jaw locked. "Remain calm. Orders are to wait."

Wait. The word hit me like a slap. Behind me, someone screamed as water surged into a lower corridor. The sound carried—unmistakable now. A child began to cry. Another man slammed his shoulder into the gate, rattling it hard enough that the steward flinched.

"Open it!" someone shouted.

I looked up the stairwell again. The difference between decks felt obscene—not luxury and poverty, but air and drowning. I felt something harden. All my life, I had waited. Waited for permission. Waited for doors meant for other people. I had survived by folding myself smaller. Not tonight.

"This gate isn't here to save anyone," I said softly to Madeleine. "It's here to control us."

Her breath caught. "Henry—"

"I'm done with that."

Another surge pressed forward. Someone fell. Water roared louder.

"We're not surviving by obeying a system that's already chosen who gets to live," I said.

"They're not opening it," Madeleine told me, as if the

realization had now fully sunk in. "We're going to be trapped here. Oh, God. This isn't right. We're going to—"

"No," I said, already pulling her back. "There's another way."

She turned to me, confused. "What?"

I leaned close. "Oliver once showed me a crew passage, one they use when they're avoiding the passenger corridors. It's narrow, and it's not meant for us, but I think we can get to the service stairs that lead to the boat deck."

"Where?"

"We have to go back. All the way to the midship galley."

She didn't hesitate. "Then let's go."

We turned and pushed against the tide of confused, frightened passengers still moving toward the locked gate. Most didn't notice us; they were too focused on finding some way up. Too desperate to stop. The deeper we went back into the belly of the ship, the more things changed. The floor's pitch was worse now; every step tilted us slightly forward. The lights flickered once, briefly dimming before glowing again with that strange, artificial brightness that felt more like denial than power. And then we turned a corner and stopped dead.

Water. It was seeping into the corridor like a slow-moving tide, black and slick. It wasn't high yet, but it moved with purpose, licking against the metal walls and rushing over our boots in an instant.

Madeleine gasped as it reached our knees. "It's freezing."

"It's seawater," I said, teeth already chattering. "And we're in the middle of the ocean."

I held on to her tighter, forcing us forward. The water surged past our legs, dragging at our steps. My thighs burned with the effort of wading forward, and every breath felt sharper than the last. The cold was a living thing now, not just a temperature but a force, crawling up our legs and stealing their strength with every step. Each time I lifted my foot, it felt heavier, like something below was trying to pull me under. The hem of my coat floated around my knees, soaked and clinging. Madeleine stumbled once, catching herself on the wall, her face pale and drenched with sweat.

"It's coming in fast," she murmured, voice trembling. "God, Henry, this ship is really about to sink."

I didn't answer. I couldn't. I just kept moving. The corridor narrowed ahead, and the dim overhead lights flickered as if the ship itself were gasping for air. The groan of metal echoed through the walls, deep and terrible, like the sound of the *Titanic's* spine beginning to bend. Somewhere behind us, something crashed. A door giving way. Or a bulkhead. We didn't look back.

My hand gripped Madeleine's tighter, knuckles white, and I leaned into the slope of the floor that was no longer flat. The ship was tilting, just slightly, but enough to make every forward step feel like climbing a hill that was trying to collapse beneath us. Somewhere between one stairwell and the next, I stopped thinking about survival. Not because I didn't want it—but because I understood, suddenly, that survival was not neutral. I had always imagined it as something clean.

You lived or you didn't. You made it or you didn't. A

simple line drawn between before and after. But now I saw the truth of it, sharp as the cold air burning my lungs: If I lived through this, I would not come out unchanged. Every step upward tore something loose inside me. Each cry we passed, each hand reaching for help we couldn't give, lodged itself somewhere deep and permanent. These moments were not going to fade. They were carving themselves into me. I thought of New York then—not as a place, but as an idea. Familiar streets. Tenement windows. A life waiting to snap back into shape if I let it. That life no longer fit. I could feel it shrinking even as the ship expanded into chaos around us. The boy who had boarded the *Titanic* believing he could fold himself small enough to survive any room—that boy was slipping away.

If I lived, I would remember this. I would remember the locked gates. The way rules hardened into cruelty. The moment love became a choice instead of a feeling. I didn't know what kind of man would come out the other side of this. Only that I could never be the same one again. I tightened my grip on Madeleine's hand. Whatever survived would have to be honest. And still, the water kept rising. Ahead, I spotted a faint glimmer of light. That should be the corridor junction—a way out. I didn't know what waited for us there, but I knew what was behind us now—death, with salt on its breath. And it was catching up. We reached the narrow, steel-lined service hallway, just beyond the bakery, and I found the door Oliver had once led me through. I reached for the latch with shaking hands. It burst open before I could touch it. And there he was.

"*Henry!*"

Oliver's eyes widened as he saw us, dripping, pale, soaked to the waist, and without thinking, he grabbed me and pulled me into him. His arms wrapped around me in a fast, fierce embrace, cold soaking through both of us, but neither of us cared.

"You're all right," he whispered, then pulled back. His hands grabbed my cheeks and drew me in, his lips colliding against mine. The kiss was laced with relief for us both, and it felt like, ever since the collision, I could breathe for the first time. A moment later, he pulled back and looked at Madeleine, grabbing her hand.

"And you? Are you all right?" Madeleine nodded, shivering hard. "You both need to listen to me. The ship is sinking." He didn't dress it up. He didn't soften it. He just said what everyone already knew.

Madeleine's breath caught. "How long do we have?"

Oliver glanced down the hall behind him. "An hour. Maybe less. Most of the flooding is already below deck. The bow is taking on water faster than they can pump it out."

"And the lifeboats?" I asked.

"They're being loaded now. First-class passengers are already being led to them. But space is tight. Officers are turning people back. If we don't get up there soon, we won't get on." He looked at us both, eyes hard. "You have to move fast. You can't stop. I'll take you the rest of the way through the crew passages, but once we get there … I might not be able to stay."

My heart dropped. "What?"

"I'm still assigned to first class," he said. "If an officer sees me wandering off post, I'll be forced back, or worse. But I'll get you to the boats. I swear it."

Madeleine stepped forward. "We're not going without you."

Oliver's eyes flicked to mine. "We'll try. But first, we get up there. Together."

A lump formed in the back of my throat—not just because the ship was sinking, but because of the thought of him not coming with us. I wasn't sure I could bear it. "Oliver, you need to promise me that—"

"No time for promises," Oliver cut me off, shaking his head. "We have to go. Now." He didn't give me a chance to argue. Instead, he pulled us forward, forcing us to move. The words stayed lodged in my throat, refusing to come out. My eyes burned. This *couldn't* be happening.

Oliver led us into the narrow passage, our soaked boots squelching against the metal floor. The water kept rising behind us, but so did we. The ship groaned. I had Madeleine's hand in mine, gripping her tightly as we followed him through the crew corridors. My mind, surprisingly, was entirely blank, focused only on the survival of all three of us.

"Stay close!" Oliver shouted over his shoulder. "We're cutting through the second-class companionway. It's faster than the main stairs!"

We raced past linen closets, dumbwaiters, and bulkhead doors. The air smelled like damp metal and burnt coal, and behind us, the distant rush of water echoed through the lower decks, chasing our heels. Every stair we climbed tilted a little more than the last. By the time we reached the second-class foyer, the floor felt like it was leaning forward, pulling us toward something we didn't want to see. We passed through a corridor lined with polished wood and patterned carpet. A piano stood tipped at an odd angle against the wall, as if it had tried to stand its ground and failed. A few second-class passengers stood there, frozen, clutching bags or each other. One woman was sobbing quietly, her knuckles white around her child's shoulder.

"Keep moving," Oliver urged. "Don't stop."

Madeleine stumbled once, catching herself on the brass railing of the staircase. "My legs—my knees feel like they're slipping."

"They are," I said. "The angle's worse than it was."

The lights above us flickered again, then steadied, humming slightly louder, like they were fighting to stay alive. We pressed on. The hallway narrowed as we turned down another passage, ornate wall sconces rattling faintly with every deep groan from the hull. Oliver's voice cut through the air again. "Just a few more turns. We'll reach the upper stair near the purser's office; it should still be clear."

We passed a sitting room, its grand settees and potted palms thrown to one side, teacups shattered across a silk rug. A man stood in the doorway, frozen, muttering a prayer under his breath in a language I didn't recognize. He didn't follow us. He just watched.

"Why aren't they moving?" Madeleine gasped, glancing back.

"They don't know where to go," Oliver said. "Or they're waiting for someone."

He slowed slightly at the end of the next corridor, checking the junction before waving us through. The brass trim along the paneling was slick with condensation. Somewhere overhead, we heard a dull bang, followed by the sound of running footsteps, too many of them, too fast.

"Officers?" I asked, breathless.

"Probably," Oliver said. "Or stokers trying to get out from below. They'll be flooding those boiler rooms by now."

Madeleine turned sharply. "Flooding?"

"Flooding faster than they thought," he muttered. "She's going nose-first. That's why everything feels like it's tipping forward."

We kept moving, shoes slipping on the now-slanted floor. At one point, I reached out and caught a painting that had fallen from the wall—a pastoral countryside, cracked in its frame—then let it fall again. At the next junction, we passed a steward covered in sweat. He rushed by without a word, nearly crashing into the wall as he rounded the corner behind us.

"Oliver," I said. "They're panicking."

"I know. That's why we have to be faster."

The corridor opened into another staircase, this one steeper, narrower. The brass railing was already warm from the frantic touch of dozens of hands before ours. As we climbed, my calves burned, and my breath came short. Madeleine slipped again, catching herself on the rail with a sharp gasp.

"Are you all right?" I asked, steadying her.

She nodded quickly. "I just—my boots are soaked. I can't feel my toes."

"We're close," I lied. "Almost there." Oliver glanced back. He knew I was lying, but he didn't correct me. And then, somewhere below us, water slammed into metal with a hollow roar.

Madeleine turned sharply toward the noise. "What was that?"

Oliver didn't hesitate. "The bulkhead. Or a door giving way. Come on!" He led us through the narrowing passage, his breath short but steady. He paused at a junction, glanced down a dim crew corridor, then turned left.

"This way," he said. "It's quicker. We'll cut through here and loop around to the aft stairs."

The hall was darker, the lighting dimmer, flickering slightly above our heads. The air smelled stronger now, salt and rust and something sharper, like wet steel. My heart was still hammering from the climb, but something in my chest tightened further.

"We're close," he said. "It should open into the pantry corridor. Just past that, there will be a stairwell to the boat deck."

He reached for the latch of a metal door and opened it. A wall of water slammed into us, cold and brutal. The wave hit him full in the chest, knocking him backward. Madeleine screamed, and the current surged into the hallway, sweeping all three of us off our feet. I barely had time to shout before the corridor became a torrent, dragging us like paper in a storm. I crashed against the far wall, my shoulder erupting in pain. Madeleine was spinning beside me, hands reaching, mouth open in a silent scream. Oliver vanished, then reappeared, clawing for grip on a broken pipe jutting from the wall. The water rose fast, dark and churning. We tried to swim, but the current carried us, flung us down a long, narrow hall, crashing us against walls and fixtures. My lungs burned. My legs kicked uselessly. We were being funneled until we hit a dead end. We collided with it hard, the three of us tangled and coughing. I reached blindly for Madeleine, pulled her up. She was shivering violently, soaked, and gasping.

"Are you all right?" I shouted.

She nodded, teeth chattering. "Henry, this isn't the way. We're trapped!"

Oliver was already inspecting the space, treading water now up to his chest. "There, maintenance hatch!" he called, spotting a small, iron-rimmed door above the waterline, half hidden by a collapsed locker. He swam to it, threw the latch, and shoved it open with a grunt.

"Madeleine, go! Now!" he shouted. She didn't hesitate. I lifted her, felt her boots scrabble at the metal as she pulled herself through the tight opening into the blackness beyond.

"Henry, your turn!" Oliver shouted. The water surged again, lapping at my chin.

"I'm not leaving you—"

"Go!"

"No!" I shouted, shaking my head. "I will not—"

"Henry, for the love of everything holy, *go*! We don't have time for this!"

I hoisted myself up, my limbs numb, the freezing water clinging to me still. My elbows burned as I dragged myself through, gritting my teeth and gasping from effort. Then I turned back and reached for the man I loved. Oliver leaped, grabbing the edge. I grabbed his arm and hauled him. His legs kicked, one boot slipping, but I held on. With a grunt and final push, he scrambled through, collapsing beside me in the tight steel shaft. We slammed the hatch behind us just as the corridor below vanished under a second flood. We lay there in silence for a moment, our ragged breathing echoing off the metal walls.

Madeleine's voice trembled in the dark. "That … that was—"

"I know," Oliver said softly. "I didn't know it was sealed. That passage should've been clear."

"You saved us," I said, reaching for his hand.

He didn't reply, but he didn't let go either. The crawl-space above us groaned faintly as the ship continued its slow descent.

"We need to go," he said at last. "Come on." The stair-well narrowed, the ship's pitch steeper now. We clung to the railing, boots slipping on the smooth brass runner as we reached the final landing, and then we saw it—the base of the Grand Staircase. What had once been *Titanic's* crown jewel, the sweeping marvel of polished oak and gilded or-nament, now looked like a cathedral caught in collapse. The elegant carpet had ripped loose from parts of the floor, bunching at strange angles. Chairs had slid to one side of the room. A potted plant lay shattered near the base of the stairs. And the clock, still reading just past 1:20, loomed silently above the landing, its carved cherubs watching the chaos below. But it was the water that stopped us cold. A dark sheet of it was rising from the bottom of the staircase, pouring in from the lower decks. It moved with eerie silence at first, lapping over the steps like a slow tide, but you could see the current, the force behind it. This wasn't a trickle. It was coming in fast.

"*Mon Dieu*," Madeleine whispered.

Oliver stepped forward, gripping the banister. "It wasn't supposed to reach this far yet."

The water was already climbing the lower steps—step by step, inch by inch. And behind us, the ship groaned again, longer and louder this time.

"We have to go now," Oliver said.

I turned to him, heart hammering. "Is there another way?"

He nodded, pointing up the staircase. "This leads directly to the A Deck landing, just off the boat deck. But we have to move. Once this fills the foyer, we won't make it."

Madeleine looked at the water, then at me. "Can we outrun it?"

"We don't have a choice."

We started climbing. The steps tilted beneath our feet. Madeleine grabbed the railing, pulling herself up as the incline grew worse. Oliver stayed just behind us, urging us forward. My legs burned, soaked socks squelching in my boots, every breath sharp in my lungs. I glanced back once. The water was chasing us now, roaring. It hit the base of the staircase with a wave, sending a chair tumbling backward in its wake. The carved railing cracked somewhere below with a sickening snap.

The *Titanic* was no longer holding herself upright. She was falling, and we were running out of time.

By the time we reached the top of the staircase, our lungs burned and our legs felt like they'd been dipped in molten iron. My hands gripped the banister as if it were the only thing keeping me upright.

"Here," Oliver said, breathless. "This way."

We turned the corner into a wide, sweeping corridor, and he pushed open a heavy set of double doors that gave way with a low groan—the first-class dining saloon. Even with the world tilting, even with panic clawing at our heels, it stopped us. It was massive. Soaring columns stretched across the length of the room, painted white and lined with gilded trim. The ceiling hung low but lavish, bordered in soft floral plasterwork and carved medallions. Crystal chandeliers dangled from above, swaying gently as the ship continued to shift. Endless rows of linen-covered tables spread across the saloon, each one set with china, silverware, and glass that glimmered in the failing light. Some settings were half finished, crumbs on plates, napkins folded beside empty wine goblets. Others were pristine, untouched. It looked like the ghosts of a hundred dinners had been frozen mid-bite. We stood in silence for a moment, surrounded by the faint clink of a spoon sliding across a plate as it shifted from the tilt.

I looked toward the far end of the saloon. A plate slid gently from its charger and shattered on the floor. None of us moved.

"I need a minute," Madeleine said, sinking into one of the chairs, gripping the table to steady herself. "Just a minute."

Oliver looked at me, as if he wanted us to keep on running, but I shook my head. Madeleine needed a moment; I knew her well enough to know that. In turn, Oliver gave a slight nod, and that was it. We let her sit. Oliver and I leaned against one of the pillars near the wall, catching our breath. Below the eerie quiet of the room, we could hear the distant sound of chaos creeping closer, muffled shouting, hurried footsteps, and the unmistakable echo of something sloshing.

"Do you hear that?" I asked.

Oliver nodded grimly. "It's the water."

Madeleine looked up sharply. "It's here?"

"Not yet. But it's coming from below, and from through the ship. The forward compartments are already flooding faster than they guessed. The pitch is worse now—feel it?"

I did. The whole room leaned forward slightly, tilting the chandeliers to a disturbing angle.

"They served oysters in here," Oliver said suddenly, shaking his head as if the thought now seemed rather ridiculous. "And squab. And soups I can't pronounce. The night we left port, there was music. Four violins. Laughter so loud I could hear it through the service doors." He looked at me. "And look at all of it now."

"I don't want to die in a dining room," Madeleine said

at last, standing again, pale but composed. "No matter how expensive the chairs are."

"Neither do I," I said.

Oliver straightened, reaching for the door. "We're almost there. A few more corridors and we're on the boat deck." He turned to us, steadier now. "When we get there, don't stop. Don't wait. If you see an opening, take it."

"With you," I said. Oliver looked at me then, his expression impossible to read, but it no longer mattered. This was the one thing I would not give up on. Even with death staring me straight in the eye, I would refuse to move without him.

CHAPTER 22

The Boats Lower Away

HENRY

The final stairwell opened into darkness. This was not the kind we were used to down below, flickering electric lights and steel bulkheads, but the open, empty kind that wrapped around your skin and pressed into your lungs.

We stepped out onto the boat deck, and the first thing I noticed was the cold. The second was the music. The band was playing. Somewhere near the first-class entrance, faint but unwavering, strings rose above the wind in soft, melancholic harmony. Slow and graceful, like the end of something beautiful. It didn't fit what was happening around us, but maybe that was the point.

The scene before us felt like a dream unraveling. The wide, pristine deck—once quiet and polished, lit by white lamps and whispers—was now full of motion. People swarmed along the railing near the lifeboats. Officers shouted orders, their voices growing hoarse as they tried to maintain control. Stewards herded passengers into lines, separating families by language and class, with urgency in every gesture.

Long, white lifeboats were lowered one by one into the black sea, filled as quickly as order allowed. Some boats were already gone. Empty davits hung like arms reaching out over the edge, ropes swinging in the wind. Others were half full, lowered slowly, creaking and swaying as they dropped into the ocean below.

We should have felt relief, but instead, we were met with a chilling truth. There wouldn't be enough space in the lifeboats for everyone. That much was already clear. The *Titanic* had been the very symbol of power, declared unsinkable. No one had ever truly believed the lifeboats would be needed.

"There aren't enough lifeboats," Madeleine said, turning to face us. She was right. I didn't say it, but we all knew. There were never enough.

"Women and children only!" a voice bellowed from the port side. "Step back—men, step back!"

We moved closer, joining the line of confused passengers already being corralled near boat 12. The first-class lifeboats had already been mostly launched. Now, second-class and the few third-class passengers who had made it this far were trying to follow. A woman sobbed behind me, clutching a baby to her chest, while her husband argued with an officer to let them on together. The officer wouldn't budge.

"Where do we go now?" I asked.

"They're loading from the forward davits now," he said. "We might have a chance if we—"

"Women and children!" another officer shouted. "Only!"

Men were being pulled back—gently, but firmly. Some resisted. Others gave in with broken expressions, stepping away from wives, daughters, and sisters, never turning around. A boy, maybe fifteen, tried to step forward with his mother. He was stopped and told to go back. He looked too old to be called a child.

The panic was still mild for now.

A quiet current of understanding was beginning to ripple through the crowd, threading between sobs and questions. Not everyone was going to make it. I turned to Oliver. He didn't meet my eyes right away.

Then he said, softly, "They won't let me on. Not yet. The passengers have to get on first."

"But we'll find a way," I said. "We can—"

"You need to get on a boat," he interrupted me, gripping my arm. "You and Madeleine."

Madeleine looked at us both, saying nothing. Whether her face was already wet with wind or tears, I couldn't tell.

"No!" I said. "Not without you."

He held my gaze, firm and steady, but there was a crack in it now. "Henry. Please. You have to do this."

"No! Absolutely not! I'm not going anywhere without you!" I shouted, tears burning in my eyes. My heart slammed against my ribs, and I struggled to breathe. How was any of this fair? I had only just found him. I had only just found meaning in my life ... and now it all threatened to be torn away.

The music played on. The wind bit harder. The ship groaned beneath our feet. And behind us, more lifeboats began to lower into the dark. The deck had gone from tense to frantic. The boat ahead was nearly full. Its ropes creaked as they strained under the weight of passengers and gravity. An officer in a white coat and revolver holster barked orders at the line.

"One more woman—now! Move!" He pointed toward us. Madeleine froze.

"No," she whispered, instinctively stepping back.

The officer pointed again. "You! Step forward, now!"

For half a second, I thought she might refuse. I saw it in her shoulders—the way they squared instead of yielding. The way her feet shifted backward, instinctively, toward us. Madeleine had never been afraid of danger. What frightened her now was leaving. Her eyes found mine, wide and blazing. "I won't go without you," she said. The words cut clean through the noise of the deck. Around us, the lifeboat lurched as weight shifted inside it. A woman screamed when the ropes jerked. The sea below looked impossibly far away—black, endless, waiting.

"You have to," I said, forcing the words out past the tightness in my chest. "You're not choosing between us. You're choosing life."

"And what are you choosing?" she demanded, her voice breaking even as it sharpened.

I couldn't answer her. Oliver stepped forward then,

placing himself beside me—not between us, but with us. His face was pale, his jaw set with a resolve that made my breath hitch.

"Madeleine," he said, steady despite the chaos. "Listen to me. You live. That's the only rule that matters right now."

Her gaze snapped to him. "And you?"

He didn't hesitate. "I stay."

The simplicity of it knocked the air from my lungs. Madeleine shook her head violently.

"No. No, that's not—this isn't how it's supposed to—"

An officer grabbed her arm. "Miss—now!"

She looked back at us one last time, fury and terror and love all crashing together in her expression.

"I'm not leaving you," she said again, softer now, like a plea.

And that was when I understood that if I didn't move her, the moment would pass. The sea does not wait for courage.

Without hesitation, I shoved her forward. Madeleine frantically shook her head, trying to step back closer to us. Her face was pale beneath the flickering lamplight, her eyes wide and brimming. "I'm not going without you!"

"You have to," Oliver said, already nudging her forward again.

"You're getting on that boat!" I shouted, the back of my eyes burning.

"I'm not—," she choked out. "No. I'm not leaving you both."

"Madeleine, listen to me. This is what they're giving us.

You take it. You take the seat. We'll find another way. We have to!" I shouted at her. My heart pounded inside my chest painfully, but this was the only way.

She shook her head, tears spilling down her cheeks now. "What if there's no other way?"

"There is," I lied. "You don't have to worry about us!"

She looked between us again. Her lips trembled. "I don't want to die up there, wondering if you're still down here."

"You won't," Oliver said, stepping beside me. "Because we'll be right behind you."

I pulled her into a tight hug, pressing my cheek against hers, my voice breaking. "You're the strongest person I've ever known. You've never let anyone stop you. Don't start now."

She sobbed once, hard. I could feel it in her ribs.

The officer was shouting again. "Now! The next seat, take it, or we lower!"

Madeleine pulled back, her hands trembling as she touched both of our faces, one after the other. Then, like something in her gave out, she nodded. She turned. A steward took her arm and helped her toward the edge, where the lifeboat was swaying in its davits. She climbed in clumsily, life jacket stiff, her shawl still wrapped tight around her shoulders. She looked back just once—just long enough for me to raise my hand. And then the boat began to lower, creaking over the edge of the ship, into the black sea waiting below.

The rope creaked like it was alive. Madeleine gripped the edge of the lifeboat as it began its descent, her knuckles burning white against the frozen wood. The ship rose above her—impossibly tall now—its lights glaring down like unblinking eyes. She craned her neck, searching the rail where she'd last seen me. Where she'd last seen both of us.

The boat lurched, and a woman beside her screamed. Another crossed herself so fast her fingers blurred. Someone dropped a shawl into the black, and it vanished instantly. Madeleine barely noticed. She could probably still see my face—tight with fear, furious with love, refusing to let her perish without a fight. And Oliver beside me, steady even as the world broke, pushing her forward as if her survival was the only thing that mattered. The guilt must have struck like a physical blow. She was going down while we stayed up. The rope slid faster now. Cold rose from the water in visible breath, sharp and metallic. Ice. She had smelled it earlier. She smelled it now, stronger, closer.

"Henry," she whispered, though the wind tore the name from her lips before it could reach me.

The lifeboat hit the water hard. The impact jolted her spine and knocked the breath from her lungs. Freezing spray soaked her skirts instantly, the cold cutting straight through wool and skin. The sea was black—so black it looked solid.

"Row!" someone shouted.

The oars dipped. The boat began to move away from the *Titanic*, slow and reluctant, as if the water itself resisted the separation. Madeleine twisted around, watching the ship recede. It was beautiful. That was the worst part. The lights still burned. Music drifted faintly across the water, thin and unreal. People moved along the railings like shadows, clinging, slipping, shouting into the dark. And somewhere up there were the two people she loved most in the world. Her chest tightened until breathing hurt.

If I live, she thought, I will remember. Henry's stubborn courage. Oliver's quiet resolve. The way they had looked at each other like the world made sense for once. She would carry their names if no one else did. The lifeboat pulled farther away. The angle of the ship grew steeper. Someone gasped. Someone prayed. Madeleine wrapped her arms around herself, shaking violently—not just from the cold, but from the knowledge settling deep in her bones. Survival was not mercy. It was responsibility.

I didn't realize I was crying until I felt Oliver's hand close around mine.

"She's safe," he said, though his voice wavered. "That's what matters."

We stood there, watching the empty ropes sway where Madeleine's boat had been. The space she'd occupied felt louder than any scream. The ship groaned again beneath our feet, deeper now, angrier. Around us, men were being pushed back—hands raised, voices breaking as officers enforced rules that suddenly felt medieval. A husband tried to follow his wife and was yanked away by his collar. A teenage boy was stopped because his voice had dropped. A man in a wool coat knelt on the deck, forehead pressed to the boards, whispering something over and over like a prayer gone wrong. I grabbed Oliver's sleeve.

"Come on." He frowned.

"Where?"

"There," I said, pointing toward another lifeboat still loading. "If we move fast—if we don't draw attention—"

He followed me without argument. We slipped into the edge of the crowd near the davits. The boat rocked as women were helped over the rail. A steward reached for another passenger.

"Miss—this way!"

I shoved Oliver forward, heart pounding.

"Now." The officer's gaze snapped to us instantly.

"Step back," he barked. "Men are not permitted."

"He's with me," I said, breathless, gesturing uselessly. "He's—"

"I don't care who he's with," the officer snapped. "Step back, sir."

Oliver's hand tightened on my arm. "Henry."

"No," I said, louder than I meant to. "You don't understand—"

"I understand perfectly," the officer replied, resting his hand on the butt of his revolver. "Move."

The crowd surged, separating us for a moment. I felt Oliver's fingers slip from my coat.

"No!" I shouted. He shoved his way back to me, face pale but resolute.

"Stop," he said fiercely. "Don't do this."

"Do what?" I demanded.

"Let you die?" His voice dropped.

"Let you live." The words landed like a blow. "You think I'm leaving you?" I whispered.

He leaned close, foreheads nearly touching despite the chaos.

"If one of us gets off this ship alive," he said, voice shaking but certain, "it has to be you."

I shook my head violently. "No. No, we stay together."

He smiled—a terrible, tender smile.

"We already are. That doesn't change just because the world is ending."

Another officer shouted. The boat began to lower.

Oliver gripped my shoulders. "Promise me something."

"What?"

"Don't freeze," he said. "Don't wait. If you see a chance—take it."

I couldn't speak. My throat had closed completely. He pressed his forehead briefly to mine. "I love you." Then the crowd shoved us apart again. And this time, the space between us did not close.

"She's my best friend," I whispered. "Like a sister. She's family."

He squeezed my hand tighter. "Then we survive. And we find her again."

CHAPTER 23

Hold Tight

OLIVER

Behind us, another boat was being loaded. And ahead, the night stretched on. The ropes creaked louder now. We stood at the edge of the deck, just behind the officer still shouting commands, and watched boat 12 descend, inch by inch, into the darkness below. The wind tore at Madeleine's shawl as she sat stiffly near the stern, her hands gripping the edges of the lifeboat like they might come apart. She looked up once, her eyes searching the railing, and I raised my hand again.

Then the boat dipped out of sight, swallowed by the black curve of the ship and the sea. Henry didn't say anything. He just stood beside me, shoulders tense, breathing steady, watching as the rope cables snapped back up empty, swaying in the wind. Around us, the deck had transformed. Panic had taken root. The band still played, unbelievably, something soft and delicate, but it was a distant backdrop now, almost drowned out by the sound of voices cracking, of orders being barked, of goodbyes spoken like confessions.

"I love you."

"Take the children."

"Promise me you'll tell her I tried."

A woman sobbed into her husband's chest as he kissed the crown of her head, then lifted their child into a waiting boat. Another man pressed a ring into someone's hand, closed her fingers over it, and turned away before she could see him cry. The deck's tilt had worsened. You had to lean backward to stay upright, as if the ship were slowly trying to dump us all into the ocean. Chairs had slid. Luggage had rolled. Someone's cane had clattered across the floor and vanished over the side.

"It's getting worse," Henry murmured.

I nodded grimly. "She's nose-down now. It'll only get steeper."

People were shouting behind us. A lifeboat filled too quickly. Another one launched half empty. A woman refused to board without her husband and was dragged away. Children clung to their mothers. Old men stood back, coats buttoned, faces pale, as if waiting for someone to tell them it had all been a mistake. I felt cold creep into my bones, not from the air, but from the grief surrounding us like fog. We were standing in the middle of history's last chapter, and no one knew what the ending would be. Henry turned to me once more.

"I can't—," he said, shaking. It was freezing—blistering cold that cut through our coats, our life jackets, our skin. My face was raw, my fingers stiff, and my teeth wouldn't stop chattering, either. "It's too cold. Just for a minute, let's get inside."

I looked around the boat deck, my jaw clenched as the groaning tilt of the ship deepened. The deck was slick with frost and sea spray. People were still boarding lifeboats in clumps, but the line had grown erratic. The order was slipping.

"Alright," I said. "Come on. Just for a minute."

We moved quickly, heading toward the first-class entrance, past a line of stewards who were shouting to "stay calm," though their voices cracked with the effort. We ducked inside, into the grand reception area—and it hit us like a punch to the chest. The temperature shift was immediate, but so was the noise. People were running now, clothes half buttoned, voices rising, and footsteps pounding against the tiled floors.

At the far end, the Grand Staircase was flooding. Water poured down its polished steps like a black tide, rushing faster than I could have imagined. The carved wood gleamed under the lamplight, soaking, breaking, and groaning under the weight of the water now rushing in from below. A chandelier above the lower landing had begun to sway violently, its chain straining as the pitch of the ship increased. One of the cherubs above the clock had already been swallowed by the rising flood. People screamed. Some froze. Others turned and ran, not knowing where to go, only knowing they had to get away. I grabbed Henry's arm as another rush of passengers pushed past us.

"We have to move," Henry said. "That's coming fast."

I couldn't bring myself to move. For once, I had no plan, no idea what to do next. Madeleine was as safe as she could be—she was a woman. Henry and I didn't share that fortune, and there was no way of knowing what would happen to us.

My mind ran through the calculations again and again. Once all the women were aboard, they would start taking men. First class first, of course. But even then, there was no telling how many men would make it onto the boats. And there was even less certainty that Henry and I would be among them.

"Oliver?" Henry shook me gently, snapping me out of the train of my thoughts. I turned to face him.

"I don't know where to go," I admitted. "They're only letting women and children in the boats. We've seen men pulled away from their wives. Officers are turning them back at gunpoint. And the lifeboats, Henry … there aren't enough. There never were."

"But there has to be something," Henry said, gripping my hand. "You've gotten us this far. We'll find a boat, or a door, or a—something."

I swallowed the lump that had formed in the back of my throat. Despite the chill around us, it felt like I was burning with doubt from the inside out, with no way to know what to do.

"I'm supposed to know every inch of this ship," I said at last. "But right now I feel like I'm standing in a building I've never been inside before."

The sound of the water filled the room now—rushing, splashing, roaring. The ship tilted again, sharp enough to make people stumble and slide across the tile. Henry reached out and took my face in both hands. "Then we figure it out together."

I nodded once, tightly.

And then we ran back into the corridor, away from the water and toward whatever might still be left above us. Somehow, with Henry by my side and his words of reassurance, my mind began to clear. Plans began forming. We needed to get to the back of the ship. The bow was going under, and the stern was higher. If there were any chance left—any collapsible boats and any debris that floated—they'd end up there. It was our best shot.

"We need to go to the back of the ship," I said, pulling Henry by the arm as another wave of voices crashed around us. Henry didn't question me, and instead, he followed my lead. We pushed through the crowd that now swarmed the boat deck in full chaos. No more lines. No more polite orders. Just the unfiltered panic of hundreds of souls realizing the water was no longer coming—it was here.

A man was weeping into a steward's chest. A woman clutched her daughter to her side and screamed at anyone who got too close. A crewman tried to direct passengers to lifeboat 4, only to be shoved aside by a man wild-eyed with terror. We passed a couple—an elderly man and woman—sitting on a bench, holding hands. Calm. Still. As if they'd made peace with what was coming. I couldn't look at them for long.

I kept my grip tight on his wrist as we wove between bodies, slipping past crates, benches, and abandoned luggage. The deck was tilting harder now—enough that people had to brace themselves against walls or railings. A few had fallen. One man's legs had given out entirely. He crawled across the planks on his hands and knees. The ship was groaning, louder now, deep within her hull. The steel was flexing and bending, with a sound I could feel in my chest more than hear. We reached the aft section of the boat deck. A small crowd had gathered around the final lifeboats—collapsible D had already launched, but collapsible B was still being loosened from its lashings, tilted, and clinging sideways to the deck like a broken rib.

"Is that going in the water?" Henry shouted.

"They're trying," I shouted back, eyes fixed on the struggle ahead.

Several crewmen were swarming over the boat, trying to unfasten it and lift it to the davits. A few passengers stood nearby, waiting for a signal, but there was no order anymore. One rope snapped. The whole thing nearly tipped over the rail.

"We're too late," Henry said.

"No," I growled. This couldn't be it. I wouldn't allow it. I *had* to find a way. If not for both of us, then for Henry, at least. "We're not."

We pressed forward, but were soon stopped by a man who grabbed me by the coat and shouted, "Where's the captain?! Where are the officers?!" His face was filled with fear, but I somehow managed to pull free.

"Gone, probably! Help those men or get out of the way!" I shouted.

To our left, a young boy, maybe twelve, was crying as

his mother tried to get him into a life jacket too large for his shoulders. She met my eyes. Her lips trembled. She didn't say anything, but I saw everything she wanted to say.

The tilt grew steeper. The stern was now angled upward, the bow pulling down into the black. The deck was no longer a place to stand. It was a place to climb. I grabbed the edge of the railing, panting.

"They're going to get it down—they have to. If we can stay near it, maybe ...," I mumbled, interrupted by another crack—metal against metal. One of the davits bent, and the crowd scattered. The collapsible boat tipped, spilling tools and ropes onto the planks. Dozens of lifeboats dotted the ocean now, floating lanterns of safety on a sea that offered none. Voices called from them.

I turned to Henry, eyes glassy. "We're not going in a lifeboat, I don't think."

"No," he said. "But we're not dying on the deck either."

I nodded. We were either going to survive or we'd die trying. There was no way we'd stay here and not do anything. Around us, people were choosing, too: jump, run, pray, or hold on. Some threw themselves into the sea, arms flailing. Some sat down and cried. Others climbed, looking for higher ground, as if height could save them.

I gripped Henry's hand again, hard. "We stay together. No matter what."

"No matter what," he echoed. And with the ship groaning beneath our feet, and the stars still impossibly bright above us, we turned toward the very end of the *Titanic*. Where the last of the hope was floating just out of reach.

The stern had risen so high that the deck now slanted beneath our feet like a rooftop. People were crawling, climbing, slipping backward into the dark. Every bench, every post, and every bolt in the deck groaned under the stress. The wood cracked. Screams echoed. Someone near the rail lost their grip and vanished with a splash I never saw—just heard.

I grabbed hold of a thick iron grating near the ventilation shaft—a fixed part of the ship's framework. Just wide enough for us to cling to. Just strong enough, hopefully, to hold.

"Henry, here!" I shouted, and he spun toward me. A moment later, he ran to me, boots scraping, and clutched the metal with both hands. I reached out and pulled him close, locking an arm around his back as if my body alone might keep him tethered to the world.

"Don't let go," I said, voice ragged. "No matter what happens—don't let go."

"I'm not going anywhere," Henry responded, pressing his forehead against mine. At that moment, his words held so much conviction that it was the only thing in this world I could hold on to.

His breath was hot in the cold air, his lips trembling—not from fear, but from the chill that surrounded us like death made wind. All around us, passengers clung to whatever they could. A man prayed aloud in German. Another wept openly, whispering names I didn't recognize. A group near the very rail was singing "Nearer, My God, to Thee" with voices thin and shaky and full of surrender.

We weren't praying, though. We were holding on.

"I'm here," I whispered, tightening my grip on his soaked coat. "I'm with you."

Henry buried his face in my shoulder. I felt his breath stutter. His hands were shaking. So were mine. The ship let out a new sound then—not a groan, but a scream. A high, metallic screech that tore through the air like the sky itself was splitting apart. The stern lurched. We screamed as we were lifted and tilted sharply forward. Screams rose like a tidal wave. People slid past us, tumbling, grabbing railings, and grabbing each other. But I held Henry tighter, and I wouldn't let go.

"I've got you!" I shouted. "I've got you, Henry!"

If we were going to die, we were going to die holding on to each other. And at that moment, above the roar of water and the crack of steel, for the first time in years, I didn't feel alone. Not for a second. Henry and I clung to the iron grating, arms locked tight around each other. My muscles burned, my fingers stiff and useless, but I didn't let go. I couldn't. If I did, I knew I'd fall not just into the sea, but away from him.

"I've got you," I whispered again, over and over like a prayer.

"I've got you, too," he responded.

Around us, the ship groaned like something alive and dying all at once. The deck was nearly vertical now. People above us screamed. Some lost their grip and slid past, vanishing into the black below with cries that were cut short by silence or the sickening sound of water. And then, the lights flickered, just once.

Everything on deck—the fear, the motion, and the voices—stopped for a second. Then the lights flickered again, sputtering like dying stars, and they went out. Darkness swallowed everything. No glow from the chandeliers. No warmth from the wall sconces. The mighty *Titanic*, queen of the sea, was suddenly a ghost, adrift in silence and cold. Then came the sound. A rumble, deep and monstrous, rose from the belly of the ship. It started low, almost like thunder, and then grew, grew, until it was a roar that shook the very air around us. A sound like the earth itself was splitting apart. Steel screamed. Rivets snapped. Bulkheads collapsed deep within the ship's bowels, where none of us could see. I could feel it in my chest, my bones, my teeth. It wasn't just sinking now. It was *breaking*.

I clutched Henry tighter. "This is it!" I shouted.

The deck beneath us shivered, lurching violently. We both screamed as the world tipped forward again, harder, faster. Far below, somewhere in the void, we heard the explosion of water as it forced its way into places it was never meant to reach. There was no light now, only starlight above and blackness below.

"Oh my God," I gasped. The stern tipped violently forward, then slammed back down into the water with a deafening crash that knocked us from the railing. It hit with such force I felt it through my ribs. A wave of freezing seawater shot skyward and came raining down around us, black and frigid. I grabbed Henry, hauling us both toward a section of grating just as the ship steadied again, briefly, floating oddly upright in the chaos. The deck groaned. People were sobbing. Screaming. Praying. Climbing.

"Henry, hold on!" I shouted, dragging us toward the rear deck rail as the ship began to rise again, slower now.

She was going up. The stern lifted—higher, higher still, like something divine was plucking it from the sea by its tail. And we, clinging to the remains of a railing, were going with it. The deck was nearly vertical now. What had once been a grand staircase, a polished deck, and a place for walking and laughter was a ladder to the stars.

I looked at Henry. At that moment, one thing became as plain as day. Ironic, given that I may not live to see another one of those.

"I love you!" I shouted, breath catching with the cold. I choked, my heart thudding louder than the screaming all around us. "I love you, Henry!"

His eyes widened. He didn't have to say it back; I could feel it in my bones that he felt it, too. "I don't want to—"

"We won't get separated!" I shouted over the cold, the metal tearing itself apart. But just as the words left my mouth, a new shriek split the air, and the ship gave another sharp jolt. And then, my grip slipped.

The deck was no longer a deck. It was a wall. We clung to the iron grating, bodies pressed together, boots scraping uselessly against metal that had forgotten how to be horizontal. People slid past us screaming, hands clawing for purchase that didn't exist. The air was full of prayer and terror and the sound of steel tearing itself apart. I wrapped one arm around Henry's back, anchoring him. My other hand locked into the grating beside his.

"Don't look down," I said.

He didn't. He looked at me instead. His face was pale, lashes rimmed with ice, hair plastered to his forehead. And still—still—his eyes were steady.

"If we make it through this," I shouted over the roar, "I don't want a life built on hiding anymore."

"What?" he gasped.

"I want mornings," I said. "I want to wake up without fear. I want a place where I don't have to pretend I'm invisible." The ship screamed. "I want New York," I continued, breathless but determined. "I want you."

Henry's heart broke open.

"You'll have it," he shouted. "You'll have all of it."

I smiled then—real and unguarded.

"Promise?"

"I promise," he said.

And he meant it with every atom of himself. A violent jolt ripped through the stern. People above us lost their grip all at once, bodies sliding past like falling stars. Someone slammed into my shoulder and vanished. Another scream cut off midair. I tightened my hold.

"Oliver—"

"I've got you!" I shouted.

"I know," he said. "I know." The ship lurched again, harder this time. The angle grew impossible. My boots slipped. The iron burned my palms. And then—

"No—*NO!*"

I lost my footing. The slick, wet metal gave way beneath my boots, and I tumbled backward, arms flailing. Henry reached for me, grabbed air. Nothing.

"*HENRY!*" I screamed, my voice ripping from my throat.

And then, nothing. Just water. Cold, endless water.

CHAPTER 24

Into the Freezing Sea

HENRY

"*OLIVER!*" I screamed, my voice breaking, my heart with it. Gone.

The ship surged again, pointing to the stars. I clung to the rail, eyes burning, throat raw, my whole body shaking—not just from the cold now, but from the empty space where he'd been. He'd said I love you. And I never got to tell him that I loved him, too.

All I could do was hold on and pray he survived the fall. The screams were everywhere. They came from all directions—above, behind, and beside me—blending into a chorus of raw human panic, unfiltered and primal. Men and women cried out for God, for loved ones, for mercy. Some didn't scream at all. They just wept, or stared wide-eyed into nothing as they clung to the railings around me, their hands slipping from the frost-covered steel. I clung to the same rail, my chest heaving, my arms burning from the weight of holding on. The deck beneath me trembled, groaning like it was alive, like it resented being torn apart inch by inch.

"*OLIVER*!" I shouted again, throat raw.

Nothing. Just shapes—dozens of them—flailing in the freezing sea. I blinked away the sting in my eyes, but it wasn't the wind. He was gone. The boy who kissed me in the smoking room, who led me through the ship like he was guiding me through a dream, and who told me he loved me just moments ago was gone. The grief cracked through my chest like the hull splitting apart.

The stern began to rise, slow at first, then faster, steeper, until we were no longer standing—we were climbing. The deck tilted up to forty-five degrees, then steeper still, until it felt like we were clinging to a vertical wall. I was panting now, dizzy, every breath a knife in my lungs. My arms screamed with the effort of holding on, my fingers stiff and bloodless on the rail. And then, ninety degrees. The ship was standing on end. The bow was gone, fully swallowed by the sea, and the stern stood like a tower piercing the stars. People hung from railings, staircases, light posts—anything. Some still climbed. Most couldn't anymore.

Then, a great groan—the sound of the final bulkheads giving way. The entire structure shivered. I looked down. Blackness. Below me was nothing but the endless, churning dark.

This was it.

If I stayed, I'd be dragged down with it. If I jumped, I might not survive the fall. But either way, it was time. I whispered, "I'm sorry," to no one and everyone, and I climbed over the railing. My heart thundered. One last look at the stars, and then I let go. I fell. Wind screamed past my ears. My body twisted in freefall. I had just enough time to pray that Oliver had made it into the water.

That somehow, he was out there, still fighting. And then, the sea rose to meet me. A thousand knives pierced through me, and every inch of me seized at once. The cold wasn't just cold; it was consuming. It punched the air from my lungs, stole the scream from my throat, and turned my blood to ice and my muscles to stone. I couldn't breathe. I couldn't think. I was underwater. And the ship above me groaned one last time. And then, I rose. Gasping, freezing, and alone.

The cold stole thought before it stole breath. It hollowed me out, scraped me clean from the inside, turned my limbs into dead weight. I screamed, or tried to, but my body could barely remember how.

"Oliver!" I choked.

The sea answered with screams of its own. Bodies thrashed around me, arms flailing, hands grabbing, voices begging. Someone clung to my life jacket, dragging us both under until I kicked free in blind panic. Another body struck mine and vanished again.

"Oliver!" I cried, voice tearing itself apart.

The ship was gone now. Just black water and stars and the sound of people dying. My muscles burned, then stopped responding. The cold crept higher, stealing sensation inch by inch. I couldn't feel my feet. Then my calves. Then my hands began to fail me. This is how it happens, a distant part of me realized. This is how people stop fighting. I floated there, gasping, screaming his name until my voice was nothing but a rasp.

"Please," I whispered. "Please."

A man nearby went quiet mid-cry. His mouth remained open, eyes glassy. He drifted past me, face tilted toward the stars. I wanted to follow him. But then I saw something. Not a lifeboat—too low, too wrong—but canvas, half submerged, men clinging to it like barnacles. An overturned collapsible, barely floating, barely there. My body screamed no. My heart screamed yes.

"For him," I told myself. "For Oliver." I kicked.

Each stroke felt like dragging myself through stone. The sea slapped me under once, twice. I swallowed water and came back up coughing, vision blurring. The boat drifted closer—or I drifted closer to it. I didn't know which. "Help!" I croaked. A voice answered. Hands reached. And I fought.

Screams struck me all at once. The air was filled with them. They came from every direction, rising and falling, hundreds of voices howling into the night. Men, women, children. Crying for help. For God. For anyone. I treaded water, arms and legs heavy and useless, the life jacket forcing my head above the waves. My teeth chattered so hard I thought they'd break. My hands were numb. My feet were blocks of ice. The cold was inside me now, crawling deeper with every second.

The ship was gone. Only the stars remained, along with the screaming. The water around me surged, pulling me under again with the ship's final gasp. I went under for just a second—maybe two—but it felt like forever. I kicked, coughed, and came up spitting salt. Bodies thrashed in every direction. Some were already motionless, floating on their backs. Some were still fighting. Some climbed onto each other to stay above the surface. A man clawed at my shoulder, trying to grab hold of my life jacket. I shoved him away. He disappeared beneath the waves without a sound. A woman nearby screamed a name over and over.

"Oliver!" I shouted. My voice was hoarse, shredded. No answer. "*OLIVER!*"

The lifeboats were far now—dim silhouettes in the distance, lit only by stars and the occasional flicker of a lantern. The screams didn't stop. They went on and on.

Above it all, I floated, barely alive, heart frozen, lungs burning, and eyes searching. I was praying that somewhere in the blackness, he was searching too.

I didn't know how long I'd been in the water. Seconds felt like hours. Minutes, like years. My body was numb, no longer shivering. My fingers wouldn't bend. My legs moved only because they had to. The screams were starting to fade. Some had stopped entirely. And I was beginning to wonder if I was next.

A shape then bobbed low in the water. Not a full lifeboat—it was smaller, closer to the surface. Canvas sides, half collapsed, slumped as if dropped rather than lowered properly. It floated awkwardly, barely upright, and it was crowded—at least a dozen men clinging to it, legs in the water, arms over the side, too many bodies for a boat that wasn't meant to carry that much. A collapsible lifeboat. Collapsible B. And it was close. Twenty yards. Maybe thirty. Far, but not impossible.

A voice in my head whispered, "Swim."

Another part answered, "You can't."

But then I saw one of the men on the overturned boat wave an arm—just a flash of movement, and I heard it.

"Over here!"

I didn't know who had shouted, but I started swimming. Each stroke was agony. My arms felt like they were made of stone. My legs kicked, but barely moved me. I went under once and surfaced again with a cry. The Atlantic didn't want me to reach it, but I didn't care.

Oliver, I thought. *Please be there. Please be somewhere.*

The boat drifted slightly, pushed by the swells, and I adjusted my course, gritting my teeth. My vision tunneled. My lungs ached. My fingers could barely keep hold of the surface when I reached a broken oar drifting nearby. Then, finally, my hand struck wood.

"Grab him!" someone yelled.

Two arms reached out and pulled me forward. I flopped against the side of the boat, half over the edge, half in the water. My body was dead weight.

"Come on, hold him—he's in!"

Another push. Another pull. And I was on top of the canvas-covered hull, clinging with the others. Legs still in the water. My cheek pressed against the soaked edge. I coughed up saltwater. I sobbed without sound, but I was alive. And I'd made it.

"You're all right, lad," someone said beside me, patting me on the back. "You're all right now."

The cold was no longer sharp—it was complete. My body had stopped fighting it. Now, it just endured. Around me, the others clung the same way—men packed shoulder to shoulder, some murmuring prayers, some whispering names, some completely silent, staring blankly into the dark. No one had room to sit. We just held on, breath by breath.

"*Oliver …,*" I whispered, lips barely working.

No answer.

I blinked up at the sky. The stars were still there. The sea stretched out, black and infinite, broken only by the occasional lantern glow from distant lifeboats, flickering like dying fireflies. The screams were quieter now. Still horrible, but not as many. At first, they'd been everywhere—an endless wall of voices crying for help. Now, it was one voice here, another there, thin and scattered.

The ocean was claiming them—one by one, and we could do nothing. My hands slipped slightly from the boat's edge. I jerked them back, panic flaring. The numbness had now spread to my wrists. I couldn't feel my fingers.

Someone beside me mumbled, "Don't fall asleep … don't fall asleep."

I didn't know if he was talking to me or to himself. I looked again at the men to my left and right—still no sign of Oliver. My throat closed. What if he didn't make it? What if I missed him? What if he's still out there, dying, and I can't see him?

"Oliver," I whispered again. "Please … please be here."

I stared into the darkness, praying, but all I could hear was the sea swallowing the last of the voices. And the slow, steady silence of the dying night. No answer. I blinked up at the sky.

No. No, I thought. *Not like this.* I forced myself to sit up. My arms screamed. My chest burned. My vision tunneled, but I blinked until the black dots cleared.

"We have to go back," I croaked. No one answered. I raised my voice. "We have to go back! There are still people out there!"

One of the men near the front turned, his face barely visible in the dim light of the stars. "We can't."

"We have to," I insisted. "My—" I caught myself. "There's someone out there. He might still be alive. If we row just a little closer—"

"Son," another voice said. "If we go back, they'll swamp us. This boat is already half underwater."

"Please," I begged. "He's out there. He's smart—he would've found something to float on. We have to try."

The man closest to me shook his head. "We barely pulled you in. We take on one more body, we go under with them."

I looked around. No one moved. They all just held on. They were survivors now. And to stay that way, they couldn't afford mercy. But I didn't care about logic; I cared about Oliver.

"I can swim out," I said. "You can hold the line—I'll go alone."

Someone laughed bitterly. "You can't even feel your legs."

"I have to try!"

No one handed me a rope. No one offered a word of hope—just the cold silence of shared guilt.

"I can't leave him!" I shouted, louder than I meant to. "I won't—" But I already had. And I was too weak to go after him. I collapsed forward, fists curled uselessly against the canvas. My chest heaved. My shoulders shook. I felt a hand rest gently on my back.

"I'm sorry," someone said. "We all lost someone."

I didn't answer. Because he wasn't someone; he was everything. I pressed my forehead to the edge of the boat, the salt drying on my skin like a second, bitter ocean. A sob escaped my lips as I tried to hold on. I couldn't bear the guilt that struck me, all at once. We promised we wouldn't let go, but we did.

"Please," I whispered again, to no one. To the sea. To the sky. To the stars that had watched it all and said nothing. But the sea had made up its mind, and it would not give him back.

CHAPTER 25

The Long Night

HENRY

I wasn't shivering anymore. The others still clung to the overturned collapsible like I did, but some had stopped moving altogether. Their eyes were half-lidded, their lips blue, their hands slack on the canvas. I kept blinking and forcing myself to breathe so I would stay awake. The cold had become something else now—not pain, but emptiness. Like I was already drifting out of my own body, floating above this cracked moment in time, above the ocean that had taken so much and left so little behind.

Every now and then, I whispered his name. "*Oliver* …"

But even that had become quieter.

The sky had shifted from black to deep blue. Dawn was coming. You could see it on the water—light touching the surface like it wasn't sure if it was allowed to. Someone behind me gasped. "Look …"

I turned my neck, slowly, painfully. There was a ship in the far distance—a small black silhouette against the sky, smoke curling faintly from its funnels.

"Ship!" someone yelled hoarsely. "There's a ship!"

More voices took it up.

"It's coming!"

"It sees us—it sees us!"

The strength broke in me like a dam. I sobbed—a sound so raw and guttural I didn't recognize it as mine. I held tighter to the edge of the boat, whispering *thank you* to anything and everything. My lips cracked. My throat burned. But I didn't stop.

The ship grew larger as it neared, gilded in gold from the rising sun. RMS *Carpathia*. A name I hadn't known before, but now it meant everything.

Around us, lifeboats floated like forgotten shells—some half full, others sagging with people who looked more like ghosts than survivors. Their lanterns had died out hours ago, but now the morning lit their faces—pale, streaked with salt and grief. And beyond it all, there was ice. As the sun climbed higher, I saw them. Hundreds of icebergs, towering, jagged, and magnificent. They were floating in eerie stillness across the open sea like monuments to everything we had lost. Some were the size of buildings. Others, sharp as blades. One just beyond the *Carpathia* was streaked red where the light hit it—not blood, I knew, but the color made me look away.

The water around them was so still and so beautiful that it made it worse. This was what killed all those people. This was what took Oliver.

The *Carpathia* came closer—hope, at last, sailing into the wreckage. And as the sky bloomed with light, the sea began giving back its dead.

"Take his arms—careful!"

The voices above me barely registered at first. They were muffled and distant, as if coming through fog. My eyes fluttered open. In front of me was a haze of wool coats, breathless faces, and smoke-stained air.

"He's alive—he's got a pulse!"

Hands gripped my arms, and suddenly I was moving, my body rising from the canvas and the water that had swallowed so many and spit me out. Pain flared in my shoulders. My legs dragged, numb and useless. I felt every inch of soaked fabric clinging to my skin, every bit of my life jacket frozen solid. Voices surrounded me, sharp and urgent.

"Wrap him up—blanket, now—"

"Get that off him—his boots, his coat, we need dry clothes!"

I collapsed onto the planks, the texture of the wood scraping my cheek. I barely noticed. A blanket was thrown over me. Hands were working at the buckles of my life jacket. Someone pushed a cup of hot broth toward my mouth. I tried to sip, coughed, and spilled half of it down my chin.

"Where—," I managed, my voice nothing more than a rasp. "Where is he?"

A woman knelt beside me. Her eyes were red, her coat too large for her frame. She pressed a hand to my shoulder.

"You're safe now," she said softly.

I didn't want to be safe without him. I turned onto my side and dragged myself toward the rail, ignoring the shouting behind me. I pulled myself upright, gripping the edge with trembling hands, and looked down into the ocean below.

Lifeboats still floated there, some drifting further away, some being pulled in by ropes and rescue lines. The water reflected the rising sun in broken shards.

"*Oliver* ..." I slumped back, knees buckling. A man caught me and lowered me gently to the deck again. A coat wrapped around my shoulders. Around me, more survivors were lifted on board. Children sobbed for fathers who never made it. Wives wept for husbands they'd watched vanish. Every face told a different version of the same story.

The ship creaked softly beneath us. And the Atlantic stretched out beyond the rail, full of the names we would never see in front of us again.

CHAPTER 26

The Survivor

OLIVER

I knew I was falling before I felt myself slip. The ship tipped violently, a shudder cracking through its hull, and the deck pitched like the world itself had come unhinged. I clawed at the railing, my knuckles whitening as I hung suspended between sky and sea. Behind me, someone screamed; ahead of me, only darkness waited.

Henry's voice cut through the chaos. *"OLIVER!"*

My name tore from him with a force that made my heart lurch. I reached for him blindly, my fingers searching through the air. For a fleeting instant, I felt his skin brush mine. Then gravity wrenched me away. The wind roared in my ears. The deck vanished. Cold air wrapped around me like a fist and pulled me downward. I didn't even have time to scream before the ocean swallowed me whole.

The cold stunned me so violently I couldn't tell if I had lungs anymore. I sank fast, boots dragging me into the dark. For a moment, the ship's hulking shadow blotted out the faint glow of the surface, and all around me the water churned with debris and bodies. I kicked upward, but my legs felt wooden, numb to the bone. I flailed uselessly, drinking in seawater that scalded all the way down.

Just as blackness crowded the edges of my vision, my head broke through the surface.

I gasped and sucked in another mouthful of salt. The ocean stretched in every direction, lit only by the intermittent flash of dying lamps on the sinking ship.

Screams rose around me—raw, frantic, everywhere at once. People were thrashing through the waves, their silhouettes thrown into broken relief by the ship's few remaining lights. Somewhere above, metal shrieked as the vessel twisted further, the sound splintering the night.

I tried to yell Henry's name, but it came out as a cracked whisper.

The current tugged at me, insistent, pulling me back toward the ship. Fear shot through me. If I didn't get distance, I'd be dragged under with the rest of it. I kicked harder. Every movement burned.

A wave crashed over my head. I went under again, disoriented and half-conscious, until something brushed my hand—a plank, thick and splintered. I lunged. Missed and lunged again. My fingers closed around the wood. I surfaced with a gasp that felt like a sob and clung to the plank with both arms, chest heaving, the salt stinging my eyes and lips. I didn't dare let go.

The cold gnawed its way inward—first through my skin, then my muscles, then deeper still. My thoughts slowed.

The screaming thinned around me until it became distant, almost unreal. But one memory stayed sharp.

Henry's hand brushing mine in those final seconds. Henry turning toward me, eyes wide with fear. Henry's voice rising above the roar—my name, breaking in the middle.

I held the plank tighter. I wasn't ready to let that be the last moment we had. *Keep kicking*, I told myself. *If he's alive, keep kicking for him.*

A faint amber glow flickered across the waves. For a moment, I thought it was a hallucination—the mind conjuring false hope to soften the end, but then it brightened, swaying in the wind. It was a lantern.

I lifted my head. Beyond the next swell, a lifeboat rose and fell with the sea, crowded with families and sailors. Voices drifted toward me. I forced air into my lungs and began to swim, each stroke a battle against a body that no longer wanted to obey. The plank bumped against my ribs with every kick, but I used it to stay afloat.

"Hello?" I tried to shout. My voice cracked on the second syllable. The lantern paused and turned.

"Over there!" someone yelled. "Man in the water!"

The boat shifted course. Oars dipped in frantic unison. *Don't stop*, I told myself. *Don't you dare stop now.* My arms shook violently. My breath came in shallow gasps. A wave lifted me—then dropped me so deep the light vanished entirely before rising again. But the boat was close enough for me to see the outline of a woman clutching her child. A sailor leaning over the side. A boy whispering into his hands.

"Reach for me!" someone shouted.

I extended a trembling arm. Our fingers skimmed, slid apart, and then found each other again. A hand clamped around my wrist with startling strength.

"I've got him!" the sailor yelled. "Pull!"

I felt myself rise. My chest scraped against the boat's edge. Two more pairs of hands grabbed my coat, hauling with all their might. There was one final heave, and I collapsed into the lifeboat.

I curled onto my side, coughing until my ribs ached and my throat burned. Water poured from my clothes, pooling beneath me. Someone draped a blanket over my shoulders, and another rubbed my back with a steady hand.

"You're all right," a woman whispered. "Just breathe."

But I couldn't. Every breath came tight and choked.

Someone asked, "Was anyone with you?"

The question pierced me like a blade. *Henry.* Henry on the deck. Henry reaching for me. Henry disappearing in the chaos. A sound tore from me—half sob, half gasp. I hunched forward, pressing the blanket to my face to muffle the broken noise.

Around me, the boat was full of grief. A child cried softly against her mother's chest. A man murmured prayers beneath his breath. The oars dipped and rose, carrying us farther from the wreck.

The ship behind us groaned, louder than before. A final shudder ran through its frame. The last of its lights blinked once, then vanished beneath the waves.

Someone squeezed my arm gently. "Don't give up hope," she said. "Not tonight."

I swallowed hard, my throat raw, my chest tight with cold and dread. I didn't know if Henry was alive. I didn't know if he had made it off the ship. But I held on to the smallest, fiercest spark inside me. I had kicked through the dark for him. I had survived for him. And somewhere out there—somewhere in that vast, merciless sea—I prayed he was fighting just as hard to survive for me.

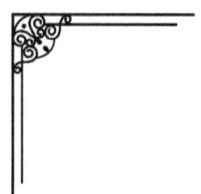

CHAPTER 27

Carpathia

HENRY

I wasn't warm. The coat they'd wrapped around me helped. So did the hot drink, and the blanket. But the cold inside me that had sunk into my chest somewhere between the lifeboats and Oliver's name echoing into the sea hadn't left.

And beneath that—twined through it like another ache—I felt the sharp, gnawing absence of Madeleine. I hadn't seen her since the deck, since hands had pulled us apart and voices had shouted over one another. I knew she'd made it into a lifeboat. I'd seen her there, alive, before the ship tore us apart. But after that—nothing. I didn't know where she'd been taken, if she was already on this ship or still out on the water somewhere. The not knowing pressed against my ribs just as hard as Oliver's name did.

I didn't wait to be told. As soon as I could stand, I left the blanket behind and began moving across the *Carpathia's* deck, legs stiff, breath leaving me in fragile bursts of fog. Still, amid all the chaos and terror, there was hope. I couldn't let go of it. A more selfish part of me claimed that this couldn't be how our story ended.

Our stories, I corrected silently. Oliver's. Madeleine's. Mine. The three of us bound together by accident and choice and a ship that had refused to carry us safely to shore.

The sun was rising, but the air still bit at every exposed inch of skin. Survivors were huddled along the railings and benches, wrapped in blankets or each other. Eyes stared out without seeing. Mouths moved without sound.

I moved from face to face, searching for him with only one thought in my mind. Please. Please let him be here.

And then, just as urgently: *Please let her be here too.* Madeleine with her dark hair and sharp wit, Madeleine who had laughed with me even as the ship had begun to die. I searched for her familiar posture, the tilt of her head, the way she always seemed to hold herself upright even when afraid.

Each face, I passed a line of third-class passengers pressed together for warmth. A steward I didn't recognize handed out cups of tea with shaking hands. A child cried softly into her mother's coat. A man sat by himself, whispering names under his breath.

I wondered how many names Madeleine might be whispering, if she was somewhere nearby. I wondered if she was whispering *mine*.

I kept moving. Where are you? Where are you, Madeleine? Where are you, Oliver?

I pushed past two officers speaking in low tones. Past a lifeboat being hoisted up by ropes that creaked under the weight. Past a coil of line left slick with seawater. Past a group of men huddled together with their backs to the wind, staring out at the horizon as if the ship might rise again if they looked hard enough.

I scanned each cluster not just for Oliver's mouth, the curve of it when he smiled softly, but for Madeleine's familiar silhouette. Each time my heart lifted, it fell again just as quickly.

Nothing on the *Carpathia* felt real. The deck was too solid beneath my feet, the air too full of living breath. Even the smell was wrong—coal smoke and wet wool, hot tea and the sour tang of fear. I kept expecting the ground to tilt, to drop away, to become the shuddering incline of the *Titanic* again. My body didn't know the difference between danger and memory.

Memory brought Oliver's hands to mind. It brought Madeleine's voice—dry, amused, brave even when she'd been terrified. The three of us had survived so much already. Surely we hadn't been torn apart now.

Every time the *Carpathia* groaned, I flinched like metal was splitting under me. My hands shook so badly I could barely keep the coat closed. Someone had wrapped it around me—some officer, some sailor, someone whose face I wouldn't remember. They'd pressed a tin cup into my palm and told me to drink. I did. The liquid burned my tongue, and then I couldn't feel my tongue at all. My throat seized and I coughed, and the cough turned into something that sounded like a sob, though no tears came. Not yet.

"Sit," someone said as I moved past.

A firm hand tried to catch my elbow. I jerked away, startled, sudden panic blooming hot in my chest.

"No," I said too sharply. "I—no. I can walk."

The man's eyes softened. "You shouldn't—"

"I can walk," I repeated, as if saying it would make it true.

If I sat, I would stop. If I stopped, the sea would catch up to me. It would reach through the planks of the deck and pull me down like it had pulled the *Titanic*, like it had pulled Oliver. Oliver. His name beat in my skull in time with my pulse. And then Madeleine's followed, relentless, insistent. *She told me she'd meet me. She wouldn't leave without trying to find me.*

I kept moving. Where are you? I forced my eyes to do what my mind could not—take in faces, one at a time, as if I were counting the living. Some were wrapped in blankets like shrouds. Some had been given dry coats; they wore them with the stunned stiffness of people who hadn't yet realized they were wearing something belonging to someone else.

A woman sat on a crate with her hair hanging in soaked ropes around her shoulders. She stared straight ahead, her lips moving soundlessly. Beside her, a child blinked slowly, as if each blink required permission. A man near the rail suddenly shouted a name into the wind. When no one answered, he shouted it again, louder—raw, cracking—until someone pulled him back and made him sit.

A cluster of first-class women stood together like pale statues, their expensive furs damp and limp. One of them clutched a small dog to her chest, whispering to it with trembling lips. A third-class boy watched her from a few feet away, eyes huge and hollow. His hands were bare, red and swollen, and he held them out in front of him as if he couldn't understand why they didn't work the way they had yesterday. Yesterday. The word landed wrong.

Everything was wrong. Time had broken with the ship. I scanned the deck again, my gaze snagging on every dark head of hair, every set of shoulders that might have been Oliver's or Madeleine's. I stepped around bodies lying beneath blankets—still, too still. I couldn't bring myself to look at their faces. If I looked, I would see him. If I looked, I might see her. If I looked and it was neither of them, then I would have looked at death and called it by the wrong name.

"Have you seen—," I began to ask a passing sailor, then stopped. My voice failed. I cleared my throat, tried again.

"Have you seen a man—dark curls, green eyes—he was a steward—"

The words tangled in my mouth, and I nearly added, *or a young woman from Paris, sharp-eyed, stubborn, alive*, but the fear of hearing *no* twice was too much.

The sailor's expression tightened. Not cruel. Just exhausted.

"Crew are being kept together below," he said gently. "If he made it, he'll be there. You need to go down and warm up. You'll freeze on deck."

Freeze. As if freezing were something that could still happen to me after what I'd already survived. As if the ocean hadn't done its worst and found it insufficient.

"I can't," I said, and the sailor moved on, already pulled toward another crisis.

The wind pressed through the gaps of the coat, needle-sharp. My skin was rubbed raw from salt and rope and panic. I was still damp beneath the layers; the cold lived there, a stubborn animal curled against my ribs. The hot drink hadn't reached it. Nothing could.

My stomach heaved suddenly, a violent twist that made my knees buckle. I grabbed the rail, coughing again, more forcefully. A taste of bile rose in my mouth. I swallowed hard.

Across the deck, someone was being carried toward the infirmary. Their head lolled to one side, hair clinging to their cheek. The person carrying them murmured something soothing. The carried body didn't respond. A woman followed close behind with her hands pressed to her mouth, eyes wide with the kind of terror that had no sound left.

I watched them pass and felt something inside me crack—not fully, not all at once, but a hairline fracture spreading through a place I'd been holding together by sheer will. Because it wasn't just Oliver. It was Madeleine too. It was the possibility that I might find one of them and not the other—and that survival could still come with loss sharp enough to split me open. It was the realization that the world had continued. That this ship moved through the water as if ships had the right to do so. That the sun rose, indifferent, and glinted off the ice like scattered glass. That people spoke in normal tones about coffee and blankets and the number of survivors, as if words could tame the scale of it. A laugh sounded nearby—high, sharp, wrong. It cut off abruptly and turned into sobbing.

I turned and saw a young woman sitting on the deck with her knees drawn up to her chest. She rocked back and forth, murmuring, "No, no, no …"

Her hands were covered in blood that wasn't hers. A man knelt beside her and tried to pry her fingers apart from whatever she was clutching—something small and dark and sodden. I forced myself to look away, throat burning. My eyes found the sea.

Beyond the rail, the Atlantic stretched out, deceptively calm, a flat gray-blue sheet. Icebergs floated like silent witnesses. And in the water—far enough away that the details blurred, close enough that the truth was unmistakable— dark shapes bobbed among scattered wreckage. Bodies. My vision tunneled.

For a moment, the deck seemed to fall away. My hands clenched hard around the rail as nausea surged. The sea still held them. It had taken the ship, taken the lights, taken the music, taken the certainty of tomorrow—and it still held them, as if refusing to admit it could ever be full.

I closed my eyes. Oliver's voice rose in my memory—soft in the stateroom we'd stolen, low and careful in the Turkish baths, teasing in the corridor when he dared to brush his fingers against my wrist. Oliver laughing quietly into my shoulder. Oliver whispering my name like it was a promise. And then Madeleine—her laugh cutting through fear, her hand squeezing mine on the deck, her voice telling me not to look back, to live.

I opened my eyes again and stared at the ocean until it blurred.

"I'm sorry," I whispered, not sure if I was speaking to him or to her or to the dead or to myself.

The words didn't mean anything anymore. They were too small. A wave slapped gently against floating debris far below. It sounded like a hand against wood, like a distant knock. I couldn't breathe. I forced air into my lungs anyway and turned back to the deck.

I moved again because moving was the only thing keeping me upright. Face to face. Blanket to blanket. Eyes that didn't see me. Hands that trembled. People walking like ghosts who hadn't realized they'd died.

Where are you? *Where are you both?* If you're here, I will find you. If you're gone—

My mind refused to finish the thought. My body couldn't survive it. I stumbled forward, blinking hard against the sting in my eyes, and pushed past another knot of survivors. My shoulders brushed someone's arm; the contact startled me so badly I nearly jumped.

"Sorry," I muttered.

They didn't react. They were staring at the horizon like it might give them answers.

I pushed past two more men, then stopped abruptly.

A pile of blankets lay near the base of a lifeboat cradle, damp and heavy. A woman knelt beside them, sorting through them with careful hands. A small silver locket had fallen onto the deck. She picked it up, stared at it as if it were a strange object from another planet, then clutched it to her chest and began to cry.

I couldn't help her. I couldn't help anyone. The only thing I could do—the only thing keeping me from collapsing into the same endless grief—was search.

"Henry!" She was already running before I could answer.

I spun around as Madeleine's voice echoed behind me. She was wrapped in a navy blanket, hair tangled, face streaked with salt and tears. But she was there, and the moment I saw her, I crumpled.

She ran to me. Her arms wrapped around my shoulders, pulling me in so tight I couldn't tell where her heartbeat ended, and mine began.

"You're alive," she whispered, her voice cracking. "You're alive."

I buried my face in her shoulder. My hands clenched into fists at her back.

"My God, it's good to see you," I sobbed, not releasing her. Up until this point, I had somewhat kept my composure and tried to keep going, but now, in her arms, I broke down entirely.

I didn't mean to. I wanted to stay standing. I wanted to be strong. But I couldn't anymore. All the things I had held in since the moment Oliver slipped from my hands came pouring out of me like a storm that had waited too long to fall.

Madeleine didn't speak. She just held me tighter, her fingers running through my damp hair, her chin resting on the crown of my head.

"I couldn't save him," I choked out. "He was right there. And I couldn't—I couldn't hold on. He's gone. I don't know if he's alive, or—"

She pulled back just enough to look at me. Her eyes were full of tears. "I know," she said. "I know you tried. You tried your best. He did, too."

"I love him," I whispered. "I *love* him." It was the first time I had ever felt that way—the first time my feelings for another person ran that deep. The first time I wanted to surrender to them completely. The first time the world seemed to stop spinning, leaving me suspended in the moment. And it was gone—just like that, after a few short days that I knew would change my life forever. I didn't even get a chance to say it back.

"I know," she said again. "He knew too."

I nodded against her, but the pain didn't stop. It pulsed, deep and hollow, a wound with no shape and no bottom.

Around us, the *Carpathia* sailed through a field of ice and ghosts. But in her arms, I let myself mourn. For the first time, I felt the weight of all we'd lost.

CHAPTER 28

If He Is Here

L ater, we sat in silence. Madeleine and I had found a small refuge near the rail of the *Carpathia*, hidden behind lifeboats that hovered above the sea like pale, uneasy spirits. Around us came the shuffle of weary feet, hushed voices, and the slow drag of boots across damp wood. No one spoke above a whisper. No one laughed. Laughter felt like something that had sunk hours earlier, swallowed with the ship.

A steward—one of the *Carpathia's*—came by with a tray of bread and something like broth. He offered it to us without speaking, eyes downcast, moving with the careful gentleness of a man who had spent the last hours stepping around grief. Madeleine took a piece of bread with trembling fingers. She held it for a moment, staring at it as if it might vanish. Then she forced herself to bite. Her throat worked as she swallowed, and tears slid silently down her cheeks. I tried. The bread was dry and tasteless in my mouth. My jaw felt stiff, as if the cold had settled into the bone. I chewed because it was expected. Because it was what living people did. But my stomach rebelled. After two bites, nausea climbed my throat again. Madeleine noticed immediately.

"Don't," she murmured, voice low. "Don't make yourself."

"If I don't eat, then …" I didn't know how to finish.

If I didn't eat, then what? Then it would mean I was still on the water, still fighting, still waiting for rescue that might not come. Eating felt like admitting the fight was over. Like admitting the story had ended without him. Madeleine reached for my hand. Her fingers were icy despite the blanket around her shoulders. She squeezed once, firm.

"We're alive," she said, and it sounded like a question she didn't want answered.

Alive. Somewhere nearby, a child coughed wetly. A woman hushed him, whispering something in a language I didn't recognize. Another voice rose, angry and hoarse— someone demanding to see a list, demanding to know if a name was on it, demanding why no one could tell them anything.

"Where are the doctors?" a man shouted. "Where— where is anyone?"

A *Carpathia* officer answered, calm but strained. "We're doing what we can. One at a time. Please."

As if grief could be processed like luggage. The deck around us had shifted. The frantic motion of rescue had dulled into a heavy, exhausted stillness. People sat wherever they could—on crates, on coils of rope, on the deck itself— wrapped in borrowed blankets, eyes unfocused. Some stared at their hands. Some stared at nothing. A few slept, but it wasn't real sleep. It was collapse. Every so often, a sound would tear through the quiet—a sob, a scream, a laugh that turned into sobbing. Those sounds made everyone else flinch. We were all raw nerves.

I watched a young man stand near the rail with his mouth open as if he might speak. He didn't. He simply stood there, swaying slightly, until another survivor guided him gently to sit down. Madeleine leaned her head against my shoulder. I could feel the tremor in her body. She was trying to be strong, trying to be my anchor, but she was drowning too.

"I keep thinking," she whispered, "that the ship is still there. That we will look back and see her lights again. Isn't that terrible?"

"No," I said, voice rough. "It's not terrible. It's—normal."

Nothing about this was normal. But the mind needed something—anything—to cling to. A *Carpathia* nurse approached, a tired woman with sleeves rolled up and hair escaping from its pins. She knelt in front of us, her gaze moving quickly over our faces.

"Are either of you hurt?" she asked.

Madeleine shook her head. "No. Just—cold."

The nurse's eyes flicked to me. "You're pale," she said. "You should come below. There's a warm room. There's—"

I swallowed hard. "I need to find someone," I managed. "A steward. Oliver. He—he was with me on the ship."

Something in the nurse's expression changed—not pity exactly, but recognition. The same recognition I'd seen on too many faces already: the look of someone who had heard that sentence in twenty different forms.

"I can ask," she said gently. "But the crew survivors—some are injured. They've been moved below. If he is here, he will be recorded."

Recorded. As if love could be reduced to ink on paper.

Madeleine straightened. "Please," she said, voice firm in a way mine couldn't be. "If you hear anything—anything at all—will you tell us?"

The nurse nodded. "I will," she promised.

Then she stood and moved on, already being pulled by another cry for help. The hours after that blurred. Someone gave us a place to sit that was out of the worst wind, behind a stack of lifeboat gear. Someone else pressed another cup into our hands—tea this time, bitter and scalding. The warmth felt like an insult at first. Then it felt like a mercy. At some point, the sun climbed higher. The ice glinted. The sea looked almost beautiful, and that made my stomach turn. The ocean had no right to beauty.

The *Carpathia's* engine throbbed steadily beneath our feet. The sound was oddly comforting and unbearable all at once. It meant motion. It meant forward. It meant leaving behind the place where Oliver had vanished. I tried to keep my eyes open, to keep searching. But my body betrayed me. Exhaustion pressed down like a physical weight. My eyelids fluttered. When I did slip into something like sleep, it lasted only minutes before I jerked awake again, heart hammering, convinced I had heard my name being shouted across the water. Each time, it was only the wind. Each time, I tasted salt and panic. Madeleine watched me with quiet worry.

"Henry," she whispered once, "you have to rest."

"I can't," I said.

Not while he was somewhere unknown. Not while my last memory of him was his hands slipping away, his eyes locked on mine. Rest felt like betrayal. So I stayed awake and stared into the crowd until my eyes ached, until every dark curl on the deck looked like Oliver's, until hope became a kind of torture. And still, I didn't see him.

Morning came cold and merciless. The air felt scoured clean, scraped of the smoke and oil that had choked the night before. Beyond the railing, the Atlantic lay unnervingly still—an expanse of gray-blue silence. Icebergs drifted in every direction, catching the thin winter light and throwing it back in shards. They rose jagged and immense, too perfect in their stillness, beautiful in the way all lethal things were.

We didn't speak. There wasn't anything to say. Madeleine's hand slipped into mine, and I held it tightly, anchoring us both. I couldn't feel the warmth in her palm anymore, but I felt the intent behind it—the need to connect, and to be tethered to something that hadn't been swallowed.

Around us, survivors murmured names. Some whispered prayers. Some sat with their backs to the rail, eyes glazed, as if the ocean had taken not just their families, but their voices too.

"Do you think there's a chance he's still alive?" I asked

finally. I had to say the words out loud, even though I didn't want to.

Madeleine looked at me, her face serious. We had never lied to each other. Even when the truth hurt, we always told it.

"I don't know," she said, slipping her arm around mine. My chest tightened, but I was used to that feeling by now. "I wish I could give you answers, Henry. But I think we'll just have to wait and see."

The last time I had seen him played over and over in my mind. It *couldn't* have been the last time. I wouldn't accept that.

I kept searching the crowd. My eyes moved from group to group, face to face, but I wasn't truly seeing any of them. Not really. Until suddenly, I did. A flicker.

A silhouette at the far end of the deck moved slowly through the survivors—one step at a time. A figure bundled in a dark coat, soaked and hanging crooked from one shoulder. A man with curls matted against his forehead, arms held slightly away from his sides like they didn't know what to do. He looked as if he'd been pulled from the sea and stitched together by sheer will.

I sat up straighter. My breath caught, lodged in my throat like a stone. I blinked hard. And then, he turned. My pulse stuttered. *Oliver.* He looked smaller than I remembered, thinner, like the night had carved something out of him. His eyes searched the deck with slow, tentative focus. He was searching for me.

I stood. My legs ached, and my body resisted, but

somehow I was on my feet before Madeleine could say a word. She turned to look at me, alarm flickering in her eyes.

"Henry?"

I took one step forward. Then another. The rest of the world narrowed. My ears rang with the rush of blood. He hadn't seen me yet. He was still looking, weaving his way between groups of shivering passengers, his steps careful but unsteady.

He was alive.

My throat burned. I could see him clearly now—the slope of his shoulders, the sharp line of his jaw, and the way his hand drifted to his chest as if checking whether his heart still belonged to him. His uniform was gone, reduced to scraps and salt-stiff cloth.

Our eyes locked across the deck, and air deserted my lungs. He went still, and every trace of movement arrested. A breath caught visibly in his chest. His mouth parted, as if he were trying to speak or simply trying to believe.

And then he began to walk toward me.

I didn't move. I couldn't take another step. I needed to see him take those steps as proof that he wasn't some grief-born apparition. At that moment, the world collapsed into a single narrowing corridor.

He reached the open stretch of deck. He broke into a stumbling run, the effort obvious in his stiff posture. His face, until now blank with shock, crumpled. He didn't even shout my name. He simply reached for me.

I met him halfway. The impact was jarring, solid, and real. His arms, still cold, wrapped around my waist, and my own hands shot up, gripping the back of his soaked coat. He buried his face in my neck, and the low, broken sound he made was the most beautiful thing I had ever heard. It wasn't a cry of grief, but of absolute, overwhelming survival.

I felt his body shaking—not from cold, but from the aftermath of terror, exhaustion, and sudden, unbearable relief. I held him tighter than I had held on to anything in my life, anchoring myself to his weight, his scent of salt and wool and life.

"Oliver," I finally choked out, the name tearing from my throat, a testament to a love that had defied the ocean. "I thought … I thought you were gone. You scared the hell out of me."

He pulled back just enough to look at me, his eyes wet, brilliant, and utterly focused. "I held on to the railing," he rasped, his voice rough and thin. "I went under, then came back up. I found a piece of debris. I just … I kept kicking, Henry. I kept kicking for you."

He hadn't stopped fighting. The man I had seen slip from my grasp was now clinging to me, whole and alive. The deep, hollow wound inside me began, slowly, to fill. The sheer, devastating warmth of this impossible reunion was pushing back the cold inside.

Behind us, I heard Madeleine gasp. I didn't turn. I simply held Oliver, burying my face in his damp hair, closing my eyes, and letting the shock wash over me. The world was still full of ghosts, but for this moment, I was holding my future, and it was warm, breathing, and impossibly, wonderfully, here.

CHAPTER 29

New York

HENRY

The sheer force of relief was paralyzing. I didn't know how long we stood there, locked in that desperate embrace on the deck of the *Carpathia*. Minutes stretched into an eternity defined only by the rise and fall of Oliver's chest beneath my hands. The world had shrunk back to the width of his shoulders, the sound of his ragged breathing, and the unbelievable, glorious certainty that he was alive.

When we finally broke apart, it was not because we wanted to, but because we were too exhausted and stiff to maintain the grip. Oliver looked worse up close than he had from a distance. The dark coat—clearly borrowed—hung loose, and his face was pale, almost translucent, smudged with soot and grime he hadn't managed to clean off. His lips were blue.

Madeleine stepped forward, her hands flying to her mouth. She didn't speak a name; she just made a soft, choked sound of pure wonder, before she launched herself toward us, wrapping her arms around Oliver tightly and not letting go.

"Madeleine," Oliver rasped, his eyes widening in recognition. A small, faint smile touched his lips. His own arms gripped her tightly, and they lingered like that for a long moment. "You're safe."

"*Mon Dieu*, I can't believe this. You're alive. *We're* alive," she said, her voice shaking violently. She reached out and touched his cheek, tracing the line of his jaw that I loved so much. "We thought … Henry said you slipped."

Oliver looked from her to me, a flash of memory crossing his eyes. "I did. For a moment. The suction was terrible. But I came up near a piece of the railing—a big chunk. I clung to it. Then, later, I got pulled onto one of the lifeboats that was barely afloat. It was full of people. They thought I was dead until I coughed." He shuddered, pulling the coat tighter around himself.

Madeleine looked around before she wrapped her arms around both of us and pulled us forward. I was glad that she did. Standing in the middle of the crowded deck, visible to everyone, felt too exposed, too much like flaunting a miracle in a place defined by loss. She guided Oliver toward the sheltered space where we had been sitting, near the library entrance. He walked with a noticeable limp, favoring his right leg.

"You're hurt," I said, putting an arm under his left, supporting his weight.

"Just bruised, I think," he mumbled. "Everything's bruised. The deck came down on me when she went vertical, but I managed to roll clear. I'm just … cold."

He swayed as he said it—barely, but I felt it through the

arm I had under him. The motion was small enough that anyone else might have missed it. I didn't. I tightened my grip instinctively. Oliver's body was rigid with cold, muscles locked as if he were still fighting the sea. His breath came shallow, every exhale a faint tremor. When I looked closer, I saw that his lashes were still wet—whether from seawater or tears, I couldn't tell. His lips were blue, and there was a raw split at one corner where the salt had cracked the skin.

"Cold," I repeated softly, as if saying it gently would make it less true.

Oliver tried to straighten. Pride flickered behind his eyes—stubborn, familiar, protective. He had spent so long being the one who moved with purpose, who knew the ship's corridors and rules. Now he stood on a strange deck in a borrowed coat, a steward without a uniform, a man without a place.

"I'm fine," he insisted, but the words were thin.

They didn't have weight. They didn't convince even him. Madeleine hovered at his other side, hands half lifted, uncertain where to touch. Her face looked carved out by grief and relief all at once. She kept staring at Oliver as if he might vanish again if she blinked. Around us, the world continued. That was the strangest part. People moved across the deck carrying blankets. A *Carpathia* sailor shouted an order. Somewhere near the stern, someone cried out a name in a voice already hoarse from repeating it. The ship groaned softly as it cut through the water. And survivors stared. Not all of them. Many were too lost in their own suffering to notice anything else. But a few turned their heads as we stood there—this impossible little cluster of three, alive in a sea of loss. Their eyes were not unkind. Some were simply blank with exhaustion. Some were sharp with envy, as if our embrace were a theft. I felt their gaze anyway. It crawled over my skin like cold.

Oliver must have felt it too, because his shoulders drew in slightly. He pulled the coat tighter around himself, not just for warmth, but for cover. His jaw clenched the way it did when he was forcing himself not to show fear.

"We should sit," Madeleine said gently, voice careful.

Oliver opened his mouth to object.

"No," I said, firmer than I meant to.

Then I softened it, because I could see how fragile he was. "Please. Just for a moment."

Oliver's eyes flicked to mine. For a second, I saw everything that lived behind them—terror, guilt, love, the echo of the water. Then his gaze dropped, and he gave a barely perceptible nod. We moved slowly, inch by inch, as if walking too quickly might tear the moment apart. I kept my arm locked under Oliver's, supporting more of his weight than he would have allowed if he weren't so exhausted. His boots made a dull sound on the wet deck. As we passed, a woman stepped aside to make room. Her cheeks were streaked with salt and tears. She watched Oliver with a strange intensity, then whispered, "Thank God," as if she were speaking to herself more than to us.

Another man—older, hollow-eyed—looked at our hands where they touched and stared for a long beat. His gaze drifted up to my face, then to Oliver's, and something in him shifted. He looked away quickly, as if ashamed of witnessing a kind of hope he no longer believed in. I guided Oliver toward the small shelter near the rail where Madeleine had been sitting earlier. The wind was slightly calmer there, blocked by stacked equipment and the curve of the ship's structure. It wasn't warm—nothing was warm—but it was less cruel.

Oliver lowered himself onto the crate with careful slowness. The moment he sat, his composure cracked. His shoulders sagged. He pressed a hand briefly to his thigh, wincing, and then he did something that made my throat tighten with love and grief: He tried to hide the wince, tried to swallow it down, tried to pretend his body hadn't been through hell.

"You don't have to do that," I whispered.

Oliver's eyes lifted. "Do what?"

"Pretend," I said. My voice shook. "You don't have to pretend with me."

A muscle jumped in his jaw. He looked away, blinking hard.

"I thought you were gone," he said quietly, so quietly that the words almost didn't exist. "When I hit the water, I—" He swallowed. His hands clenched on his knees. "I kept looking for you. I kept thinking … if I see you, I'll know I didn't fail. And then I didn't see you."

The guilt in his voice hit me like a physical blow.

"You didn't fail," I said immediately. "Oliver, you didn't fail."

He gave a short, bitter exhale. "Tell that to the people who didn't make it."

I didn't have an answer. None of us did. So I did the only thing I could: I sat beside him, close enough that our shoulders touched, and I took his hand in mine—openly, without thinking. His fingers were still cold, still stiff. But they curled around mine as if my hand were the last solid thing on earth. Oliver's eyes fluttered closed for a moment, and when he opened them again, they were wet.

"I'm here," I whispered. "I'm not going anywhere."

He nodded once, almost imperceptibly, and leaned the tiniest fraction toward me—an unconscious movement, a surrender of strength he didn't want to admit. Madeleine watched us with her hands pressed over her mouth, tears slipping down her cheeks again. She looked like she was trying to memorize every detail—our faces, our hands, the simple fact of us sitting together—so she could believe it later when grief tried to rewrite the truth.

"I'm going to get you something warm," she said suddenly, voice thick. "Tea. Anything."

Oliver tried to protest again, but his voice failed. He only nodded. As Madeleine hurried away, I kept hold of Oliver's hand. And for the first time since the *Titanic* had begun to die beneath our feet, I let myself believe that we might live long enough to figure out what came next.

Madeleine came back at a near run, a steaming mug clutched carefully in both hands, her breath fogging the air as she approached us. Even now, even after everything, disbelief still flickered across her face—like she was afraid that if she stopped moving, one of us might vanish.

"Come here," she said softly, urgency and wonder

tangled together in her voice. What were the odds that all three of us had survived?

I couldn't begin to calculate them, only knew that somehow the stars had tilted in our favor.

We eased Oliver down onto the bench, his movements slow and stiff. Without hesitation, Madeleine shrugged off her own blanket—thick navy wool still damp at the edges— and wrapped it around him, tucking it securely over his legs with careful, almost reverent hands. Only then did she press the mug into his palms.

"Drink," she urged gently. "It's hot."

The tea steamed between us, fragrant and grounding, a small miracle passed from stranger to survivor. And for the first time since the ocean had tried to claim everything we loved, we were sitting still—together, breathing, alive.

Oliver took the mug with both hands, the warmth seeping slowly into his fingers. The three of us sat together: Henry on one side, Madeleine on the other, flanking Oliver, and forming a small, insulated unit of impossible survival.

"When I got in the lifeboat," Oliver said quietly, staring into the tea, "I kept watching the water, waiting for *you*." He lifted his gaze to meet mine. "I was sure you were still down there. I told myself you were a strong swimmer, but …" He didn't finish the sentence. The despair he must have felt was mirrored by the despair I had carried until an hour ago.

"I found a collapsible, too," I explained, "one of the ones that were floating free. I was dragged onto it by a steward, just before I lost consciousness. We were picked up maybe an hour before dawn."

We existed in a strange state of temporal suspension. The past—the terrifying, agonizing night—was too close. The future—New York, what came next—was unimaginable. All we had was this perfect, fragile present: three lives miraculously spared. For a long moment, it was all we could hold on to.

The gradual, heartbreaking cataloging of loss marked the early morning hours on the *Carpathia*. Officers, grave-faced and weary, began moving among the survivors, attempting to take names, compile lists, and match the saved with the missing.

A commotion started near the rail. A woman, elegantly dressed despite her soaked, torn garments, recognized a man wrapped in a blanket. She screamed, "Robert!" It was a scene of momentary, explosive joy, quickly followed by the crushing question, "Where is Thomas? And the children?" The deck was filled with these sharp peaks of reunion and vast, deep valleys of realization.

Oliver shivered again as he drained the last of his tea, his hands trembling faintly around the cup. I rubbed his shoulder, trying to lend him warmth through the damp wool.

"I saw the boat tip," he murmured, voice frayed, eyes unfocused. "I saw people fall from the very top." He wasn't speaking to me anymore; he was receding into the memory, into the dark water that had nearly taken him.

Madeleine rose at once, keen enough to catch the shift. "I'm going to find the doctor," she said gently. "Your leg, Oliver—and the shock. Tea isn't enough."

She looked at me, like she was silently asking for

permission, and I gave it with a small nod. I fought the urge to smile for the first time in what felt like forever. Madeleine never asked for permission to do anything … yet now she had. I watched her thread her way through the clusters of survivors, grateful for her unflinching practicality. In chaos, she always seemed to find the ground beneath her feet.

When she was gone, the silence changed. It thinned, stretched taut between us—heavy with everything that had happened and everything we had nearly lost. I reached for Oliver's hand. It was still cold, but he didn't pull away.

"I didn't stop looking for you," I said quietly. "Even after Madeleine found me. I walked the deck twice. I couldn't accept it. It felt like … the world had ended."

Oliver turned toward me. His eyes found mine with a faint, rekindling spark. "When I saw you," he whispered, "I thought I was dreaming. Or dead. I thought you were … a ghost. Something cruel."

"No ghost." I tried for a smile and managed something soft, shaky. "Just a fool who can't keep hold of a railing."

A breath of something—almost a laugh, almost a sob—escaped him. Whatever we were before the sinking, we had survived something absolute. And we were still here.

He leaned his head on my shoulder, and then mine rested on top of his shoulder. We stayed like that for a long moment, just taking in each other's presence. I wanted to drown in it and lose myself in him completely.

It wasn't long before Madeleine returned with a middle-aged doctor from the *Carpathia*, a kind-faced man who looked like he hadn't slept in days. He examined Oliver, brisk but gentle.

"Shock," he said finally. "And hypothermia. The worst seems past, but he needs rest, dry clothes, and food. A proper meal, not just tea." His eyes flicked to me. "And you, son? Hurt anywhere?"

"No, sir. Just exhausted."

"You both look like you've come through a war," he murmured. In his voice, there was no exaggeration. "Most of the surviving men are being placed in the public rooms, but your friend needs warmth and quiet. I'll see if I can secure a corner cabin."

Madeleine stepped forward without hesitation. "Please, Doctor. He's my … cousin. We're traveling together. If he could be near me?"

Her lie was seamless, heroic in its simplicity. A young woman vouching for a male relative would grant Oliver privacy and dignity that a common steward would never be offered—especially one stripped of his uniform, his position, and his place in the ship's rigid hierarchy.

The doctor nodded. "Very well. Give me an hour. I'll return."

When he left, the new shape of our situation settled around us. Oliver was safe, but the world that had defined us had been shattered. He was no longer a steward; I was no longer a passenger. Whatever rules had held us apart had sunk with the ship. We were just two men who had found each other again against odds that should have broken us.

The next hour passed in a kind of quiet sanctuary. We

stayed close, talking about small, inconsequential things: the scratch of the blankets, the taste of the tea, and the persistence of the human heart. The noise of the deck softened. The horizon blurred. The icebergs lost their sharp edges.

We were safe. We were together. A fragile, flickering light amid the cold wreckage of everything we had known. Our impossible dawn had come.

The doctor made good on his promise, securing a tiny, repurposed cabin far below decks for Oliver. It was cramped, windowless, and smelled faintly of brine and boiler oil, but it was warm, dry, and private. Madeleine spent all her free time with us, sitting guard and fetching provisions.

The *Carpathia* turned south, leaving the iceberg fields behind, steaming toward New York.

Sleep came in fragments and dragged the sea with it. Oliver woke gasping, hands clawing at air that wasn't there. The cabin walls felt too close. The floor too steady. He sat up, breath shaking. He had lived. That fact weighed heavier than the water. I slept nearby. The sight hurt in a way Oliver couldn't name. Why us? Faces surfaced when he closed his eyes. Screams that never faded.

"I thought I was going to die," he said quietly.

I stirred. "You didn't."

The atmosphere aboard the ship shifted from panic and initial shock to a deep, pervasive weariness. The days melted into one another, marked only by the repetitive routine of eating simple meals, sleeping fitfully, and the endless, low murmur of survivors sharing their stories or, more often, sitting in stunned silence.

Oliver slept for almost twelve hours straight, with a feverish, heavy sleep of exhaustion. When he woke, his color was better, and his limp less pronounced. He was hungry, and the simple fact of watching him eat a thick bowl of soup felt like a victory that transcended the sinking itself.

Madeleine and I took turns talking to him, piecing together the events of the sinking from our respective viewpoints. It was a macabre and necessary puzzle.

"The stern was almost vertical," Oliver recounted, his voice still low, but stronger. "I saw the captain. He was standing right on the bridge wing. Just … holding on. He didn't try to save himself. He looked like he was watching a final curtain fall."

Madeleine shared her experience in lifeboat 12. "The sea was like glass after the sinking stopped, Henry. Just silence, and then the awful sounds of people dying nearby. We kept shouting to keep the others awake. The stars were magnificent, the sky was black, and the water was freezing. It felt like we were the last people on earth."

We processed the trauma slowly, segment by segment, like unwrapping a wound. It was only by sharing the horror that it became manageable. In the confines of that small, dark cabin, we became three people bound by an unspeakable secret: the intimacy of having shared an apocalypse.

$$\approx$$

As the *Carpathia* pressed through warmer, calmer waters, the question of what came next grew heavier than the blankets on our shoulders. The nearness of land didn't soothe us—it sharpened everything. Choices. Consequences. The danger we carried with us.

Madeleine broke the silence first, sitting upright on the edge of the cot like someone preparing to address a jury. "We need a story," she declared. "A simple one. Tight. Unshakeable."

Oliver blinked at her, weary and still pale. "A story? Madeleine—we're survivors. Isn't that enough?"

"No," she said, her voice low, steady. "Not for you. You're the crew. Or you used to be, at least." The word hung there like a sentence. "You don't have a cabin or papers or even a uniform anymore. When we dock, the American inquiry will pull every surviving steward aside. They'll want to know why you lived when so many didn't. And your employer will want you back on the next available ship."

Oliver looked away, jaw tight. He knew it was true. The crew didn't get mourning or respite. They were expected to return to service.

I rubbed my hands together, trying to think through the rising panic. "So he needs a reason to be with us. A reason to leave the ship with us."

"Exactly," Madeleine said. Then she took a breath—one of those breaths that precedes a plunge. "He's my cousin."

Oliver choked on absolutely nothing. "Your what?"

"What? There are worse things you can be than my cousin, Oliver." Madeleine arched her brow, staring at me. "Besides, that title has already secured you a cabin." She gestured around.

"It can hardly be called that," Oliver pointed out. My lips tugged upward as I fought back a smile.

He was getting his spirit back. That was good.

Madeleine rolled her eyes. "You're my distant cousin. A struggling artist from the English countryside. Traveling second class on a ticket his late father bought him. And when the ship went down, he saved my life." Her eyes gleamed with a fierce kind of loyalty. "Then he went back to help others. That is why he was separated from me. That is why he has no belongings. And that is why he belongs by my side now."

"That's quite a leap," Oliver muttered, though a faint, incredulous smile tugged at his mouth.

"It's also the only thing that protects you," she shot back. "A steward who survives is interrogated. A brave young man who saved a lady is … heroized. And no one questions a lady's claim to her own kin."

I exhaled, tension easing just enough for hope to slip through. "And if he's your cousin, Madeleine … then he leaves the ship with you."

Her gaze flicked between us, reading the fear we didn't voice. "Yes," she said. "He leaves with me. With us. They won't separate family."

The plan grew roots from there. We wove it carefully. Supposedly, Oliver had been sick during most of the voyage—too ill to spend time in public rooms. And when the disaster struck, Oliver's instincts had driven him to protect Madeleine, returning to the decks after securing her place in a boat. My presence was the simplest to explain: a friend of Madeleine's, grieving and shaken, with no reason to question the existence of a shy, artistic cousin.

The *Carpathia* kept steaming toward New York—toward inquiries and headlines and the rigid world waiting to reclaim us. But for the first time, the three of us had something stronger than fear: a story that could keep us together. A lie that felt more honest than the truth the world demanded. A chance to step off the ship as one. And not let go.

As the days passed, the sense of unreality began to lift, replaced by a nervous anticipation. The *Carpathia* grew cleaner, the passengers more organized, the atmosphere subtly shifting from raw despair to something like expectancy. Land was coming. Decisions were coming with it.

Oliver was walking more steadily now, color returning slowly to his cheeks, but with every step regained, a new worry seemed to take its place. One evening, while the sun bled orange along the horizon, he leaned against the rail beside me and exhaled shakily.

"God, I can't wait to have ground beneath my feet. I'm sick of the ocean," he said, shaking his head.

I smiled. "New York isn't that far away. Don't you worry."

Those words seemed to trap his mind with another worry. "New York is … massive," he murmured. "A city that swallows people whole. Where do I go, Henry? Who am I supposed to be once we dock? Even with Madeleine's story, I'm still just a man dragged out of the sea with nothing. No papers. No references. No home." He swallowed. "I don't know anyone but you two."

I turned toward him, the wind tugging gently at the loose strands of his hair. "You know two people you *need* to know," I said softly. "And that's enough."

Oliver's eyes lifted to mine with a quiet, heartbreaking uncertainty.

So I took a breath, the kind one would take before saying something they'd been carrying too long.

"Come with me," I said. "To my mother's house."

He blinked. "Henry—"

"I mean it." I stepped closer, lowering my voice as if the sea itself might overhear. "My mother lives in New York. There's space. More than enough. She's … complicated, but she's kind. And she loves me. She'll help you if I ask."

Oliver shook his head slightly, overwhelmed. "But Henry, you can't just bring home a … a stray man from the wreckage of a tragedy and say—"

"I'm not bringing home a stray," I cut in gently. "I'm bringing home the man I …" The words caught, but I forced them through. "The man I nearly lost. Twice."

He stared at me, breath unsteady.

"I can't do that again, Oliver," I said. "I can't lose you again. Not to the sea, not to an inquiry, and not to the cold streets of a city that doesn't care who you are." My hand found his. "You said once you didn't know where you belonged. Well … then belong with me. For now. Until we figure out the rest."

Oliver's fingers tightened around mine, tentative at first, then with a desperate sincerity that left no doubt.

"But Henry … how?" he whispered. "Where would I sleep? What would I tell her? What would we be?"

"We'll say you're Madeleine's cousin," I murmured. "A young man who helped her, who lost everything, who needs a place to land. It won't be a lie she can't live with. My mother has a heart for actual strays, and you're far more dignified than any of the creatures she's rescued over the years."

He let out a startled laugh, soft and bewildered. But beneath it, fear still glimmered.

"And after?" he asked. "What happens when I'm well enough, when I find work? When the world stops being … this?"

I stepped in close, close enough to feel the warmth of him through our coats. "After," I whispered, "we see who we can be—together. Without secrets. Without the ship or our roles between us. I love you, Oliver." The words finally slipped from my lips so effortlessly that I didn't even register them at first. "I love you," I repeated them once more, allowing myself to taste them on my tongue. "I think I've loved you since the first moment I spoke to you."

A single tear slipped down Oliver's cheek. He didn't hide it.

"You'd really take me home?" he asked, voice breaking.

"I'd carry you there myself if I had to," I said. "Whatever comes next, we'll face it together. As long as you stay."

Oliver leaned into me then, just slightly, but enough. Enough to make the future feel possible. Enough to make it clear he wasn't going anywhere.

The final evening aboard was taut with nerves. The

lights of the mainland flickered on the horizon—soft, golden, almost unreal. They shimmered like a promise and a warning both: The nightmare was ending, but what waited beyond it had teeth of its own. Madeleine slipped into the cabin for one last council, closing the door behind her with a quiet click.

Oliver stood slowly, fastening the dark coat Madeleine had found for him. It hung loose on his still-recovering frame, but somehow gave him a solemn dignity—like armor before a trial.

"Thank you," he told her softly, taking her hands in his own. "For everything. I owe you my life."

She shook her head softly. "We saved each other. All three of us." Her gaze lingered on Oliver—tender, steady, almost fierce in its resolve. Then she looked at me with that same unwavering clarity. "Whatever comes next, we face it together."

Before either of us could speak, she pulled us both into her arms. It was clumsy, cold, and desperate—our coats still damp, our breaths still trembling—but the moment she held us, something inside me loosened. Oliver let out a quiet, broken laugh against her shoulder, one that sounded like relief and gratitude tangled together. Her embrace tightened, binding us in a single knot of shared survival. When she finally released us, there were no instructions. No warnings. No timeline. Just her warm, resolute presence beside us. "Stay close," she murmured. "Both of you."

And we did.

Night fell heavily as the *Carpathia* crept toward New

York Harbor. Rain slicked the decks, blurring the horizon into a trembling watercolor of shadows and fractured light. Through the downpour, the city emerged slowly—its jagged skyline rising from the darkness like some vast, indifferent sentinel. Fog clung low over the water, parting only when broken by lanterns along the distant shore. A collective gasp rippled across the deck.

Boats—hundreds of them—crowded the harbor. Ferries, tugs, private crafts, each painted with the colors of grief and awe. Their horns let out long, aching wails that echoed across the water. The docks churned with people—families craning forward, reporters shouting, and strangers gathering simply to witness the surviving fragments of catastrophe.

The sound was thunderous: bells clanging, sirens crying, voices colliding into a single, overwhelming roar.

Oliver's hand slipped into mine, the pressure urgent. "We made it," he whispered, breath trembling.

Madeleine stepped closer on my other side, her shoulder brushing mine. "We did," she said quietly.

The gangway lowered with a heavy thud, wood slamming against the pier. Shouts erupted, orders barked, ropes tightened, and officials scrambled for what little control the moment allowed. The three of us didn't wait for instructions. We moved with the crowd, folded into the flood of bodies pressing toward the gangway. Wrapped in borrowed coats, hoods low, we passed through the chaos like ghosts—unremarkable and unnoticed. No one asked for names. No one checked the lists. In disaster, anonymity became its own fragile form of mercy.

Our boots hit solid ground for the first time since the night the world had cracked open. Oliver let out a shaky exhale, as if grounding himself. Madeleine brushed her fingers against mine before looping her arm through Oliver's, anchoring all of us.

New York rose before us—untamed, brash, and unknowable. It was a place where a man could vanish into a tenement, where a woman could reinvent herself beneath a new name, where three survivors could disappear into the swirl of the city's relentless pulse.

We stepped forward together, swallowed by the cacophony, the steam, and the cold kiss of river wind. We were nothing but three figures held close by circumstance and choice—alive, unmoored, terrified, and fiercely determined. Whatever waited beyond the harbor, we would face it together. Shoulder to shoulder. Breath to breath.

A new beginning carved out of wreckage. A fragile, defiant hope carried into the streets of a city that would never know our names … or our stories.

CHAPTER 30

A Love That Refused to Sink

HENRY

The city did not slow down for the dead. That was the first lesson New York taught us. The docks were loud with shouting, carts rattling over wet stone, steam hissing from pipes, and the constant press of bodies moving somewhere urgent. Reporters called questions into the crowd that no one answered. Names were shouted and swallowed by the noise. Some people cried openly. Others walked with terrifying calm, as if their bodies had decided grief would have to wait.

Oliver walked beside me, still unsteady, his arm linked through mine more for balance than affection—though I welcomed both. Madeleine moved slightly ahead, carving a path with purpose. She looked like someone who had made a decision and would not be diverted from it.

I felt unreal. Every step away from the harbor felt like theft. As if I were stealing time that belonged to someone else. The ground beneath my boots was solid, but my body still expected it to tilt. Every loud sound made my chest tighten. Every sudden movement sent my heart skidding.

Oliver stopped abruptly on the edge of the crowd and looked back toward the water.

"They're still there," he said quietly.

I followed his gaze. The harbor was crowded with vessels—tugs, ferries, small private boats—all jostling like mourners who didn't know where to stand. Somewhere out there, beneath the gray surface, the *Titanic* rested with her secrets and her dead.

"Yes," I said. "They are."

He swallowed, his throat working. "I keep thinking I should be able to hear them."

I didn't answer. There was nothing I could say that would make that thought smaller. Madeleine returned then, her face flushed from cold and effort. "Come," she said. "Before someone asks us questions we don't want to answer."

She led us away from the docks and into the city proper. The streets narrowed quickly, buildings pressing in like curious onlookers. New York smelled the same as it always had—coal smoke, damp stone, refuse, and life piled too close together—but now it felt sharper, almost aggressive, like the city was daring us to survive it.

Oliver glanced up at the buildings, then down at his hands. They were still mottled with cold, knuckles raw and red.

"Do they always loom like this?" he asked.

"They do if you let them," I said. "They stop feeling so tall eventually."

He gave a faint smile. "Good."

We walked in silence for several blocks. My mother's neighborhood was still familiar enough that my feet knew the way even when my head felt far away. The tenements leaned close together here, windows fogged, laundry lines sagging overhead. Somewhere, a radio crackled faintly through an open window. A woman laughed. A baby cried.

Life. Just … life.

When we reached the building, I stopped short. The door was open. My stomach dropped.

"Henry?" Madeleine asked.

"I—" My voice stuck. "I didn't expect anyone to be up."

We climbed the stairs slowly. Each step creaked the same way it always had, but now the sound felt unbearably loud. Halfway up, I heard my brother's voice.

"Not yet. No word yet."

I froze. Oliver's hand tightened on my sleeve. We reached the landing. My brother stood in the hallway, hat in his hands, his face drawn and gray. When he saw me, his mouth fell open.

"Henry?"

For a second, neither of us moved. Then he crossed the space in three strides and grabbed my shoulders.

"Jesus Christ," he breathed. "We thought—"

"I know," I said hoarsely. "I know."

He pulled back, eyes searching my face like he was afraid I'd vanish. Then his gaze flicked to Madeleine, then to Oliver.

"Who—"

"This is Madeleine," I said quickly. "And this is Oliver. They were with me on the ship."

Something shifted in my brother's expression at the word *ship*. His jaw tightened.

"You'd better come inside," he said.

My mother was awake. She sat propped against pillows, thinner than I remembered, her hair gone gray at the temples, her eyes too large in her face. When she saw me, she stared as if I were a trick of the light.

"Henry?" she whispered.

I crossed the room in two steps and dropped to my knees beside her bed.

"I'm here," I said, my voice breaking. "I'm home."

She reached out, her hand trembling, and cupped my cheek. Her skin felt fragile, almost translucent.

"They said the ship—" Her breath hitched. "They said—"

"I know," I said. "But I'm here."

She cried then—quietly, with the restraint of someone who had spent her life holding herself together. Madeleine moved to her side at once, slipping an arm around her shoulders, steady and familiar. I took my mother's hand, warm and trembling in mine, and let her cry until her breathing finally evened out.

Madeleine gave her shoulder a gentle squeeze, murmuring something soft and reassuring before stepping back, her presence a calm anchor in the room.

When my mother lifted her head again, her gaze drifted past me and settled on Oliver, who stood awkwardly near the door, wrapped in a borrowed coat, unsure whether to move closer or fade into the wall. Her eyes sharpened—not with suspicion, but with quiet, thoughtful curiosity.

"And who is this?" she asked.

I took a breath, feeling Madeleine's steady presence just behind me.

"This is Oliver," I said. "He saved us."

My mother studied him for a long moment, the way she always had—seeing more than people expected. Then she reached out her free hand.

"Then you're welcome here," she said simply. "Anyone who brings my son home is welcome."

Oliver hesitated, emotion flickering across his face, before taking her hand. His voice was rough when he spoke.

"Thank you, ma'am."

Madeleine smiled then—small, relieved, and proud—and for the first time since the ocean had tried to take everything from us, the room felt like it might truly hold us all.

She squeezed his fingers with surprising strength. "You look half frozen. Sit down before you fall."

Something loosened in Oliver at that—some tension he'd been carrying since the water. He sat. That night, we ate soup in chipped bowls. My brother talked too much. My mother watched Oliver with quiet attention. Madeleine washed up and then sat cross-legged on the floor like she had nowhere else she wanted to be. No one asked for details. The world had taken enough.

Later, when the apartment had gone quiet, Oliver stood by the window, looking out at the city lights.

"I'm not sure how this works," he said after a moment.

"How what works?" I asked.

"Being here," he said. "After everything."

I stepped closer, our shoulders brushing.

"We'll figure it out," I said. "As we go."

He turned toward me, studying my face in the dim light.

"You really mean it?" he asked. "About me staying?"

"I do," I said.

"Yes."

He leaned forward and rested his forehead against mine.

"Then I'll stay," he said. "For as long as you'll have me."

That night, there was no ceremony to it. The apartment settled into its own quiet, the kind New York offered when it finally grew tired of itself. A carriage rolled past below. Somewhere down the block, a door opened and closed. Life continued, unconcerned with what we had survived.

Oliver and I shared the narrow bed without discussion. We turned toward one another naturally, as if our bodies had already agreed on the arrangement. He slept with one arm wrapped firmly around my waist, his face tucked against my neck, breath warm and steady. I rested my hand against his back, feeling the slow rise and fall there, grounding myself in the simple fact of him.

Madeleine slept in the bed beside ours, curled on her side with one arm thrown over her pillow, breathing deeply at last. For the first time in days, none of us were listening for alarms, for water, for loss.

Sometime before dawn, Oliver stirred. He didn't pull

away. He didn't rush. He simply opened his eyes and stayed there, watching me like he was confirming something important. Then he leaned in just enough for his forehead to touch mine and whispered, so softly I almost thought I imagined it, "I love you."

My eyes opened slowly. I tightened my arm around him and breathed him in.

"I love you too," I murmured.

We stayed that way as the light shifted, neither of us needing to say anything more.

Morning came gently. Pale sunlight crept through the thin curtains, touching the floor, the edge of the bed, the dark spill of Madeleine's hair. The city sounded different in daylight—less threatening, more curious, like it was waiting to see what we would do with it.

Madeleine woke first.

She sat up, stretched, and looked at the two of us with a small, knowing smile.

"Well," she said, "you both look far better than you did yesterday."

I smiled, still half asleep. "High praise."

She swung her legs over the side of the bed, her expression shifting into something thoughtful.

"I've decided something," she said. "I'm going to look for him. The painter. The man I met in Paris. The man who was supposed to meet me when we docked."

I nodded. "You'll find him."

She pulled on her coat, paused at the door, and glanced back once more.

"Don't wait for permission," she said. "None of us sur-vived for that."

When the door closed behind her, Oliver and I lay there quietly, sunlight warming the room, the bed still holding the shape of all three of us. Outside, New York waited. Inside, I held the man I loved. And for the first time, I knew we weren't going anywhere.